M000080459

GIRL WARRIOR

By Carmen Peone

ISBN-13: 978-1-7323356-0-8
ISBN-10: 1-7323356-0-5

© copyright 2018 Carmen Peone

All rights reserved.

This book or parts thereof may not be reproduced in any form, stored in or introduced into a retrieval system, or transmitted, in any form, or by any means (electronic, mechanical, photocopying, recording, or otherwise) without prior written permission of the copyright owner and/or publisher of this book, except as provided by United States of America copyright law.

This novel is a work of fiction. Names, descriptions, entities, and incidents included in the story are products of the author's imagination. Any resemblance to actual persons, events, and entities is entirely coincidental.

Cover design and formatting by Rossano Designs
Photo credits: Carmen Peone
Published by Painted Hill Press

DEDICATION

For Luanne Toulou Finley—
you inspire, encourage and enlighten.

Art by Katlyn Watt

CHAPTER 1

2015 San Poil, Colville Reservation, Washington State

When the bus rattles to a halt in front of the Republic High School, my tummy knots. Will he be in school today? I drag myself off after everyone else unloads. My hand hovers over the door handle until I finally push through the glass entrance. Jocks, who act as if the hallway's their private football field, slam me into one of the glass trophy cases. I catch my breath and allow my gaze to hone in on one of the few art projects inside, hoping my idea for this year's project will speak volumes.

Something in my life has to matter.

I drop my backpack off at my locker and head for the elementary building where all grades share the cafeteria. The smell of boiled eggs and sausage patties fills the brick-walled room. I grab one of each and add a strawberry yogurt, hoping it will help untwist the knots. This morning the tan walls feel cold and dreary while the checkered floors spin my head. Where is she?

"Hey look, it's Charnaye Toulou!" Hagan's voice echoes off the walls. "Horse racin' Indian princess. I saw you in Omak this summer eyeing the hill. Suppose next you'll try and take on the suicide race." He laughs. "A bunch of your racing buddies seem to think you could handle it. Can you?"

I cringe, nausea bubbling up my throat.

A small group of students gathers around us. Why can't people mind their own business? What makes me the target? Does the color of my skin really matter?

"But you don't have the guts for something that big, do ya. A scrawny thing like you might as well stay on the small fair tracks." He takes a step closer.

I step back and hunch my shoulders into a protective stance. This year can't get over quick enough.

"What's your shirt say today?" Hagan Hurst's eyes drop to my green Native Pride T-shirt. "Come on, worn-out cowboy boots? Where's your moccasins and buckskin?" He looks at his friends and they all laugh. Even some of the girls giggle. "At least you got the braids right."

"Get a life." My face scrunched, I spin around and shoulder out of their inner circle.

"Where is she?" We need to discuss our art project. My heart races as I zigzag around the students. *I hate him!* Our lack of money shames me.

"Char!" Jill Lamore's voice sounds behind me.

She waves her arm. The green bow in her short, flaxen hair matches her eyes. Her flip-flops snap with each step. We find a couple of empty seats in the corner and settle in. "Should we paint or do photography for our project?" Her long, slim fingers stroke the air.

Hagan's bigotry makes me shudder. I clear my throat, shaking away the moisture pooling in my eyes. "Whatever we decide, our project needs to be good enough to highlight the display cases. There needs to be more than sports trophies in there." I swallow the boulder lodged in my throat. "I'm sure we can come up with something that will take it up a notch in class."

"Art. Let's create something with a little kick in it. Something that includes peace and hope…and harmony…for everyone—of any race." Jill lifts a brow and takes a long swallow of milk.

"Harmony, huh?" Hagan leans over my shoulder. His sulfur-like breath brushes against my neck.

I elbow him. "Get away from me!" Sick of years of his racial comments, I feel like I'm at the end of my rope. But for my family, I'll hang on.

He claps me on the back and strides away. "Catch you later, Miss Native Pride." He stops and turns, his sharp, gray eyes boring into mine. "See you next week in archery." He smirks and flicks his head to the side. Red locks the color of flames from hell flip off his freckled forehead.

His laugh bounces from wall to wall as his cowboy boots click down the hall, his posse slinking behind like dogs on a leash. The rainbow of the "Six Pillars of Character" banner hangs on a wall. I shake my head.

Trustworthy: not at all. Respect: they don't know the meaning. Responsibility: they no doubt think theirs is to trash girls and Natives. Fairness: this makes their eyes cross because they have no idea of the meaning. Caring: not a thread runs through their iced veins. Citizenship: the cowboy way, not exactly how I was taught. Worthless culls. Every one of them.

"Don't pay any attention to him. He's such a creep," Jill says. "You're beautiful and talented. Best jockey around."

Heat tingles up neck. "I won't." I open my yogurt and dip in the plastic spoon. "What a jerk. *Loot hamink e he hahoolawho.*"

Jill stares, mouth open. "There you go, talking Salish again when you're mad. What does that mean anyway?"

"I just called him the snake he is." I lick yogurt from the spoon. "Creator listens to me when I speak my language." Plenty of females have entered and qualified for the Suicide Race. Why can't I? It'd be the perfect way to prove myself, a rite of passage after all. The money I'd earn could spruce up our rickety shack. Lift the heavy weight that seems to bear down on Mom's shoulders.

"I bet He does. I'll be praying Hagan finds the end of himself…in a steaming heap of you know what. He's sure got something coming his way. Hope it stings." Jill taps her pen on the table. "You look like you didn't get much sleep."

"Precalculus, U of W application, Gates scholarships, the pressure's getting to me—it's too much."

"The price you pay for brains." Jill's expression softens. "Sorry the fair got canceled. You would've won all your races."

I stir the yogurt and let it slide off the spoon. "Thanks. I still have the Okanogan Fair and a couple weeks to prepare. Things'll work out. They always do." Or was I simply trying to convince myself it would? I finish my yogurt and push my tray aside.

"Let's get back to the art project. How about this girl-warrior thing? I can see a Native woman, such as yourself, with bow and arrow, Hagan's head as the target…" Jill gives me a wide grin.

I chuckle. "Idnit! I like your idea."

The bell rings.

I sigh. "Ready for AP History? More about the 1600s and colonies and war, oh joy. These weekly exams are gonna kill me."

CHAPTER 2

After school I saddle Stimteema and hit the scorched trails. She's my rock, named after my mother's mother—a horsewoman who herded cows alongside the old-timers. Some say she should have been a boy because she rode like one. We weave in and out of blackened trees, a cloud of ash spiraling behind us.

It feels like death.

The knot in my belly unravels at a snail's pace as we track a few cows and pick our way through downed logs with white needles before starting up the hills behind the ranch. As we follow an old logging road, suicide entertains my thoughts. Is that the only way to get away from him? Tears slide down my cheeks. I wipe them away.

I urge my mare into a jog. Floating ash makes me cough so I slow her down. I rein her back into the woods, and we weave through honey-colored larch at a walk. What's left of black moss hangs down like tinsel from outlining trees that missed the flames. It makes me feel I'm back in the old days when elders used to steam and eat black moss. When life seemed simpler. No internet. No cell phones. No bullies. Or was there?

An eagle passes low overhead. Stimteema darts to the side. I clutch the saddle horn and pull myself back into the saddle. The charred forest seems void of wildlife, save an occasional bird. As we drift through the trees, there's no sign of life. I feel like the forest looks—dead inside.

Stimteema stumbles, and I flinch. "You waking me out of my daydreams, girl?" I rein her back on the logging road, sit up and off her back, and ease her into a gallop. It doesn't take long to eat miles of ground, leaving an ash trail behind.

When my lungs can't take the ruin any longer, I bring her down to a walk. Hagan's words slips through the cracks and I shudder. *I suppose next you'll try and ride down the suicide hill.* His venomous laugh replays in my mind. *You don't have the guts for something that big.* What if he's right? What if I choke? I sit up in the saddle and lift my chin. "I have the right to come down that hill. Times have changed. It's not just for guys anymore. Girls can be warriors, too." Stimteema's ears flick back toward me. "I know I can win." I pat her neck. "All I need is the right horse."

You might as well stay on the fair tracks, that's more your speed. I shove the thoughts away and switch my focus to how it felt to watch the race from the Okanogan River last year. The rush of horses barreling down the hill and plunging into the water. How the water felt lapping against my thighs after they'd passed by. Goosebumps break out on my arms. *It's in my blood.*

I turn around and head for the barn, tears spilling down my face as an image of my father in his wheelchair imprints my mind. Everything is broken—just like me. I wipe my face with the hem of my shirt, fighting back the threat of fresh tears. Should I end it all? What would that do to my parents? Kari? Grandfather? I stiffen. *The barn needs new doors. Dad needs a new ramp into the house. We need to get rid of the mold. The car needs fixed. Mom's not safe in that old, brown jalopy. Neither is Kari.* "Do I have what it takes?" Stimteema's ears flicker back and forth.

A nine-year-old should feel protected and happy, not victimized. The knot returns and wads in my gut. Kari should be playing with her friends, not in weekly counseling sessions and combating nightmares. Mom should be gardening, watering her flowers, singing while she cans, not working so hard to keep what little food we have on the table. Fresh tears tumble. I have to hold on.

I stroke my mare's neck. Her black mane blends into a light brown neck with splotches resembling shadows. *Where else will we get more money?* I sigh, again brooding over ways to scrape more money from the cracks.

When I reach our ranch Sshapa's bent-over, feeding a bottle calf a can of grain. He waves, his eyes showing signs of weariness. "How was your ride?"

"Good!" I choke on my words.

He studies my face. "The black streaks say otherwise."

I wipe my face with the back of my hand. "Did a lot of thinking is all." I flee to the barn, anxious to avoid further scrutiny. I unsaddle my mare, brush her, and toss the horses hay, lingering for a while to consider my options.

By suppertime I step into the kitchen. Dirty plates are scattered on the table. "Chase and Sshapa went to fix fence in the south pasture," Mom says. "You're dinner's in the microwave."

Outside, cows bawling for their young seem deafening. Too many times, calves crawl under the fence and wander off. My heart hurts for them. Inside, Kari's snuggled under a dark brown blanket the color of her hair on the couch, reading Mom's old, worn *Black Beauty* book, bangs in her eyes. Dad watches the news, waiting for the weather report. Sweat still beads his forehead with each forecast. Some nights I hear him in his room praying for rain.

News stations continue to replay the horrid summer forest fires we've had for the past three months. Most of the smoke has cleared out down low, but at higher levels, flames continue to devour the land. Dad grunts and rolls his wheelchair down the hallway with swift jerks. The creak of our scarred wood floor makes me cringe. I have to find a way to get more cash. *This house is a battered shack.* The only way to score enough money to help my dad get around better is to enter and win next year's Suicide Race. But they can't find out.

After I've eaten, I slip into to my room. Five years of Omak Stampede and Suicide Race posters hang on my walls. All I have to do is find the right horse. I sigh and tug off last year's frayed jeans and replace them with worn sweats. When Mom calls for me, I stumble out of my room and bump into Dad, nearly sitting on his lap. His scrawny legs wouldn't feel it, but mine do. My hip bone crashes into the metal armrest. I scrunch my face and hold in a moan.

Mom sits across from me with a cup of coffee. She pours in a bit of caramel flavored creamer and slowly stirs until it blends brown. Her eyes glance at the couch. She sighs. In her early forties, Mom is small-framed but can buck bales with the best of them. Despite her quiet ways, she's a tiger inside. Always there for me, fighting for a better life, with wise words and a soft touch.

"How's your senior project coming along?" She rubs her temple.

I herd bread crumbs to the center of my plate. "Which part?"

"Any of it." She rests her chin in her hand, elbow on the table.

Lines crease her face that weren't there last year. Dull gray hair has replaced shiny black locks. It frames her small face and petite nose. I smile at her and wave a hand. "There's too much to do."

"Like what? Where's your list. I'd like to help." She takes a sip.

I shrug. "In my room. I have to figure out where I'll earn my eight hours of community service, complete a resume, fill out a job application packet, FAFSA—heck, I have no idea what that is—not to mention my ten-page 'high school and beyond' paper…" Fresh frustration simmers within me as my body tenses.

"How about picking one item off the list."

"Which one? I have to do them all."

Mom takes another sip, sets her cup on the table, and fingers the handle.

"I think there's a FAFSA meeting for parents and students come January. The resume and job application I can help you with, plus there are lots of online examples of resumes."

I sigh and lay my fork on the table.

"Do you know who you want to do your community service with?"

"No. Maybe. I was kind of thinking either at the Wild West Farm and Garden or Eich's Mercantile."

"Eich's has ice cream." Her brows lift.

I smile. "Yeah, that's what I was thinking."

Mom fingers the table. Like she does when her mind is miles away, but she's trying to relax and be a thoughtful, concerned mother. I know she's got a lot on her plate. I like that she's sitting with me, talking. We don't get much time together lately. Not for the last couple of years.

"But K Diamond K is closer. I thought of them, too," I say.

"Another great option. Either way, one day's work is all you need. One Saturday. I'm sure any of these places would love to have you. When you figure it out you can take my car." She pauses. "Since you want to be a lawyer, have you considered one of the local attorneys? I'm sure Jim Sam is available."

I nod. "I'll need him for my high school and beyond paper. For my hours, I want to do something fun."

Mom downs her last bit of coffee. "Don't blame you." She clears the table. I do dishes so she can grade papers.

After everyone has turned in for the night, I sit on my bed and tackle a Precalculus lesson. My mind struggles to wrap its fingers around $3(x - 1) + 2 \leq 5x + 6$. I scan $2(3 - 4z) - 5(2z + 3) = z - 7$. My brain hurts tonight and these equations don't help. Footsteps shuffle in the kitchen. No doubt Sshapa can't sleep either. I find him bent over, head in the fridge, scrounging for his before-bed snack. It's like clockwork.

"Sshapa?"

He turns to me, gnarled fingers gripping that jar of peaches. "Hello, Granddaughter. How's your homework coming?"

"Fine. I'm fiddling with numbers and letters again."

He nods. "I quit being interested in numbers when they added letters. Don't need to add letters to count heads of beef." He gives me one of his teasing smiles. The kind where his eyes twinkle like holiday lights. He motions me to the table.

I get him a fork and bowl and set them in front of him.

"Thank you, dear." He watches me sit down. "What is on your mind?"

I hesitate as butterflies dance, bumping into one another in my stomach. Why am I so nervous to ask him? It's only for history, right? Shivers wash down my limbs. I set my jaw and open my mouth. "Well…" a hitch catches in my throat. "What do you know about the suicide race?"

Sshapa chokes on his peaches. He wipes his mouth with his shirtsleeve. I get him a glass of water.

Oh, crap! I pat him on the back.

He takes a sip and clinks the glass on the wood table. "Why do you ask?" His words are no more than a croak.

"It's for history." I pass him a napkin. "We have new books that include Natives from our perspective, not whites attempting to describe our way of life. I figured I'd do my senior report on the Suicide Race."

He stares at the table for a moment. "It does not matter who writes in the history books as long as it is the truth."

"I just want to find out where and how the race began. Who started it? Which band? What kind of horses did they ride? Things like that. All I know is it's in Omak and it didn't start there."

Sshapa takes another bite of peaches. Swallows. Watches me. "This race is not safe. I think you should do your report on something else. Something that matters.

Like ranching or being a lawyer or teacher." He pushes from the table and shuffles to his bedroom, face dark.

Why did he cut me off? What does he know? Did something happen? Someone he knew? I'll find out. Eventually, he'll tell me. He's got to.

CHAPTER 3

My eyelids blink open to my brother standing over me with a water gun inches from my temple. I groan, knock it out of his hand, and roll over. The floral quilt my Tima made for me years ago slides off and hits the floor. I lie still, hoping he'll leave. But I don't hear footsteps.

"Holy! Get up, Charnaye," Chase says. The quilt drops on my back in a heap. "Time to feed."

I roll over and my eyelids make an attempt to lift. "You do it."

Footsteps dash to the bathroom. The mirror reveals puffy bags under my eyes. I sigh.

What's Sshapa hiding from me? What is so bad about the suicide race? *Suicide.* What was I thinking? Shame ripples through me. *Creator, please, never again.* The race, I've watched it almost every year since I was a small girl. It's safe. Horses get cut by barbed wire, kick each other in the pasture, heck, they do more damage to themselves than a human ever could. Good grief, how often do they die from colic? I splash cold water over my face and head back to my bedroom.

Water stains blemish the ceiling, making my throat ache. I cough, rub my eyes, pull on sweats and boots and go feed. It's still dark at 5:30. As fall creeps in, my mind fights it. I trot down the worn wooden ramp neighbors threw together after the car wreck, tripping over a loose board. There are no arm rails, so I end up in the dirt. I roll up to my feet and kick the side of the ramp. "Freak! Piece of crap." My hands grow stiff by the time I'm in the barn. My jaw hardens. My body shivers against single digit temperature as fall creeps in.

My fingers jerk away from the half-pound coffee can of grain. I pull my sleeves down and cover them, shielding against the frigid tin. Stimteema's low whicker courses through the walls of our old barn—a series of add-ons that groan with the wind. The wood is old and gray, yet sturdy. It reminds me of my grandfather.

My gaze catches the trees beyond the barn, now a burnt forest covered in black soot and leafless trees.

"You gonna feed these horses?"

I jerk around and drop the grain.

"Sshapa, don't sneak up on me like that!"

He grins. "Don't let your guard down, Char. That's how we get into trouble." He pauses. "That's how Coyote gets into trouble."

I salvage what little grain is left, add more, and pour the richness into Stimteema's handmade wooden feeder. She nudges my hand away as if to punish my tardiness. I stroke her nose and wait for a story. It doesn't come. But something unexpected does.

"You asked about the mountain races in Keller last night. I cut you off." Sshapa strokes Stimteema's neck.

I divide flakes of hay, anticipating my grandfather's continuation.

"I hesitate to share this with you."

I toss a couple flakes in Shorty's feeder, my father's Appaloosa horse. "Why is that?" Butterflies swirl inside my belly before fluttering out and down my throat.

"What are your motives?" His voice is low, filled with concern.

"I told you, Sshapa. It's for history. They always talk about Columbus and Cortes and Montezuma and the Spanish Conquest of Mexico. So much is about the whites and the Atlantic Coast. We can write about whatever we want for our first report. I want to write about the West. About Native events. I'm tired of hearing about war. I want to write about warriors. Our warriors."

"I see." He eases down on a bale of hay, tugs out a piece of hay, and fiddles with it.

Something in his voice tells me he's not convinced. "Sshapa, I thumbed through the pages of our book. They mention Red Cloud, but he's Sioux. Our book covers treaties, policies, the Indian Removal Act. They mention the Pacific Coast Indians, two whole paragraphs...say we are hunter-gatherers of fish and nuts and lump us all into the Salish or Chinooks. It's nice to mention we once used huge cedar trees to dig out canoes. How thoughtful." My blood boils. "Just think, this is AP History. They're stupid."

Grandfather nods when I give him a sideways glance. He slides the strand of hay between his coffee-stained teeth.

I drag hay-mixed dirt in circles with the toe of my cracked boot.

Sshapa nods. "I'm happy you care so deeply."

I grunt, wishing he'd hurry so I don't miss the bus.

"What else is in that history book of yours?" Sshapa chews on the hay.

I toss more flakes of Timothy into feeders and pick up the end of a string of three hoses that attach to our house. Nothing spills out. I chastise myself for forgetting to turn the water on before walking to the barn. I toss the end to the dirt and drop to the bale beside Sshapa.

He pats my knee with the motion of a ninety-year-old man and he's only in his mid-sixties.

"They always have the most famous people, mostly men, although they were kind enough to add Pocahontas, and the most famous tribes like the Sioux and Iroquois. I looked up the Colvilles. Nothing. I looked up the Palouse. Nothing. I looked up Salish…well, I already told you they mentioned us, but really only the coastals. I want to talk about the Okanogans." I take a breath and exhale a groan. "I want people to understand the right of passage and what it means." I want to believe my speech is the truth. But know it's not.

He nods. "I see."

I see? Really? What do you see, Sshapa? I pluck hay from a bail and twist it around my finger.

Silence stretches longer than my patience allows.

I stand. "Have to water the horses."

"What does the rite of passage mean to you?" His tone sounds challenging.

I turn and lean against a stall door and gather my thoughts. "A journey from childhood into adulthood, but more. Kind of like the vision quests our people used to take. But it's not just about becoming an adult. It's more about becoming a warrior. Strong. Dedicated. Honoring the Creator and our heritage. Our traditions are dying a strangulating death." I give him a hard look. At least my words hold honesty this time. "Isn't that what you always tell me?"

He stares at me with penetrating eyes. "The races began in Keller." Sshapa tosses his piece of hay to the side and pats the empty space beside him.

I settle back on the bale and lean against the wall, thankful he's willing to share.

He pulls his collar up and his hat down and shoves his hands deep in his pockets. "The terrain was rugged. Rocky. Men swooped down like they were on fire. It was a quarter-mile vertical drop. They would gallop across a dry channel of the San Poil River and stampede into the rodeo arena."

I sigh and wait, my leg gently bouncing up and down.

"This took place during salmon runs in the spring. There were games for kids. Our people fished, danced, gambled, sang…honored Creator for his gift of fresh salmon. Winters dragged along at a turtles pace. By spring everyone was sick of dried meat. Dried roots and berries. Our bellies were hungry for fresh food." He stares at the forest through an open stall door as though reliving old times. "They were dark, cold days as my grandfather described to me. Everything was dried. Stiff. Fresh meat revived our spirits. Salmon meant Creator was caring for us once again. After all, He'd brought them to us."

My muscles relax as the butterflies find a new place to play. I lean back against the wall, one heel on the bale.

"Men showed their strength and courage by racing horses. They came off the hill near the Keller Park, on the west side. It was dangerous." He raises a knobby finger in the air and lets it briefly linger before bringing it back to his pocket.

I imagine jockeys trembling as they broke off the hill and launched down toward the inlet. "Did any of them turn back, afraid to go down?"

Sshapa nods. "Yes. Many lost their nerve." His gray brows furrow.

"Did they ever bet?" I ask questions that would fit a report. "Before they raced?"

His eyes brighten and his thick lips break into a wide smile. "There was always betting. It was a time of celebration. Riders paraded their horses around the grounds prior to the race. Before long a heap of goods piled in the dirt. Heck, they bet moccasins, tobacco, blankets, knives, furs, traps, beads, and sometimes even wives. They'd arrange marriages once in a while from the outcomes." He chuckles and stares past the horses for a long moment. "Families would bet with loggers and miners on jockeys and horses and with their winnings bought coffee, flour, salt, sugar and the like."

I envision a bunch of excited men bidding on their favorite items, and the terror in the women's eyes when handed over to their promised grooms. "Did the jockeys get anything out of all of this? Or just the spectators?" I struggle to wipe the horror of an arranged marriage from my mind.

Sshapa nods. "Oh, yes. Jockeys bet against each other's horses if the rider owned their own horse. Bet saddles. And of course, horses."

They'd be crazy to come off the jagged rock faces that line the south end of Keller. No way would I ever do that. I can't imagine them carving a path wide enough through the bluffs.

Sshapa squints at his watch. "You go turn the water on and get ready for school. I'll finish here and give these hay burners a drink." He smiles and motions to the house.

"Thank you, Sshapa. This helps." I smile inside until the lie twists my heart. How can I honor a man I love and turn around and fill the space between us with deception? I shove past the guilt and justify the lie with a race of pride. After Dad's accident, there's no way my family would agree to me bolting down the hill.

I stomp in the back door and shrug off my coat, dropping it on the kitchen chair. Dad sits in his rickety wheelchair, his gaze glued to the morning news. The smell of eggs and bacon fills my nose. I plop down in a chair and stare at a picture of my grandmother sitting a horse, tall and confident. I pluck it from the wall. "*She* was a warrior," I whisper.

"Your mother made breakfast this morning. It's on the table," Dad says over his shoulder.

"Is Kari up?" I hang the picture back on the wall, strengthened by Tima's determination, and fill my plate.

Dad turns his wheelchair toward me. "Should be, I'll check."

I push back from the table. "I will."

"No!" He sighs. "I can manage. I may be in a chair, but I'm not helpless. You eat." He bumps the wheelchair into the wall, backs up and takes another go at the hallway. The skinny wheels bounce down the hall as his strong arms rotate with each warped pass.

My gaze lingers for a moment before forking a bite of eggs into my dry mouth. This lie *has* to be worth it. Dad needs to function on level ground and in clean air. An electric chair would be nice, not the battered chair he sits in now. He reminds me of an old, lifeless man. The only thing thriving is his will. I fork in another bite and wash it down with milk.

He speaks softly to Kari. His tone sounds loving, encouraging. He has every right to be angry, but still, he refuses. "They took away my legs, Char, but they will never get my honor," he always tells me. He's right. The bathroom door closes. Floorboards creak as he wheels himself back to catch more news of the local weather. Updates on remaining fires fill the space. Since most are high in the mountains and ninety percent contained, talk of school shootings takes most of the airtime. That and cop killers. What is our country coming to?

"Any food left?" Dad faces me.

"Um, yeah, I'll get Kari a plate." I rise.

"Sit. I'll get it." He studies me with a scowl. "You dressed for school? Is this how you represent our family?" His grimace turns into a smile.

I look down. "Well…"

He tosses me a kitchen towel. "Clean up."

I pass Kari in the hall. Her swollen, dark brown eyes rise and fall, arms folded across her chest. I pray healing over her as we pass. A pang of guilt and sorrow hums inside of me. It should have been me in the car, not her. How selfish of me to ride that day, refusing to watch her while Dad went into town for grain. Why had I insisted on preparing for the Kennewick race? It would have been just as beneficial to work the thoroughbred when we returned. Rebellion—it haunts a person.

CHAPTER 4

The members of Board of Directors for the Republic School District study me. I never knew five people could be so intimidating. One smiles. Another leans forward, blinks, and scans the papers in her hands, her elbows resting on the table. I wipe sweaty palms on my jeans. My throat tightens. I've waited all day for this meeting. And now I sit in an empty classroom, English to be exact, knotted in nerves. All I can think about is what a liar I am. And to the man I honor the most. Images pass by of my dad's mashed truck, blood on the street, him wheeling down the narrow hall of our home. I shudder. I can do this. I have to. Kari's swollen eyes flash through my mind. Her frail, thin body. What about Sshapa…

"Charnaye, you with us?" Mr. Peterson says.

My head snaps up. "What?" They stare at me. I swallow. Saliva sticks like cotton in my throat. "Um, yes. Sorry. I was…anyway, can you repeat the question?"

Mr. Peterson smiles. "At this point, we welcome you here and are interested in what you have to propose to us. So please…" He fans his hands out in my direction.

I wiggle in my chair. "Okay, thank you." My eyes drop to my notes, but I can hardly read them through trembling hands. "I would like to switch my high school and beyond plan." I give them a small smile. Fiddle with the notecards.

Mr. Jackson clears his throat. "Charnaye, you want to be an attorney, correct? Have you changed your future plans?"

"No…no…not at all. I still plan to attend the U of W and pursue that career. I want to help those who are victims of car accidents and the like. But, well, I…for my project I would prefer to display a presentation that honors my people." I look down, knowing I'm blowing this. Using weird words that I think are impressive. *I sound like an idiot.* A photo of my grandmother sitting tall on a bay horse flashes through my mind. I take a deep breath, peer at each one of them, lift my chin in hopes they believe my lie. "My people have been warriors from the time of creation. It is displayed today through events like the World Famous Suicide Race during the Omak Stampede. I would like, if approved by the Board, to honor my people by bringing to the forefront this rite of passage from my culture and share with my school, parents, and community."

One board member gasps. I think it was Mrs. Sherman. She looks like she's about to faint. I gather the courage to look each one of them in the eye. Old Lady Sherman sits with her mouth covered, face turning white, the color of her short, curly hair. It's a bit much, if you ask me. I never mentioned I plan to race down it. The look of shock on her face makes me want to smile, stand,

and war-whoop. But I thread my fingers and lay them on my lap, take a deep breath, and smile. Hoping a look of confidence will sway the panel.

Mrs. Langley clears her throat. "Tell us more, what will your angle be? Who will you interview? What is your interest in the actual race—do you want to participate?"

Another gasp ripples through the room. Old Lady Sherman's judgmental sneer burns through me before I actually see it. "My Sshapa Wesley, as you know, is a member of the Okanogan Band, one of the twelve belonging to the Colville Tribes and knows much about the race. He has agreed to share his knowledge with me. There are also other elders in Keller I'm sure he will hook me...I mean introduce me to if needed. I'm sure I can interview horse owners and jockeys. Find out about the breed of successful horses and their training programs. I know a few of them, or I know of them. We race together at the fairs. I would like to examine and present the history of the original race in Keller and how it transferred to Omak and why. And finally, I would like to talk about what the race means to the jockeys. They're mostly men, but I know a few women have qualified and have run the hill as well." My attitude shifts from a lie to genuine interest. "This is important to our culture and what it means to be an American Indian." Should I mention the rite of passage? Or is it overkill?

Mrs. Allen taps her pencil on the table. Her stink eye makes me cringe. She puckers her lips and turns them into a slow smile that spreads wide like butter on a fresh slice of homemade bread. "I think this is wonderful. We need more young ladies like you to take the horse by the reins and kick some—"

Mr. Peterson clears his throat. "Thank you, Mrs. Allen."

She adds, "Pun intended." Her eyes twinkle under the florescent lighting. She winks at me, still tapping her pencil on the table.

The Board's mental games make me squirm.

They discuss my proposal. Words like mistake, culture, dangerous, and pride fill the room in a quiet hush. After several excruciating minutes, Mr. Peterson quiets them. He calls for the vote. Yes. Yes. Yes. Yes. No! Old Lady Sherman's squinty eyes pierce me like a freshly carved arrowhead. I nod at her, acknowledging she's been heard and even understood, but outnumbered. I resist smiling. And war-whooping.

"Well, Miss Toulou, it looks like you really love your heritage. Your commitment to being a Native American Lady is inspiring and has won us over." Mrs. Allen glances at Old Lady Sherman and frowns. "Well, at least most of us. I look forward to reading your paper and listening to your speech come May."

My heart flips in my chest. I release a breath. Smile. Stand and shake each board member's hand. I pump Old Lady Sherman's just a stretch longer. I strut out, chin up. Until I think about telling my parents my change of plans.

The *click, click, click* of high heels in the hallway sends chills down my spine. Not a slow saunter but more like a stampeding bull. The hair on my neck stands on end. A chill rushes down my arms. The clock on the classroom wall reads 4:05. *Crap, I'm late.* I sprint through the hall and come face to face with the bull—Mom.

"I just talked with Mr. Aspen." She snorts, head wagging from side to side. Imagine a bull with heels.

"Nice guy, isn't he? I—"

She points a finger centimeters from my nose. "Don't get smart with me, Charnaye Toulou. I have to come track you down, miss my meetings because you were supposed to come get Kari and make sure she got on the bus with you, no less, and get home to help Sshapa get your father into the car for his doctor's appointment." Her voice rises with each word.

My conscience pangs. "I'm—"

The bull's voice lowers, nostrils flaring, "I don't want to hear your excuses. We all have to pull our weight here, Charnaye." She folds her arms over her chest, shifting her weight. "I know this is hard on you. Your senior year and all, but I can't…I need your help. Please." She looks away.

Moisture glints in her eyes. Can't miss the dark bags under them. Or her worn-down sigh.

"I'm sorry, Mom. You're right. There is no excuse." I wait for her to speak. May as well take my tongue lashing like the warrior woman I've been bragging about for the last twenty minutes. Because I know if I dare roll my eyes, my mother will likely knock them off my face.

"I have now missed a meeting with a parent whose child is struggling in class to drive you and your sister home. I can't have this. I just can't." She swipes a finger under an eye. "That parent had to take off work, miss pay because she's part-time. Is that fair? No, no it's not." She pauses to collect herself. "Things have changed now, since the accident. I have your help one more year before you head off to college. Then it's just me with Kari."

I look down because now my eyes are watering. "You have Chase." Once out of my mouth, I regret every syllable.

Mom glares at me, lips trembling.

"Where's Kari?"

"In the car." She turns and strides out.

The *click, click, click* of her heels picks at my heart.

We pull into the driveway to swirling ambulance lights. Kari sniffs in the backseat, eyes red. I turn around to comfort her and see her face in her hands. Her body shakes as if reliving the accident all over again. Mom pulls alongside the ambulance, jerks the car into park, and hops out. I lean over and turn the key, shutting off the engine. Kari is now unbuckled and curled up like a whimpering puppy. I look out the window, but can't see anything. So I get out and help Kari into the house. I flick the TV on and slide a cartoon into the DVD player.

I step outside in time to watch the ambulance drive away. I don't see Mom, but Sshapa is left standing, watching the flashing lights fade. He glances my way before turning to the barn. Do I go after him? Explain myself? Beg for mercy? Staying with my sister is the responsible decision to make. I should have picked her up in the first place.

I sit by Kari on the couch. She rests her head on my lap, and I stroke her hair. "Dad will be okay. I'm sure this is nothing." I pull a fleece blanket off the back of the couch and tuck it around her. We sit and watch the cartoon. Or at least my eyes are open and pointed in that direction. Her steady, shallow breaths drift through the room. I hope she's sleeping because I don't think she got much last night. I lay my head against the couch and close my eyes.

The squeak of the back door awakens me. The TV screen is fuzzy. Sshapa slowly sinks into what used to be Dad's ripped easy chair that leans to one side. I don't really know what to say. Tears threaten to spill, but I force them away. Wipe my eyes. Because I don't know what to do, I stroke Kari's hair. She stirs. Looks at me and asks about our father. I'm hoping Sshapa will take it from here.

He stares at the television screen with weary lines creasing his weathered skin.

"Sshapa," I say in a quiet voice.

He looks at me.

"What's going on?"

"Turn off the TV and we'll talk."

I reach for the remote, push the off button, and toss it to the other side of the couch. Kari sits up and with sad eyes, gazes at Sshapa. He waves her over to his lap and she goes, settles herself in.

"Your father's chair tipped over when I was trying to get him in the car. His head hit the ground pretty hard. I thought we could do it. But I should have waited for help. Or canceled the appointment. I thought you were supposed to come home and help, but maybe in my old age I've gotten things jumbled up." He rocks Kari, holding her tight. "Don't worry my little *Swaskee*, he'll be all right. Your mother's with him." With a soft touch he pats her back.

His shaky tone suggests there is more, but I suspect he doesn't want to worry Kari, his precious blue jay. I lift my chin to speak, but nothing comes out. I drop my head and hug my knees. Do I come clean? Or dig the pit I'm stuck in a little deeper? The movie *Holes* pops into my head. I saw it when I was twelve. I think of all those holes in the ground that woman forced those boys to dig, looking for treasure, lying to them all about having an honest boys' home. It's the same kind of deception. Just packaged in a different box, topped with a black bow.

"Char, why don't you fix something to eat. Kari must be pretty hungry by now. You and I can talk later."

I nod, rise out of obedience to my elder, and walk numbly to the kitchen. Half empty cupboards offer a box of spaghetti and a jar of extra meaty sauce. I make dinner, not paying much attention to what I'm doing, just thinking of how I could justify my next lie. They began to stack like Legos. One lie connects to the next. *This rite of passage has to be worth it. At least the money will be. Provided I win.*

Once Kari's in bed, Sshapa calls me into the kitchen. He motions me to sit down. I do so, staring at the kitchen table.

"I know my body is old, but my mind is still sharp."

I nod. "It is. I was supposed to come home and help you. I forgot."

Sshapa takes a bite of peaches. He lays his fork on the table. Looks me in the eye. "What is this need to lie?"

"What? I'm…" I lift my hands in the air.

Sshapa studies my face. "Granddaughter, we've always been able to talk. Have we not?"

"We have." I slump in my chair.

"Why have you lied to me and your mother?"

"How did you know? You only saw her for a minute."

"It only takes a second to share a lie, don't you think?" He pauses. "Then that second turns into minutes, days, weeks, years. Before you know it, you don't know how to tell the truth. Can't recognize it any longer. It surrounds you, chokes you. Binds you so there's no escape."

I drop my gaze to my hands. "I'm sorry, Sshapa."

"Why didn't you tell me you wanted to change your senior presentation topic?"

"I figured you'd all get mad and try and stop me. Push the lawyer thing."

Sshapa smiles. "You're right. We would have fought you on it. But in the end, it's your project. You have to follow your heart." He takes another bite. Puts his fork on the table. "You didn't even try."

"Try?"

"What attempt did you make to talk to me about your desire to change your topic? What about your parents? You didn't even give it a shot."

"I'm sorry." The lie's fingers wrap around my throat, like an invisible noose. "I thought I needed to do this on my own. I'm a senior, ya know?"

"I see. Another lie?"

His eyes darken. He thinks he knows me, but he doesn't. Not really. No one does. I push away from the table and walk to my bedroom. Forms need to be filled out so I can hand in my Gates Scholarship application on time. I need to finish reading my chapter for AP History—a quiz a week. Kari, Dad, the ranch, no money, the pressure chokes me. I plop down on my bed.

The desire to toss it all to the wind temps me. Maybe I should stay home and work the ranch. I rest my head against the wall, staring at the 2010 poster of the Omak Stampede. Jockeys from the suicide race rim tipis from the encampment. The looks on their faces fill me with guilt and shame. What kind of warrior would I be if I quit? With a groan I hit the books.

Around ten mom pulls in. The engine shuts off. Only one door closes. I flick off my light, close my eyes, and curl up under my covers. I have to win.

CHAPTER 5

Kacey Musgraves's twangy voice singing *Dime Store Cowgirl* wakes me up. Am I the girl too big for her britches? I roll out of bed and wonder how I'm going to get out of all of this. Not the race, but the lies. I pull on my jeans and T-shirt and rush out the door. The cold claws at me so I go back in, find warm clothes, and circle back out. After turning on the water, I trot down to the barn and relax in the quiet. I feed the horses and sit outside Stimteema's stall, my mind replaying our wins at the North Central Washington Fair last month.

The half-mile, three-quarter-mile, and one-mile derby were easy victories. Every dollar counts. And with Chase making just under three thousand dollars off this year's steer, we should be able to buy more hay. Maybe next year he can keep the money for himself. Even though his savings account is shallow, the last couple of years he's chosen to donate the money to the ranch. It's pretty honorable really, especially for a fifteen-year-old. Guess he's earned a break. For a short time, anyway.

We're supposed to head out tomorrow for the Okanogan Fair, if we still get to go. We'll probably need the money for hospital bills, unless Indian Health covers what insurance doesn't. Winnings may only add up to twelve-hundred tops, but still. I walk over and open Stimteema's stall. Stroking her neck, I pray we win the Okanogan races. I pray for my father. I pray I can tell the truth, and have the guts to look Sshapa in the eyes.

I close the stall door and head for the house, turning off the water on my way. The tick of the clock is the only sound in the kitchen. On the table is a note next to Sshapa's truck keys. Mom's handwriting instructs me to get Kari ready and drive us both to school. I read on. *You'll be late, so I'll call and let them know why.* I grab the keys and read more. *Chase spent the night in town with a friend. Sshapa and I drove to the hospital early this morning. I'll fill you in later. Don't worry, things will be okay.* I stare at the note. Things will be okay? But why did you have to go in so early? They aren't telling me the whole story. Who are the liars now? I crumple the note and toss it in the garbage.

"Kari!" I shake her shoulder. "Wake up and get dressed. We're going to the hospital." I rummage through the cupboards and find pancake mix, eggs, and milk in the fridge and pour all the ingredients into a bowl and whip them all together. The more I think about Dad and the note and withheld information, the harder I beat the batter.

Kari pads into the kitchen, rubbing her eyes. "Why are we going to the hospital? I don't like it there. I don't want to go." Her voice pitches higher as her gaze roams the living room. "Where's Mom and Sshapa?"

I pour batter onto a hot skillet. "They're at the hospital. Come on *Swaskee*, let's get going." I smile. "Go and get dressed while I finish here."

"But I don't want to go. I want to go to school!" She sets her hands on her hips, lips pursed.

"Okay. You win. I'll drop you off before heading to the hospital. I'm sure Mom'll come find you sometime today." At least I'm guessing she will. Anything to give Kari a little peace and hope. To settle her tender heart.

Forty-five minutes later we pull into the school. Kari slides out and I watch her walk into the building, pink horse backpack slung over one shoulder. Once she's inside, I pull out, turn left, and follow Highway 21 as it winds around and up the hill to the Republic Hospital. Anger boils inside as I drive through the old mining town. They make a big deal out of me lying and they're doing the same thing. Why do adults think it's okay for them? "Nothing but double standards." I slap the steering wheel.

I turn right at the two rock columns holding the sign that reads Ferry County Memorial Hospital. The off-white, water-stained hospital looks stale. It's a small, one-story concrete building. Reminds me of a mental institution. After parking the truck, I stare at the building. They airlifted Dad to Spokane after he'd wrapped his truck around a tree like a pretzel. The only time I've been here was when Stimteema and I rolled down the hill behind our house. She scored a few scrapes and bruises, and I broke my left arm.

I pull the glass doors open and step into an empty lobby. An orange "Wet" sign alerts a warning to my right. The cramped foyer extends a help desk at ten o'clock and sitting area with a couple chairs and a few magazines to the right.

Ten minutes pass before a white-haired woman wearing frog-print scrubs appears and plops in a chair. "How can I help you," she asks without looking up.

"Sheldon Toulou's room, please." I tilt my head back and gaze at the ceiling.

Computer keys click. She tells me the room number and points the way. I thank her and turn down the hall. His room is a few yard away. But each step feels as though bricks are tied to my shoes and concrete poured into my legs. The fierce warrior attitude leaks courage with each drag of a foot. By the time I reach my father's room, there is no fight left. Eyes closed, his breath comes in raspy waves. The bed shrinks him to child-size.

Mom closes the magazine in her hands. The scrape of a chair captures my attention. Sshapa's waves me in. Hand against my throat, I tiptoe to Dad's side. An IV runs like veins into his arm. A heart monitor beeps. Mother gives me a weak smile.

Sshapa takes my hand. He motions for me to sit in the chair beside my father's bed.

My attention rests on Dad's plum-colored face. I suck in a breath as I settle in a chair and let the tears flow when I exhale. Steps squeak on linoleum outside the room. "Is he okay? Why is he here? And not in Spokane?" Shards of glass littering the ground flashes in my mine. So does the dark red stain on the pavement September rains tried to wash away. The vision shifts from dad's body twisted in the bushes to the hung-over log truck driver in cuffs.

Mom sits on the opposite side of the bed. "He'll be fine."

Fine? I shudder.

She puts a finger to her lips. "They gave him something to sleep. He bumped his head is all, Char. There's no major injury. They want to keep him here for observation." She turns and slips her husband's hand into hers. "He'll only be here a day or two." Her thumb rubs his purple skin. "Besides, I don't want him in Spokane. I know they can care for him here." She sighs. "I'm out of leave. At least here I can visit."

"There's nothing here! He needs to be flown to Spokane. This is stupid! This is no ICU. This tiny hospital doesn't have what he needs." My brain swirls leaving my body to sway.

Mom wears a worn expression on her face. "He's not critical. He doesn't need to be in ICU. He stays put. He's in good hands."

"Are you kidding me?" I glare at her.

Mom brushes her finger down his arm.

I sigh, knowing I won't change her mind. "What happened? I mean Sshapa told me he fell, but…" The lump in my throat stops the words from surfacing. My gaze travels from Mom, to the IV needle in his arm, to the squiggly lines on the heart monitor. I watch the lines on the screen dive and pitch. Dive and pitch.

"Like Sshapa said, he had trouble getting your father into the car. The wheelchair rolled back and your father was thrown to the ground. Head first. He's got some bumps and bruises and is pretty sore, but other than that, he'll be fine."

My mood softens. "How did the chair roll back? It's got brakes." I sweep my fingers across the bruise and scrapes on his face.

"I thought I had the brake set, but not sure if it got bumped or just didn't set it tight enough." Sshapa's voice sounds shaky.

"It's not your fault, Sshapa," I say. "It's mine. I should have been there instead of with the school board." *Telling a lie.* "I should have done what I was asked. I'm sorry." Tears slide down my cheeks.

"It was an accident," Mom says, her voice low. The bags under her eyes match my father's shade of purple on the side of his head.

"I better get to school." I rush to the truck, get in, and slam the door shut. Bile rises into my mouth. I bolt out of the truck and retch in the parking lot. I climb back in and wipe my mouth, searching for a sip of something to get rid of the acid taste. I pop in a hard candy that was left on the seat and start sucking. I fire up the engine and pull out of the parking lot. Instead of turning left to school, I turn right, drive nine and a half miles toward Curlew Lake, turn into the Black Beach Resort and RV Park, and pull up to a park edging the water.

Only a few cars are parked in front of the office, everything else is empty. I get out and slump onto the grass, staring at the reflection of orange and yellow trees and jagged mountains across the lake. Houses and cabins clutter the shoreline. Fortunately, this time of the year most of the tourists are gone. A thin curtain of haze hovers over the water. The smell of smoke hangs in the air and burns my nose.

I lie on my back in sparse grass and close my eyes. Only Creator knows what will happen in the next two weeks.

CHAPTER 6

"Char." Jill reaches over and taps my shoulder with her pencil. It skims my peripheral vision, but my brain doesn't connect it to the rest of me. "Char, did you hear me?"

I scowl. "What?" My focus sticks to my father in the cold hospital bed.

She shakes her head and in a whiny voice says, "What about our art project?"

I gaze down at the blank page. "What about a bay paint mare, an Okanogan girl, both she and her horse are in full regalia—blues, greens, purples, yellows." Excitement cracks my bleak mood. "It would be cool to draw the horse and girl George Flett style on old ledger paper. Have you seen his work before?"

Jill shakes her head. "You mean vintage ledger paper used for recording finances?"

I nod.

"Where do they get that kind of paper?"

"I don't know where he gets the paper, but I think some of it is from U.S. Army ledger books. His work is awesome. I saw it in Inchelium a while back. We were over there with family one year for Thanksgiving and took in a craft fair at the Catholic Church hall. I met George and picked through his drawings. I wish I would have had the guts to talk with him and buy one. I remember seeing "North American Light Company" and "Western Union" in the background of a few prints. Some of the ledger dates are early 1900s."

Jill taps her lips with a finger. "Is he Colville?"

I pull out a sheet of paper Mrs. Larson printed out for me of him wearing a blue denim shirt and blue jeans. He's posing on a chair in what appears to be a museum or art gallery. Behind him hangs three of his paintings and two pieces of men's dance bustles on the wall beside his art. I hand it to Jill.

"Hmm," She points to the bottom of the picture. " 'Rick Singer Photography.' " She gives me a judgmental look.

"I'm not selling it." I study the photo. "And no, he's Spokane." I scrunch my nose.

"Right." Jill chuckles. "His work is incredible."

"That's what I'm saying. I think we should make a drawing of an Okanogan girl our age in full regalia with a traditional bow and quiver and arrows across her back or hanging off the saddle—"

"I know, racing down the suicide hill, right?"

My mouth opens and closes like a fish on a riverbank.

Jill flicks a palm up. "I was right there when Hagan and his cronies were talking smack, remember?"

"Yeah," I say, "I like the idea. But let's have her on top of a grassy knoll. Do you like the ledger page for the background? Can you do it?" I narrow my eyes. "And no, I'm not racing down the hill." A heaviness perches on my shoulders.

"Right. Not tempted to race down the hill. I know you better than that."

"I didn't say I'm not tempted."

Jill lays the paper on the table. "Girl Warrior is a great name for this piece." She nods. "I think I can pull this off. You do realize with the ledger for the background there won't be a grassy knoll."

I shrug. "Doesn't matter."

She retrieves an easel and settles in a chair.

I get the canvas and colored pencils. "I know we talked about doing a project with all different races, but…"

"But you need to prove yourself and I get that. You ride in a man's world. So for now, we'll work on this, and do the harmony project next. I'm okay with it. I have your back, Char. You should know that by now."

"Yeah, but it feels self-centered." I hand her the pencils. "However, I do ride in a man's world with a bunch of chauvinist *coo-coos*."

Jill gives me a confused look.

"Chauvinist pigs." I imagine *coo-coos* strung up, hog-tied, and ready to butcher. Knife in hand, I volunteer to slice nice fat pork chops. Instead, my focus shifts to art class. "And I do know you've got my back."

We work all period sketching an outline on paper. There are only six of us in this class. The others have art projects, but I don't pay attention to them. After a while, my mind wanders to the image of my father lying in a hospital bed hooked up to machines, tube down his throat. It shifts over to my mom's shadowed, worn eyes. Sshapa's thin, straight lips and tired face. Out of nowhere

Mrs. Larson saunters over to me, golden curls bouncing like the tone in her voice. "How's your father, Charnaye?" Her eyebrows scrunch.

I give her a crooked smile. Jill's head snaps my way and I ignore it. "He's fine. Thanks for asking." She pats my shoulder and clicks over to the next student in her green heels.

"What's wrong with your father?" Jill says.

I shrug and tell her.

"Is he going to be okay? Why is he not is Spokane?" Her face twists.

I sigh. "Mom wants him close. She's worn out. Two years of caring for him and the ranch, not to mention my grandfather, it's too much."

Jill rests her pencil on her lap. "I'm sorry. What can I do to help?"

"Nothing!" I close my eyes, rubbing the back of my neck. "I'm sorry. I didn't mean to..." I grasp the colored pencils, put them away, and rush out, leaving Jill hurt and confused I'm sure. I head straight for the girl's bathroom and splash water on my face. I lean against the cool, brick wall and slide down the floor until my breathing slows. Walking out, I bump into Chase.

We stare at each other for a moment before I ask, "Did you see Dad yet?"

His upper lip curls. "Where were you? Why didn't you make it home to help Sshapa?"

My gaze drops to the floor.

"Man, you're selfish. But I guess you're a senior, big girl on campus. Can do what you want. I knew it was wrong to stay with Justin. Guess from now on I'll stay home and make sure you don't screw up again." The vein on the side of Chase's neck protrudes.

I open my mouth to defend myself, but my brother continues his rant.

"What's so important you couldn't get Kari? Make Mom miss her parent meeting. Oh, wait, what…instead of being a lawyer you're gonna race down 'the hill' now. Big stuff!" He pounds the wall above my head. "It's always about you!"

I flinch.

"It's all around school, warrior girl…or queen of the hill…is that it?" Chase goes to walk off, but I grab his arm and fling him around.

"What if I am? It's none of your business. And yes, I should have been there, don't you think I know that?" The volume of our voices baits teachers out of their classes. "There's more to this than you know."

"Like what?"

Mr. Shelton frowns. "Everything under control here?"

"Yes!" Chase marches off.

I'm not sure if I'm looking at concern or irritation or a mixture of both when Mr. Shelton's attention turns to me. I nod. "We're fine." I walk off, picking up speed as I jog past the English and wrestling rooms. I push out the door and down the covered walkway that leads to the sunken football field. Taking two steps at a time, I land hard on the track and run.

The vice principal must have notified Mrs. McMillan, our librarian, because as I turn the fourth corner, she is standing on the track in a yellow dress and high heels in my lane. I'm glad it's her and not Mr. Deadbeat, our school counselor. His real name is Mr. Drifface. Should be doofus for all he's worth. It's past time for him to retire. None of us can relate to some old grandpa with aged ideas and incompetent advice.

Mrs. McMillan smiles, arms out. I run into them and cling tight. She strokes my hair and lets me sob. "It's going to be all right." She puts her arm around me and leads me back to the library, her thick blond hair waving in the wind.

"Mr. Aspen knows where you are and so does your next period's teacher. We realize you're under stress with your family situation, so if you need to talk we can or you can just hang out until you feel like going back to class."

I sink in a chair by her desk. The library's deserted so I unload on her. Tell her the accident is my fault. Tell her it hurts to breathe. Tell her my dad has to pull through or I don't know how Mom will make it.

"I'm sorry." Mrs. McMillan hands me a tissue. "Does your family blame you?" She eases into her desk chair.

I shrug. "Chase does. That's why we were arguing."

She takes my hand. "We all make wrong decisions, but blaming yourself for the accident…that's a lot to carry around." She gently tucks a wisp of hair behind my ear. "Don't you think Chase hurts deep down, too? Maybe he blames himself for being gone. It's important to support each other in times like these. Blame doesn't make the accident go away. It doesn't help your father. Or your mother or grandfather. Does it?"

I study her chestnut brown eyes. "Guess not."

"How's Kari?"

"Fine."

"Is she still seeing the counselor?"

I tilt my head.

"Your mom's kept me up to date since the accident. Even grown-ups need to vent. In fact, she asked if I thought you or Chase needed to talk to someone."

"What'd you say?"

"Something like, 'Well, Arlie, you have two strong, amazing teenagers who I think will

pull through just fine. But I'll keep an eye out, make sure they don't pull any shenanigans." She gives me one of her easy-going smiles.

I nod, knowing we aren't fine. Kari's screams last night proves it. "Better get to class."

Mrs. McMillan hesitates before saying, "Is there anything else bothering you?"

I glance away. "I…"

"It's not healthy to keep it all inside."

I shrug. "Hagan keeps harassing me."

Mrs. McMillan shares her own childhood experiences with boys and what she calls strategies against bullying. We spend an additional ten minutes forming a plan of action for the next time Hagan approaches me with his threats and lies.

"Don't tell anyone yet. I want to try and handle it myself first." I stand to leave.

"For now." She gives me a stern look. "Come back and see me if you need to talk. And I'll be watching him." She holds up a finger. "One more thing, if you say you're going to do something, it's always wise to follow through. Yes?"

CHAPTER 7

Kids laugh and scream, music blares over a loud speaker, animals—they all buzz the air at the Okanogan Fair. The white edge of Stimteema's eyes flash as her gaze darts from person to person and horse to horse. While I rub her and pray for safety and protection, she cocks a back leg and lowers her head. I work my way from head to tail using gentle, slow strokes. When my fingers tire, I take a short water break and wrap her legs. Mom hands me the blanket with today's number she picked up from the office, and we tighten and buckle each side of the girth with equal pressure.

"You nervous?" Mom wiggles the saddle, making sure it's settled on Stimteema's back.

"No," I watch another rider saddle his horse over her shoulder, "it's just another race."

She arches her brow. "Okay. Be safe then." She pats my shoulder and heads for the stands.

I reach for the bridle, but it's not there. I search the tack room and come up empty. Then the truck. Not there. Stimteema's ears flicker. Footsteps approach. I tense, hoping it's not Chase.

Images of Dad in the hospital, wires everywhere, creep into my mind. Chase's accusing words sink their claws in and tear deeper. I need to find a way to shake them off before I step into the saddle. But I haven't found it yet.

"You about ready?"

I flinch at the sound of my brother's voice. "Almost." My gaze locks on the tack room.

"Joe Best is gonna pony you."

He disappears and returns with a bridle in hand. Then fits it to my mare.

I lean on Stimteema and say one last prayer, trying to release the hurt and anger that crushes my chest. I breathe and try to relax, fingers entwined in her mane. I imagine us coming out of the gate, straight, and in the lead. We round each corner and cross the finish line. A smooth ride. Or so I hope.

"Listen, I'm sorry for what I said at school. It's not your fault. I was mad I wasn't there to help Sshapa." He shifts his weight.

I nod. "Let's go."

We meet Joe Best near the track. He smiles, exposing crooked teeth. I've never seen anyone as short and squatty as him work a horse like he does. He takes wild horses and gentles them within a few hours with nothing but a soft touch and a calm voice. I shake his hand and check the girth one last time. Chase gives me a leg up. I slip my boots into the irons and tighten my grip on the rein as Stimteema prances in circles. Joe grips the lead strap and snubs her close, speaking in a low, soothing tone.

"Hey, Charnaye," Billy Beck says. "You back for more?"

"Ha! You ready to eat my dirt?" I say with a smirk. His black and orange ribbon shirt with a bear claw embroidered on the back sweetens his sour presence. His helmet has the same native print bandana wrapped around it, the back corner flapping with each bounce. His etched face twists. His thick lips and nose are as large as his ego.

"Not sure why you keep showing your face. This is a man's sport. There's no room for a pretty little thing like you. Look around, the other girls have already figured that one out. What's taking you so long?" Billy turns his horse in a few circles.

"Yeah, looks like you have great control today." *One more coo-coos to string up and butcher.*

Tone Highwater watches from the back of his horse. His gentle dusky eyes and soft face match his spirit. His turquoise blue and red ribbon sleeveless shirt reveal lengthy, muscular arms. He's been cheering me on the last couple years. Each crumb of advice he shares bumps me up a place or two. Our gazes lock and he nods.

"Hey, brother." I nod back. His courage ignites me.

Joe and I ride down the track a good clip before Chase grabs the lead strap and guides me into the starting gate. He climbs on top of the side panel and holds Stimteema's head still and straight.

"Three-quarters of a mile, this is a breeze for her." Chase pats her neck.

I stare straight ahead, grab a handful of mane, and wait for the gate to pop open. Horses bang the sides of the 2.5' X 8' cast iron stalls.

Chase leans close. Closer than he should. "Ride for Dad."

I swallow the lump in my throat.

Gates burst open. Stimteema launches forward. I'm jerked to the side but manage to hang on and keep my balance. We gain the number three position, two lengths behind the number two horse. Three lengths behind the number one horse. My focus locks on the jockey in front of me. I reach back and spank Stimteema with a crop. When we come around the corner, she sling-shots into the lead. I reach back and spank her again with my crop as we come down the straightaway in front of the stands for a second and last pass. Nose out, she stretches forward with each stride. I smile inside knowing what Billy Beck just had for lunch.

I pull my mare to a lope, happy for another win under my belt—more money toward hospital bills. Gratitude floods me as Stimteema slows. We circle our way back on the track and search for Joe. He catches us, a huge smile across his face.

"Great ride." He latches on to Stimteema's rein and pulls us to a stop. We find our way to the front of the stands for a family picture. I unbuckle the girth, letting my mare breathe freely. Mom orders Joe to dismount and stand with the family. He hands his horses to a friend and takes a spot behind her. I hear him whisper, "You got one talented girl, Arlie." She swipes a tear. I wish Dad was here. This win is for him.

Joe ponies the horses back to the barn while I walk with Chase, feather-light saddle in hand. Chase puts away the saddle and bridle. I walk Stimteema until she's breathing easy, rinse her legs to shrink tissue together, and rub her muscles down with liniment. Someone standing near the horse trailer captures my attention.

"Nice riding today," says Tone Highwater. He's got his little brother Zack with him. Zack's chocolate ice-cream covered face resembles his big brother. I fluff his hair. He giggles and offers me a taste. I look at the mess all over his shirt and hands and politely decline.

"Your colt is coming along nicely," I say. "Did you come in third in the half-mile?"

"Yep. He broke out of the gate a bit slow, but coming from last place to third isn't bad. He's quick and I'm thinking next year, we'll give you a run for your money. Ayyyz!" He hands Zack a napkin.

"I bet you will." I run my gaze over his strong arms and tight, tanned six-pack.

"Well, just wanted to come and congratulate you. Got to take this one to see the cows and sheep." He ruffles his brother's hair.

"Yep. Pigs too. You promised." Zack wipes his chocolate covered hands on his pants.

"Who's taking care of your horse?"

He grins. "My sister. We bet. She lost. Now I get to have some fun." He gives me a two finger salute.

I watch them walk away. I love how he's so into his little brother. What's not to love about this guy? Drop-dead gorgeous, nice, the perfect smile. The kind of guy I'd like to have around.

"That is such a nice boy," Mom says as she approaches.

I find myself staring at his back. "Yep, sure is. But he's too nice. Besides, he's more like a brother."

"No such thing as too nice."

I shake my thoughts away and turn to her. Mom's face appears bright as if a spark has ignited passion back in her life. Her stance is relaxed. I'm glad she came. Just her, me, and Chase. She let Kari stay the weekend with a friend. I'm guessing she hopes my sister will be forced to laugh and play little girl games. Maybe she won't have nightmares if she doesn't have to look at dad in his wheelchair for a day.

"Your father will be proud of you. I know I am." She hugs me.

"I wish he could be here."

"Me too, Char. But you know he needs to be home resting. Your grandfather's taking good care of him. I'm glad he pushed me into coming with you. I need the break. I also need an Indian Taco. Want to come find one with me?"

"Sure. Just let me change."

"Great. I'll meet you over there. I'll go stand in line, it's a long one." She gestures to the food vendors.

I hurry and slip on fresh jeans and a purple T-shirt with a horse on it and a caption that reads: Life is better when you're on a horse. Kari bought it for me two Christmases ago. I agree with the saying. My mom always tells us girls, "Horses are cheap therapy." If I could only bottle their smell. I give Stimteema a shallow bucket of water before meeting Mom. On the way I find myself face to face with Hagan.

His eyes search me like a hungry wolf. I try not to burst into hysterics. He's tried these scare tactics since he was a kindergartner. The weaker kids he can intimidate. But the rest of us, we grow taller.

"Heard you changed your senior project, from lawyer to, did I hear this right, let's see…World Famous Omak Suicide jockey. Don't you think you're taking this Native girl act a little too far?"

"It's my culture." I lift my chin and stare back at him, not flinching. "Don't flatter yourself. It has nothing to do with what you said the other day. The race is about a rite of passage, something you'll never earn."

"Really? Well, I *am* flattered." He smirks, leaning closer to me.

I smell chew on his breath. It makes me gag. "My people have been running that race for generations. It's our way." I push him back a step.

He grabs my arm.

Chase wheels him around and lands a left hook to his right cheek. "Leave my sister alone. Jerks like you have no place around our women." He pushes him and Hagan stumbles backward. Chase pushes him again. "Get out of here or I'm gonna pound your freakin' face."

Onlookers crowd toward us in a semi-circle.

Hagan scans the crowd and smirks. "Since little kids are watching I'm gonna back off. For now." His voice makes a deep, growling sound. "I'll be back, trust me."

Chase and I catch up with Mom.

"What took you two so long?" She searches our faces. "Your food's getting cold."

Chase looks away.

"Just making sure Stimteema's settled in." I glare at my brother.

Mom claps her hands. "Great! Let's eat before we load up and head home. Really, I'm in no hurry." She slathers a fry in ketchup and shoves it in her mouth.

It's dark by the time we get home. I unload Stimteema and settle her into the stall.

Sshapa's in the barn. His face lights up when he sees mine. "Hey, my horse racer. I heard you won two of your races. And third in the mile derby? That's my girl."

"I should have won the derby, but I let her get boxed in. Couldn't find an opening to get around the traffic." I hug my grandfather.

"You cannot win them all. You took two of them, two-thirds, right?"

I smile. "There you go again, math with no letters."

Sshapa forks hay into my horse's stall. We feed and water together. I turn off the water at the house and walk back to the barn. I need more answers. Grandfather is not telling me everything about the suicide race. I watch him replace a latigo on an old western saddle by the dim lights in the barn. "Sshapa, tell me more about the race. You told me how it began, in Keller. But…I think… you're holding back. What are you not telling me?"

He buckles the cinch to the new latigo strip and perches himself on a hay bale. He pats the space beside him. I know he's about to tell me what's good for me. It may not be what I want to hear, but it's always the truth. "Your Stimteema rode him down the Keller hill when she was your age." He points to his tall, bony quarter horse gelding. A blue roan with a ratty tail. Most of his teeth are mere stubs and we have to feed him beet pulp just to keep him alive.

I walk over to Old Blue and watch him eat. "Why didn't you tell me this before?"

"She didn't want us to. It was before we were married, one month prior anyhow," he said with a hitch in his voice. He wrings his hands.

"Why? What's the big deal?"

"Because she knew you had that same streak of spitfire in you that lived in her." He pops a stem of hay in his mouth. "She saw it in you as a baby."

I try and imagine her plunging down the old Keller hill. "Was she sober?"

Sshapa chuckles. “She was.”

I drop beside my grandfather. “How’d she do?”

“She held her own. Didn’t come in last,” he says. “Boy, could she ride. I tried to talk her out of it. But like you”—he places his hand over mine—“she had to prove herself to the world.”

CHAPTER 8

I shove through the high school doors just as the bell rings. Overnight, winter has whipped up icy roads and dropped a foot of snow. I thought December had buried us. January looks like we'll get dumped on even more. There are already two feet. What's a couple extra, right?

I dash down the hall and bump into Carla Comak, the new girl. "Sorry," I say.

She glares at me like I'm a piece of trash. I hear she's some fancy horse show champion and by the looks of her, she loves to sparkle. Shiny Montana Silver earrings dangle from small ears and a big brown belt sparkles in the light. She has some kind of expensive quarter horse and cleans house down in Nampa, Idaho every summer at regionals. Her long, flaxen curls and fancy snip-toed cowboy boots contrast her snarky demeanor. Her blue eyes resemble tropical water, still and peaceful.

I make my way to the library. Sam leans against a bookcase, holding hands with his girlfriend, Sally McRae. A twinge in my stomach constricts. She's a nice girl. Smart, pretty, athletic. She has hair the color of straw, big emerald eyes, and a delicate mouth. Basically everything that attracts a guy. Rumors of marriage have run rampant this year. I guess we'll see. They both hope to attend Central Washington University next year, Sam tells me. So maybe they will. They catch me staring at them. My gaze drops to the floor.

"Hi, Charnaye," Sally says.

"Hey. How's it going?" It's hard to hate a girl this pleasing. She's down to earth. Her entire family is wonderful and active in the community. I sigh. Boy, how I wish I was her. Attached to him.

"Good. Thanks. I hope you guys get a lot of studying done. I don't know about you, but this AP History is kicking Sam's butt. And you have Precalc on top of it? I could never do that." She shakes her head and turns to Sam. "See you later." She kisses Sam and bounces out the door. He watches her and I watch him. *Lucky girl.*

He turns to me and grins. It melts me like ice cream on an August afternoon. I drag my focus off him, settle in a chair, and stare at my history book. Six other students are studying as well, but their voices are low. Sam sits across from me and cracks his book open. "Want to tackle the chapter review questions?"

"Sure. What's first?" My thoughts wander back to the way they look at each other. Shivers race up my arms. I wonder if that's how my parents felt about each other when they met. I wonder if I'll ever find that kind of love. I'm not sure I want to let anyone that close. Most boys are as mean and ornery as a hungry badger. I sneak a quick glance at Sam. I find myself thumbing through the pages and not knowing where to stop.

He taps the book. "You with me?"

"Um, yeah. Sorry." I find the right chapter.

"How did U.S. presidents and Congress seek to reintegrate the Confederacy into the Union?"

"Oh, boy. Well…" I hunt for the right answer. I can't find it.

"You okay? Normally these answers come right to ya."

At the sight of him my stomach drops to my toes. I nod. "Uh-huh." By the look on his face, he's not convinced.

"What's up, Char?" He leans back in his chair. "Everything okay at home? Is your dad all right?"

I swallow hard. His round eyes weaken my knees. No way can I tell him to dump Sally for me. No way would he even consider it. I'm a fool. "Nothing, really. Let's get through this." We discuss this question and others that deal with creating and preserving a continental nation from 1844-1877. This would be meaningful if it had a local thread. My head pounds by the time we finish. But being able to talk things out helps the information stick. No matter how thin the session.

After the final bell rings, I close my book. Sam heads out, and I check in with Mrs. McMillan. I convince her things are going well. "Kari's nightmares are less and less and my father is back to his crazy, funny self."

"And your mom?" she says.

"She's…she's still upright. That student who was giving her a hard time has settled down so yeah, she's doing better. My sister seems happier, and if Mom's happy and relaxed so is Kari, she looks…well…"

"More relaxed?"

My fingers drum the table. "Yeah. And younger I guess."

"Glad to hear it. Thanks for checking in." Mrs. McMillan runs a book tag under her scanner and into the computer system.

I stand by her desk, wanting to tell her how much I love Sam. Explain how unfair life is that he's with Sally.

"What's on your mind?" she says.

I open my mouth. Shut it. Shake my head. "Nothing. Better get to archery."

I turn the corner on my way to the elementary gym when I meet Hagan, Carla, and their snobby friends in the hall. Hagan purposely slams into me. My books fly out of my arms and skid across the linoleum. I fist my hand, ready to lunge. "Oops, sorry, Charnaye. I really need to watch where I'm going." I put my hand down, not wanting to play into his head games. He looks at his buddies, a smirk on his face. They circle me like a pack of hungry jackals.

Carla snickers. "Yes, you do, Hagan." She turns to me and crosses her arms. "Nice T-shirt." Her eyes scrutinize me from head to toe. You'd think as the new girl, she'd have a few more manners. "Your hair would look great in braids. There are a lot of girls like you with pretty twisted hair in different designs. Might lighten your features." She puts up a hand like she's about to touch my hair and I slap it away. "No need to be harsh. I was just going to smooth out those loose strands."

"People like me? Sure you were." I hold her gaze.

"Burn!" One of Hagan's friends snickers.

Hagan's cronies laugh. I wonder if they can think on their own. They've been his puppets for so long now I doubt it. Probably their parent's puppets, too. The yes sir type that comes from being gutless.

"I didn't mean it like that." Carla gives me a snarky smile.

"Right. Of course not." I step closer to her.

She takes a step back. "Come on Hagan, let's go. She can't be late."

"Yes, don't be late for archery." He grabs a pretend arrow out of a pretend quiver from his back and nocks it to his fake bow, using me as the target. "See ya shortly."

Do guys really do that? What idiots. And do girls like her really think stuff like that is cool? *Losers.*

They push past me. I gather my books, not sure why her words stab me in the heart, but they do. *People like me?* What does that mean? What, because I'm Native? Because we don't have new rigs and brand-named clothes? No cell phones or internet? I don't care what Hagan says. He's no better than the muck on the bottom of my boots after cleaning stalls. Tears threaten so I duck into the laundry room just outside the gym and slam the door shut. I flip the dryer on and crouch against the wall next to the washer. I suck in a sob and let loose. It's one thing for Hagan to talk down to me, but Carla? Really? Pretty ladylike for a glitzy cowgirl. At one time I thought we might be friends. I guess not. Hagan and his herd must be rubbing off on her. When she first came, she seemed nice. What a lie.

After I get my wits about me, I turn off the dryer and walk to the gym. I hope I don't see my mom. She checks in with me every once in a while to see my progress. I'm glad she's involved and all, but not today. I don't want to talk about my feelings or anything else. And I know if she sees my puffy, red eyes she'll pull me out and try for a heart to heart. I duck into the girl's bathroom and splash cool water on my face. Long bangs would be an asset right now.

A little girl skips in. "Why are you sad?"

I hate honest little kids. "I'm not," I say with conviction. "What are you doing over here? You should be in your building."

"Yeah, right," she says and walks into the stall. The little redhead looks the size of a second grader, freckles covering her nose and cheeks. "I wanted to see what this side looks like."

I press the dispenser lever, rip off a square of paper towel, and pat my face dry. When did small children learn to speak so freely? A toddler yes, but a child that size? Normally when they enter school and have a few hard knocks, they tone down. Not her. I look in the mirror and see my eyes are still puffy. Little feet drop to the ground. Out comes the ball of fire.

"You didn't flush," I say. The mirror shows her swirl around.

She flushes and comes along side me. "I usually remember. You gonna tell me why you're sad and why you're lyin' about it." She stands on her tiptoes and flicks the water on.

"Why do you care?" I say. "Where is your teacher? She fall asleep? Why aren't you on the bus?"

She shakes her head. "A fourth grader was mean to me today. She told me I was stupid and didn't know how to throw a ball at recess." Her gaze drops to the floor, chin trembling. "I missed the bus so my dad's coming to get me."

I bend down, eye to eye. "She's wrong. You're not stupid. I'm sorry she said that. But remember, people will always call you names. Give you a hard time. You got to know how cool you really are."

Her big green gaze lifts. "I'm cool? You really think so?"

I put out my fist. "I know so."

We fist bump and I head to the gym. I hate mean girls. They're stupid and full of themselves. Like Carla Comack.

I push the gym doors open and find my bow. Hagan hovers close by, so I go to the opposite end of the gym. Arrows fill orange traffic cones. I grab one, stand sideways, my right foot at a forty-five-degree angle, and take a deep breath. I focus on the target—the black circle in the middle of the round target. Hagan's face flashes in my mind, and I replace it with Carla's. I shake my head and nock my arrow, focus on the bottom right of the target. I pull back, chest out. My fingers release the string and the arrow soars, sticking into the center of the target.

"Looks like you'll eat tonight," Jill says from behind me.

I swing around. "Where'd you come from?"

"I watched you stomp in. You looked like you were on a mission. Walked right past me. You didn't hear me say hello. What's going on with you?"

I force calmness into my voice. "I'm sorry. My mind's on the next AP History test. It's gonna be tough."

She searches my eyes before saying, "Liar!" She laughs.

I shake my head. "Ever figure out what you want to be when you grow up? You could always be a truth teller! Ayyyz!"

Jill shakes her head. "No. Maybe. I'm thinking about working some and going to a community college."

"Don't blame you." I catch of glimpse of Hagan staring at me, pointing an arrow at my head.

He walks over and crowds out Jill.

"Hey! Knock it off." Jill shoves him aside.

He doesn't even acknowledge she's there. "Want to bet on tomorrow's competition?" He's holds his bow to my face.

I grunt, sick of his ongoing intrusions. One more year. That's all I have to endure of him, is one more year.

Jill says, "No."

"I wasn't talking to you," Hagan says, his voice deep and low. He levels an evil sneer at her. "You up to it?" he says to me.

I act like I'm considering his offer. "Um…no." I take a couple steps away.

"I'll make it worth your while."

I stop and survey him. "Oh, yeah? Like you have anything I'd want."

Jill grabs my arm and pulls me to the bleachers.

"He's so full of crap," I say. But at the same time, I wonder if there is really something he could have that I want or need? Or is this just another con job? I put my bow on the rack and grab my backpack. A folded slip of paper floats to the floor as I pull my water bottle out of a side pocket. Jill picks it up and hands it to me. I unfold it, read the scribbled words, shove it in my jean pocket, and stomp out of the gym, red-faced.

CHAPTER 9

Sshapa drives me to Omak for the archery competition because he has to purchase supplies after. I'm glad because the last thing I want to do is ride the bus with Hagan, although I'm still curious about his bet. What could he offer me that I'd want? I don't care about material things like he does. Everything I need is at home. Or right here with me.

"Ready for this archery match?"

I glance over at Sshapa. Deep crow's feet outline his eyes. I shake my head and grin. "Wrestling has matches. This is a competition. Just a fun, simple contest of skill." There is a peppermint candy between us and I reach for it, unwrap it, and pop it into my mouth. The note stuffed in my backpack slips back into my mind. *Don't even think about racing. You'll regret it!* I'm sure it's one of Hagan's tricks to get inside my head. He knows I'm good, otherwise he wouldn't have said anything. *Lowlife.*

Sshapa eyeballs me. "That was my last one."

I drag my thoughts back to his comment. "Oh, sorry. But thanks, it's for good luck." I stuff the wrapper in a plastic garbage bag that hangs from his shift stick—give him a courtesy grin.

Sshapa winks. "You seem a little preoccupied lately. Everything all right?"

"Yeah." I wish people would stop asking.

Sshapa concentrates on the road. I know he's letting me assemble the nerve to spill my guts. It's his way. I've never been able to fool him. Ever. "*Steem uss spaoos*? Tell me what is in your heart."

I look at my hands. Fiddle with my fingers. Then sigh. I don't want to have to talk about this. But I know he'll pester me until it's out. So I may as well get it over with. "My workload is too much. Can't catch a breath. Kids are bothering me at school and I'm tired of it."

Sshapa nods. His eyes and hands follow each turn and twist of the highway. "What are they doing?"

"It's not so much what they do. It's what they say." I cross my arms over my chest.

"Oh? What do they say?" A frown spreads over Sshapa's face.

"They just make rude racial remarks." I go back to fiddling with my hands. I'm almost an adult and need to learn to deal with these kinds of obstacles. Yet at this moment, I feel like a little girl sitting on Sshapa's lap and crying because I fell down and have a skinned knee. Father tells me we can't change the past. I know this. He tells me hanging onto the venom and bitterness doesn't move us into anything peaceful. He says we all have to move forward. Learn from our pasts and just keep walking. Be thankful for today. He tells me to help heal the wounds by creating a bridge of harmony between

Indians and non-Indians. It's not so easy. Especially when the bridge is cracked.

"Some kids learn sour attitudes from family and beliefs. Many are spoiled and feel entitled." Sshapa lets me chew on this. "It benefits no one."

"It hurts, Sshapa. You guys have always taught us that every life is valuable to Creator. He made us and we all count. From the unborn to the old and frail."

"But?"

"But it's hard to think rotten people count."

I look out the window and watch trees speed by. Desautel Pass is beautiful this time of year. White capped branches sparkle in the sunshine. I let the windy road speak to me as we meander for miles. It tells me to be patient and trust with each corner we take.

After a time of reflection, Sshapa says, "Do you know Chief Jim James' story about the origin of guardian spirits and Sweat Lodge?"

"I know he was a Sanpoil chief. But I don't think I've heard this legend."

Sshapa has one of those looks in his eyes, the kind that takes him back to the old days. "Sweat Lodge was a chief long ago. He decided to create birds and named them, too. He went on to say people would come and tell the boys and girls what to do and encourage them. They'd be good hunters and fishermen and things would come easily for them. He told the people that whoever desires to construct him will be able to. The one who prays for him would receive their wish. They could come to him for healing and help. In this world, he was there to help the human beings."

I sat quietly and thought for a while. "Are you saying I need to sweat and ask Creator for guidance?"

Sshapa smiles. "That is always a good idea. What I am saying is there are kids who were created to heal the land with words. With kindness and love. I believe you are one of them."

Words without actions are empty. My hand lifts to my neck, and I know I need to do more than a report. The race beckons to me. Calls me by name as I hold this custom deep in my heart. I know it's not just for guys. I can earn this honor just like they do. The bad part is I'd have to lie about racing. How, I'm not sure. But it would be worth it. We need the money. Father needs a better life. Mom an easier time of things. But where do I start? Who could I contact? What horse will I ride? Stimteema's long legs run great on the flat track, but I'm not sure how'd she do coming off a drop the size of the suicide hill. We've swum water, but to plunge in like they do? Her tall legs? I just don't know.

The only thing worse than chickening out would be to qualify, get dumped in the water, and be eliminated.

CHAPTER 10

The noise of the crowd makes me dizzy. It bounces off Omak High School's gym floor. Not even the tarp drowns out the voices. We beat the bus here. So I find us a place to sit in the bleachers and wait. It won't be long. There are ten schools here for this event. Should be a good one. I think the tribe pitched in for awards: jackets, T-shirts, food, arrows, and even a Genesis bow for the highest score. It's the brand we have to compete with at state in Ellensburg.

Last year I won my division. Three of the girls that were in the top five stroll by. One is from Inchelium and two from Omak. A fourth from this area is from Curlew. I don't see her yet. She's one of the few that talks to me. Great shooter. It's funny how girls come here with pretty jewelry, acrylic nails, and too much make-up, as though here for a Glamour photo shoot.

One such girl is perched two kids down. I cover my mouth as I let loose a snort. She looks to be in middle school with Nike everything from head to toe, bright orange nails, and dark, short hair held in place by a can of hairspray. *Really?* My dirty brown Ariats squeeze my feet and make me squirm. I run my tightly braided hair through my hands and caress my unadorned earlobes. From hers dangle long, green, glittery earrings. It's stupid to wear them because the rules don't allow it. A girl on my left bumps into me, giggling and flirting with a boy behind her. I shove her off me.

Sshapa catches up on all of his man-gossip in between watching me and his partner's grandkids. He's huddled with three friends in the bleachers, their lips running.

My teammates file in. Hagan brings up the rear, strutting like a rooster. He stops in front of a National Archery in the Schools (NASP) banner hanging on the wall and appears to be posing. What a hack. Jill bounces over to me.

"Made it." Jill bumps my shoulder.

"Ready for today?" I bump her back.

"I am. But some of the bows were left behind. Guess who volunteered to share with you."

I stare at Hagan. He catches me glancing at him and tosses me a sly grin. I cringe. "No way."

"Yep. He eagerly volunteered before I could open my mouth. Then whispered something about some bet?" She tied her shoe. "Coach won't let us swap."

I shake my head. "No bet."

"He said there was a bet."

"There is no bet. He's trying to bait me. I'm not hooking." I pull out a protein bar from my pack, unwrap it, and tear off a hunk with my teeth. The crumpled up note stares back at me. What will I regret? Did Hagan write this? I study him.

"Do you even know what that bet is about?" she says. "Did he say what's at stake?"

"No." I dig in my bag and search for my leather forearm guard. "Don't care."

"Maybe you should."

I look at Jill. "What did you hear?"

"He's betting you a horse. A suicide horse that's already run and has done well. Someone needed some serious cash, dumped the horse. His dad picked it up in Omak a couple weeks ago."

"Hang on, that means his dad owns it. Not Hagan. He can't bet something he doesn't own. What a cull." I slip on my forearm guard. "I'm gonna go practice before they start calling for us." I rise.

Jill grabs my arm and pulls me back down. "He has pictures of the horse. A big red chestnut. Kind eyes. I saw them."

"I suppose everyone knows about it."

Jill nods. "Everyone."

I trot down three steps of bleachers and head for a bow dangling off its rack. I shot it last, so it will be at my draw weight, unless someone messed with it. I grab a blue bow. Hagan closes his fingers around the end of my bow and holds tight. I glare at him. "What?"

"Want the bet or not?"

"What? To a lame horse?" I shake my head. "No thanks."

"You've been talking to Jill. I knew she'd run right to you. Faithful friend."

"She is." I try and jerk the bow free, but he holds tight. "You're freakin' crazy. Stay away from me."

"Bet or no bet. Here's what he looks like." He holds out a crinkled photo of the horse Jill described.

"You okay?" a voice says.

I lift my gaze to see a tall, lean guy staring at me. He's a foot taller than I am. His face is soft and inviting with big, dark brown eyes. Perfect teeth. I swallow. I've seen this guy before. Where?

Hagan lets go of the bow. "Just having a little conversation about a horse."

I push the picture out of my face.

The hunk glues his gaze on mine. Steps closer.

The track. That's where I've seen him. "Just warming up." I tilt my head. "I'm Charnaye."

"Yeah. I know." He leans in. "Let me know if you need anything." He sits close and watches us.

Hagan shoves the picture in my hand. "Just in case you change your mind." He stands behind the bow line and waits his turn.

This horse is strong, big boned, and the look in his eyes reflects courage. His legs are straight with nice big hooves. I can't imagine how heart-wrenching it was for whomever to have to give him up. What could be more important than this big boy? Did kids need food? Did debts need to be paid? Did a rig break down that was needed to get someone to work? I shake my head. "No bet. I wasn't born yesterday." I give the picture back.

Hagan laughs. "Why not? Got a better one than the old plug you ride?" He searches my face. "No way. You're not considering riding that nag of yours, are you?"

I lift my chin. "Can't bet on a horse I've never seen, let alone ridden." I'm not taking the bait. That "old nag" is the best thing that's ever happened to me.

"If you don't believe me ask Tone Highwater. He's over there"—Hagan motions with his head—"He's ridden him. Go on. Ask him."

Tone sits on the bleachers, talking to his little brother. He's always including that little guy. I jerk the bow free. "I said no bet. Leave me alone." I reach down and grab three arrows, walk to the taped line on the gym floor, and drop the arrows in an orange traffic cone. The same orange on that girl's fingernails. Can't she see she's pretty without all the extras?

"Hey. What's got your feathers ruffled?"

I look up and see Sam smiling. "Oh, hey. Nothing. Sally here?"

"She's over by Jill." I side-step and wave to the girls.

"She shooting today?"

"No. She's been sick. Just came along for the ride. She's tired of being home bound."

"Don't blame her. Is she okay? She looks pale."

"Nice diversion, but I asked you a question. Gonna answer it?"

"Is she okay?" Hand on hip, I lift my brows.

"Yes. Gonna answer me?"

"Just want to have a good shoot." I march over to the line and pull an arrow out of the cone and nock it to my bow. I take aim, low and to the right of the round target, breathe in, chest out. I release my fingers and watch the arrow stab the target in the outermost ring.

"Nothing bothering you today, huh?" Sam takes a bow off the rack, stands behind me, pulls out an arrow from the cone, and takes aim. He releases. I watch the arrow slide into the center of the ten point circle. "Nothing, huh?"

I lift a second arrow from the cone, nock it to my bow. I aim, releasing my death grip. I suck in a breath, hold it, and focus on the right, bottom corner of the target. I release my arrow and watch it stick into the outermost ring. Again. I drop my chin.

Sam shifts his weight. "Ya ready to spill your guts? Or you gonna blow your last arrow?"

My face grows hot. "I need a drink." I turn to leave, but Sam grabs my arm.

"Doesn't all this have to do with a bet? Some horse you think is lame? Or could he win you the title?"

"How do you know?"

He glances over to the bleachers. "Jill."

"Faithful friend." I shake my head. Sam drops my arm.

I grunt. "Hagan wants to bet me a horse he doesn't even own." I shake my head. "He's freakin' nuts!"

"Apparently he does own this horse."

"How do you know?"

"I talked to Tone."

His name keeps coming up. What does he know? How? Was it his horse? No, it can't be. Someone he knows? I've never seen him ride the horse.

"I hate when you do that." Sam taps an arrow in his hands.

"Do what?"

"Think without letting me in on it. Those wheels are turning in that head of yours." He pauses. "What's going on? Are you really considering riding down the suicide hill?"

I fetch my last arrow. "No." My gaze locks on the target.

Sam laughs, head back. "Do you think you can really hide this from your family?" He shakes his head. "From me? We've been friends for a long time, Char."

"I'm not riding. Just doing a report. There's no bet." I rush off, leaving Sam hanging with his own opinions. I hate when he's right. Can't hide anything from him. But if I do take this bet, the horse can stay with Hagan and no one will be the wiser. I know Hagan will keep that horse at his place. He'll want to keep his big beak in the loop. I can hide it. I'll convince him to do so, too. Somehow.

I pluck a water bottle out of my bag and stroll over to Tone who is sitting on the bleachers. I pretend to be interested in his little brother. Ask how he's doing. The normal chatter. How do I ask Tone about the horse? Without blowing my cover? But when Zack runs to get more food, I'm left sitting there with Tone.

"I bet you want to find out about a horse," he says.

The competition is in full swing and the first set of archers line up. The succession of *thwacks* when the arrows hit the targets rips through the gym. "Kind of."

"Why?"

"Just curious."

He laughs. "Hagan already told me you want to race this year. Is that true?"

My skin sweats like a horse before the gate opens. With Hagan's big mouth, how would I ever persuade him to keep a secret? I have to find leverage. There has to be something I can hold over his head.

"Don't worry. No one else knows."

The hunk who interrupted Hagan saunters by. He smiles, making eye contact with me. His dark eyes make me shiver as a rush of heat climbs my neck.

"You gonna answer me or keep staring at him?" Tone elbows me.

"What about the horse." I watch the hunk sit down with a group of kids all wearing matching green T-shirts. "What's his name?" I motion to him with a finger.

Tone looks at him. "Tell me first. You plan on riding?"

"I'm thinking about it." I turn to him and plead, "Please don't say anything. You know how my family will react. Since my dad's been in a wheelchair, everyone's over-protective."

"Even your grandfather?"

I glance at my hands. "Especially Sshapa."

"I won't say anything." Tone scowls. "His name is Benton Marchand. I thought you knew him. He races in Okanogan and Republic with us."

"Promise?" I watch Benton rise and disappear in the crowd. "You'll keep quiet?"

"Holy! I said I wouldn't say anything."

"Say it." I clutch his arm.

"I promise." Tone nudges me with his shoulder. He leans close. "I'd do anything for you."

It would be simpler if I shared the same feelings. But I don't, so I drag him back to the bet. It wouldn't be right to lead him on. "Have you ridden this horse?" I give him the picture.

The announcer calls my name. I glance over at Tone and shrug.

He waves me on. "Better get going."

"But—"

"You're going to miss your turn. Go! We'll talk later."

CHAPTER 11

Everyone watches me as I walk to the line—the late girl. Hagan smirks and taps his palm with the pictures. My skin crawls. *Relax. Tone will keep his promise.* Hagan's words tick in my mind: *Got a better one than the old plug you ride?* I imagine Stimteema's long legs bounding off the hill, tumbling down. Over and over. Hagan's voice comes back, *No way. You're not considering riding that broke down horse of yours, are you?* I know she's not broke down, but I also know she's not a good suicide horse. I stare at Hagan, eyes narrow, and nod.

He smirks.

I line up in between the second and third place girls from last year. Two whistles blast and we grab our bows, walk to the cones, and place our bows on our toes as the rules suggest. I pull an arrow from the cone and take a breath.

"Nice you could join us," one says. She takes her stance.

The other gives me a scowl.

I fix my gaze on the target and imagine a picture of Hagan's head plastered on it. I aim my arrow right between his eyes. Sshapa's voice carries as he cheers me on. A lightness blankets me. Until the lie comes back like a stack of bricks on my shoulders. I shrug it off. My family needs the money. I need a horse. It's all good.

The tweet of a single blow from the official's whistle sounds. I nock my arrow, aim, and release.

We'll talk later. Why did Tone tell me that? He knows something. Something promising or he'd not have made mention of it. Cheers fill the room. I look down at the target, my arrow sticks the middle of it. I got Hagan right between the eyes, just like I saw it in my mind. Ten points. I look at the target to my right. Someone's been practicing. A triumphant sigh slides through her lips. I peer to my left. Eight points. A different sigh emerges. One that sounds like improvement is needed to beat the top girl.

She'll have to beat me. But they are clueless as to what I'm shooting for. It's not for a trophy. Nor a T-shirt or fancy jacket. Not even a bow. It's for a winning horse. A horse that could earn us a hefty check this summer. Cash to help my father.

That is if Hagan keeps his promise.

I snatch a second arrow out of the quiver. Place my bow on the toe of my shoe and face to my right. We wait for a single whistle to blow. Instead, five short, immediate tweets indicate an emergency. A toddler is on the floor in front of us. We stand back, put our bows on the rack. Watch as a frantic mother scoops her child from the floor and rushes to the bleachers. We wait as the side door is closed and listen as onlookers question as to how it had been open in the first place. Two whistles blast. We retrieve our bows and line back up. One whistle blasts and I nock my arrow to the bow string. Take aim with my thumb gently against my cheek. I release my arrow and watch it stick into the center of the target. Ten more points. I turn to Hagan and smile.

He lifts one finger and throws me a cocky grin.

I nod. *One more, idiot, and that horse is mine!*

But why? Why would he want to give away a perfectly sound horse? Doubt creeps in. What's wrong with the horse? Or what's wrong with Hagan? Does he have a plan to harm me? Thinks I'll make a fool of myself? Oh my goodness, I'm getting a lame horse.

I curl my fingers around the last arrow and nock it to my bow. I raise it to eye level. Aim. Release. I blow out my breath and stare at the target, not sure where the arrow landed. Could it be? Silence stirs the gym. Oohs and awes flit about the room like a hummingbird. My fingers play with the neckline of my shirt. This has never happened. My thoughts scramble to understand how. It's got to be a sign. That horse is meant for me.

Hagan's mouth hangs open. By the look on his face, he probably bet someone else I'd fail. I lift one finger and turn to Sshapa. He claps and shouts and encourages everyone else to join in and they do. My legs wobble.

My coach strolls over and pats me on the back. "Nice job, Robin Hood."

Hagan rakes his fingers through his hair. Again I lift one finger, holding a serious expression. His face turns three shades of red. I wonder how his father will react. I chuckle. No matter what, I will ride that horse.

After recording my lane teammate's scores and placing our equipment in the designated areas, I stroll back to the bleachers. Jill comes at me like a freight train. We almost topple over as she hugs me, screaming in my ear. "I've never seen that done before. Ever! That was the coolest thing."

"I can't believe I pulled it off. Now if I could only do something like that in E-burg. That would be something. We shout because the crowd is still cheering. Sshapa strolls toward me. I step away from Jill and fall into his embrace.

"Nice shot, Granddaughter." He releases me and wipes away tears forming in his eyes.

His friend pats his back. "I think Grandpa here is a might bit proud."

An arm pulls me around and I come face-to-face with Tone. He picks me up off the ground in a bear hug and we laugh. He's still holding me when he leans to my ear and says, "Hagan just lost three hundred dollars. He bet a bunch of guys you'd lose."

I pull away and he sets me down. "He bet that much? Why? What's he got against me?"

"I don't know. But he's mad. He just stomped out with a bunch of friends. Probably trying to figure out how he's gonna get out of this." Tone snickers. "It'll be fun hearing about it."

"He's probably trying to impress Carla."

"Who knows? He's not the brightest bulb in the place. You just won. A horse. An amazing ride, Char. You're gonna love him."

"Yes. I did. And you owe me a conversation about this horse."

"I sure do. Let's grab a bite to eat and I'll tell you all about him."

I search for Sshapa. He's visiting with some friends by the exit doors. "I can't. Sshapa's ready to go. We have errands to run."

"But aren't you staying for the awards ceremony?"

I shake my head. "Coach is gonna grab everything for me. Besides, my *award* is in Hagan's barn."

Tone nods. "Sure is."

"We'll talk later. I'll call you." I search the room for Benton, but don't see him.

"Okay, here's my number." He tears a corner from a napkin, scratches some digits on it, and hands it to me.

"Char!" Jill catches up to me. "You never told me what the note said."

I glance at my grandfather. "Later."

She tips her head, hands on hips.

"I promise." *Crap!* I don't know what I'm gonna tell her. I don't want anyone to know about the stupid notes. They don't mean anything. Especially if Hagan is writing them. Punk.

I catch up to Sshapa and we walk to the truck. "Nice boy."

"Yes. He is."

"I see the way he looks at my granddaughter."

I glance at him. "What? No way. He likes classy ladies, Sshapa. I'm too much of a tomboy for him."

"Tomboy or not, it's the way he looks at you. He comes from a good family, ya know."

I clear my throat. "He's more like a brother."

Sshapa chuckles. "I don't see brothers looking at sisters in that way."

I gently shove him. "Stop, Sshapa." A laugh escapes my lips.

Besides, Sam has my heart. And Sally has his.

CHAPTER 12

Jill and I sit in front of the easel in art class, staring at our work-in-progress. I like what we have so far. The horse, a black and white paint, is outlined with a young Native woman by her side. The young woman is in full regalia with an eagle feather tucked in her hair at the back of her head. Her horse's tack is beaded to match, a fringed blanket covers the saddle. I've decided to use blue, purple, red, and yellow. Jill's right to suggest the yellow. It will make the blue and purple snap.

Jill's grandpa tore out a sheet from a ledger he had from his time running the old mercantile in Pendleton, Oregon. All Jill had to do was recreate it on canvas. No easy task.

"It's not quite the Army ones George Flett used," she says, "but close enough. I figure a ledger is a ledger. Heck, I don't even know where Mr. Flett got a hold of those military ledgers he used. Or any other one he worked with. Must have known someone who knew someone. One of those deals."

"It's perfect!" I'm angry she's not considering art school. Her talent should not be wasted. I don't think she realizes how good she really is.

"All I need now is to sketch the bow and arrow. It'll be tied onto the saddle. I sketched a traditional Native saddle into the picture, so there's no western saddle horn." She points to the canvas. "The quiver will be doeskin, with rabbit fur hanging off the end. I want them to be perched on top of a hill." She turns to me. "Sound good?"

"Remember, no hill. This is turning out just as we envisioned. Well mostly you," Jill says. She gently strokes the canvas with the tip of a finger.

"You've done most of the work."

Jill grins. "You are the vision behind this project, not me."

I stare at the horse Jill sketched, wondering if Tone will call tonight and share what he knows about my new horse. Hagan has been avoiding me. I think he's a pretty sore loser. He better not renege on the bet either. I don't even know the animal's name. But now that he's mine, I'll give him a new one. Lightning. Bolt. Jasper. 007. Tad. Smokey. Please Me—because he will!

Jill clears her throat.

I look at her, trying to recall what she'd said. "I'm the vision?" I jab her in the arm. "When *you* paint this, it'll be perfect. That's your talent. I still don't see why you don't go to art school. There's a good one in Seattle. Can't remember what the name is, but I heard it's good."

"The Art Institute."

"What?"

"The name of the Seattle art school."

I throw her a look. "You know the name of it?"

"Yes, I once pondered that idea. But not for long. I'd rather fiddle with it. It's funner when it's my hobby. I can't imagine the pressure of having to finish a project by a certain time for some event I don't want to attend. Or be disappointed if a painting never sold. No, I rather just mess with it. And if I sell one—all the better." Jill mixes her paints. "You done? I'm ready to start."

"Yeah. I think two eagle feathers on each side of the bow looks good. I want it to represent harmony between Natives and non-Natives. What do you think?"

"I think I like it." Jill touches up a spot on the canvas. "By the way, I thought you hate guys?"

"What?"

"I saw the way you drooled over tall, dark, and totally hot!"

"He's taken."

"I'm not talking about Sam. I saw you and that guy checking each other out in Omak at the shoot."

"Whatever."

A hand touches my shoulder. "Hey. Nice work you two." I whisk around and face Sam. I crane my neck and peer around him. I don't see Sally.

"Thanks," Jill says.

Images of me and Sam holding hands and talking, walking down the halls blast my thoughts. I envision him with Sally in the library, snuggling close to each other. I shake my head. I rub my forehead and give him a slight grin. Sam and I lock eyes. "What's up?" I ask, trying to act normal, but feel the heat climbing up my neck.

"I have to scratch our after-school study session. Sally's pretty sick. I promised her I'd drop her missing assignments off at her house. You okay with that?"

Like he needs my permission. "Yeah, no problem. I hope Sally's okay. Tell her hi."

"Will do. Thanks. We can meet early tomorrow morning if that works."

"Sure. That works."

Sam nods, swivels, and strolls out the door, looking like every minute he's away from his gorgeous, perfect girlfriend is a wasted minute. I slouch in my chair.

"Oh…that's bad." Jill smirks.

"What's bad?"

"You like both of them."

I act like I'm focusing on the project. "No." I motion to the painting. "Your turn."

"Yes. You do. It's written all over your face. Bright eyes when he talked to you, faded when he walked away. Not good."

"Shut up. He's taken."

"I know, but still…" Jill tilts her head. "Sally might have some autoimmune disorder."

"Where did you hear that?"

"My mom. That's why she's sick all the time."

My heart sinks. "Go ahead and paint," I say. "I'll be right back." I head for the bathroom, splash my face with cool water, and lean against the wall. *Sam. Benton.* I shove them out of my head and focus on the race. I imagine myself sitting in that new saddle, "Queen of the Hill" stamped on the fenders. Once cooled off, I march out and come face to face with Hagan Hurst. Our eyes lock for a brief moment. His gaze darts away, and he ducks into another room. I open my mouth to call his name and close it. *He can't hide forever.*

"He got beat to a pulp, you know." Carla walks over to me, too close for comfort. I take a couple steps back. She crosses her arm in front of her big chest and gives me a sharp stare, tapping her shiny cowboy boots on the floor.

"Who? Hagan?"

"Yeah. He was so sure you'd lose, he bet money. But didn't have it. So the guys he owed jumped him last night in the park."

I narrow my eyes at her. "What park? I can't believe he got jumped. I can't believe he was dumb enough to bet on me."

"The park behind Eichs." Her eyes accuse me. "Isn't that the only park in town?"

"He shouldn't have bet. That's on him, not me."

"Whatever. You shouldn't have let him. You know how arrogant he is."

I didn't expect that to come out of her mouth. "So you finally see him for who he is. Why are you sticking up for him? And *let* him? He does what he wants and I don't give a crap what that is." Shiny earrings dangle from her ears. "Besides, I thought you liked him."

She lets out a creepy laugh that echoes down the hallway. "Like Hagan? No way. I like to play with boys like him. They think they're so cool. So...popular and clever. They're nothing but little boys. Easy targets." A smirk creases her face.

"He shouldn't have bet money he doesn't have. I really wonder now if he bet a horse that's really not his. But Tone says the horse has what it takes."

"Don't be stupid. You never had that horse. I thought you were pretty desperate to make a bet with a guy like Hagan."

I know that horse was meant for me. The arrows, splitting like they did. It's a sign. "Not my problem." I walk away.

I need to call Tone tonight. This isn't good. I slink past the door Hagan entered, junior high English. Not sure what he's doing in there, other than hiding out. He's not a TA for anyone. What a crap shoot. I go back to the art room. Jill has a great start on the Native woman. She takes her time. Pressure to get this done squeezes me. I want this in the glass case before spring break. Mrs. Larson said we can take our time since it is such an intense project. I want it to be perfect. With Jill adding color, it's bound to be.

"Nice job." I place a cup of water next to her so she can wash out the paintbrush. As much time as she's putting into this project, she gets full rein of the next one. Somehow, I'll have to make sure hers is exactly as she envisions it.

"Thanks," she says, keeping her focus on the project.

I don't know how she makes the beads look real, must be that toothpick of a brush she's holding. I sit in the chair and watch, glancing at the clock. Bell's about to ring. "So," I say. "Mr. Bettin' Man has a shiner."

Mid-stoke Jill stops painting and turns to me, hand still in the air. "No way!" She lowers her voice. "What? Who?"

The bell rings. "I'll fill you in next class." We rush to clean our area and place the project on top of the cupboard.

"You still need to tell me what that note said."

"I will." *Another lie.* They've become too comfortable.

It doesn't take long to grab our precalc books and take our chairs, in the back of the class no less. Too bad Hagan wasn't smart enough to be in this class, we'd have a front row view of his purple and red scraped face. I'd love to hassle him about what really happened. Mrs. Seymour gives us the assignment and I do a few problems. The teacher's grading papers so I turn to Jill. She watches me, a hurry-up look on her face. I lean close and fill her in. She shakes her head.

"You're not gonna get that horse. I think he's made a bet riding on his daddy's pocketbook." Jill made a deep, soft sound in her voice, shaking her head.

I twist my fingers together like a French braid. "That's what I'm afraid of," I say with sickness in my throat. "He better come good on this bet or I'll…"

"Oh, you'll do nothing. Harmony, remember. That's what we stand for. What comes around will boot him right in the you-know-what!"

I send her a small smile. "I know. I'd like to be the one who gives it to him."

"Yeah, I do know. I'll be praying you get the perfect horse. Be patient. It'll come your way in God's timing." Jill shakes her head. "It'd serves him right for his dad to put a shiner on the other eye." Jill points to my pack. "The note."

"Ladies, you need to be working, not chatting," Mrs. Seymour says.

I give her an apologetic expression and mouth, *later*.

My mind wanders back to Sam. I'd like to have him stick up for me. Put a third bruise on Hagan's face. It would be nice to run into his arms and feel the warmth of his kindness, holding me with tight protection. Would he kiss me? Is that wrong to dream about him when he's with Sally? It makes me feel dirty. Like I've cheated on Sally. And she's sick. I'll never get him anyway. Time to shake him loose.

My project. That's what I need to concentrate on. And call Tone to get the scoop on this horse. Tonight. I need to get a list of elders from Sshapa and call them. I wish we had internet at home. I could just e-mail them all. It would be so much easier. It can be hard to hear some of the elders as they are soft spoken. And hard for them to hear me. Although I bet most of them don't have the internet. I know Sshapa hates technology. Pen, paper, and my brain are his motto.

The clock says class is almost over. I have ten minutes and only four problems are complete. I jig my leg. Peer out the window. Can't have Sam. May lose a horse I've just won. For the first time ever, I've lost track of time and won't finish my assignment. I have no good excuse—just a list of lies to track. So what should I do?

Hide my heart. My dreams. Me.

CHAPTER 13

The house is dark when I step inside. Like my heart. "Hello?" The tick of the clock answers. "Where are you guys?" I flip on the lights. A note on the table leans against a partially drank coffee cup. Same lined paper. I freeze. The clock reads 7:00. I pick up the note and read it.

Char,

Had to run Sshapa to the hospital. We found him on the floor of the barn. Unconscious. Dropped Kari and Chase off at the Maxwell's. Please feed the animals. I'll call when I know something.

Mom

I re-read the note. This can't be right. Sshapa's the healthy one. He's strong. Did he fall? Heart attack? *No!* I read it again, scanning the pages for clues. I look at the clock again. 7:10. *Go feed.* My boots stick as if nailed to the wood floor. *Go feed!* It's the lies. I've always told the truth. Until now. I've cursed Sshapa. My lies seem to tear this family apart. Hot moisture burns my eyes. I wipe them away with my shirtsleeve. We have to make it. We need more money.

Somehow I make my way to the barnyard, shoveling snow as I go. I toss the chickens feed, and they squawk as if I'm the coyote come to tear them apart. I throw slop to the pigs. They ignore me and devour their food. In the barn, the horses hang their heads over the stall doors and whicker. I reach out to stroke my horse, but she turns her head. All I want is to have her warmth wrapped around me and inhale her healing scent. She whinnies for her food.

I fall onto the stacked bales of hay, curl into a ball, and hide my face with the hood of my sweatshirt. The wind bangs against the barn, threatening to come in and wreak havoc. I lie there and watch the moon half covered with clouds. Enough light shines through the barn door, illuminating the horses. Their shadows bounce with each bob of their head. They stare at me with accusing eyes. I pull myself from the hay and feed them. With a heavy heart, I lumber back to the house. The trees extend their haunting arms down toward me as the wind ebbs and flows. Even they seem to try and snatch the truth from me. I run into the house and slam the door shut, locking it.

I rush to my room and rummage through my bag, digging out Tone's phone number. I hesitate, feeling like I'm using him to feed my selfish angst. The truth is I am. I head to the living room and slouch in Dad's chair, grasping the phone. The quiet makes me dream about the life we used to have before the accident. I lift a finger to punch in the number and freeze. Why call Tone? Why not Jill? The horse. That's why. I need a distraction. Jill would give comfort and pray over me. But I need to find out more about the horse. I punch in the number and listen to a ring from the other end. After the third ring, I hear a voice. His mother.

"Hello?" she says.

"Um, yes, hello. This is Charnaye Toulou. Is Tone there?" My body shivers.

"Oh, hello, Charnaye. How are you? I heard about the double arrow shot in Omak, what did he call it, Robin Hood? That's fantastic!"

My neck tingles. "Yes, ma'am. Thank you. I still can't believe that happened. To me." A pathetic laugh escapes my lips.

"Well, you certainly proved yourself as a marksman. Good for you," she says. "Tone?" She yells through the phone. "Tone, Charnaye Toulou is on the line." A muffled sound carries through the line. "I think he's coming, dear. It was nice talking to you."

Faint footsteps grow louder.

"Hey, Char, how's it going?"

My voice cracks. "Okay." *Don't cry. Don't do it.*

"Hey, what's wrong?"

I can't find the words to speak at first. "Oh, nothing. Just that…" A dam cracks inside of me.

"What? You can tell me. Come on…"

"I came home to a note telling me my mom found my grandfather on the barn floor. He was breathing but unconscious. Don't know if he's okay. Don't know if he fell or had a heart attack. My father must be with them because he's not here…" I squeeze my eyes shut and hug my knees. *Should I mention the other note?*

"Oh, man. I'm sorry, Char." His voice sounds sincere.

Butterflies should be flitting in my stomach when I think of him, but they don't. I wish I could get Sam out of my head. My mind darts to Tone who is sweet and generous. Jeez, what am I thinking, he's hot! Why do I have to like someone else? Someone who has a girlfriend? I'm torn. Nothing short of an idiot. To mangle things further, Benton's enticing body creeps into the mix. Who can resist his smile?

"Is there anything I can do for you? Do I need to come over and help with chores?"

A laugh escapes me. "You live two mountain passes away. It'd be midnight before you got here." *Why does he have to be so nice?* "No. Thank you. I just got in from feeding." The clock reads 8:45. My stomach growls. It's stirred up like a hornet's nest. "I'm sure he'll be fine."

"Yeah. He's one tough, old man." He chuckles. "How are you holding up?" His voice is tender. Caring.

"Okay. Did you hear about Hagan?" I can't talk about Sshapa any longer or the crack will burst.

"No. What's with him?"

"Guess he made a bet on my archery shot he can't pay. Got beat up good."

"What? No way. What was he thinking? His mouth is bigger than his cheap promises."

"Good way to put it."

"Have you talked to him?"

"No," I say. "I wanted to choke him myself. I'm afraid he's gonna renege on the horse deal. I'm thinking he was never really gonna give him to me. Thought I'd lose. Was sure of it." I play with the TV remote. "The horse was never mine."

"Maybe I was wrong and his dad didn't give him the horse. His dad did get it for cheap. He knows cow horses, not race horses. Has no use for one. That's what Hagan told me at the shoot. I think Hagan's scared of the horse. And his dad."

"Hagan's nothing but a liar. He can't be trusted," I say. "Why do you think he's scared?"

"He told me about the day his dad brought the horse home. His old man made him jump on and the dang thing bolted. I think he's just chicken and won't admit it. He's a bronc rider, not a racer. Speed scares him." Tone laughs.

He laughs so hard, I start in. After a long moment we settle down. "Do you think I'll get the horse?"

"I don't know. Probably not."

My stomach growls. I clutch my belly, leaning back against the under-stuffed chair. A leg falls asleep, I wince as I straighten it out, tuck the opposite foot underneath. I swallow, throat dry.

My feelings for Sam fade.

"Char, you're talented. Like no other girl. I watch you race these horses, you're strong, fluid…"

"You're making me blush. Stop…" A warm sensation flows through me. I like it. Tone's easy to talk to. Better than Chase. He's like an older, protective brother. I like that he genuinely cares about people. "But now I'm back to square one. No horse. How am I gonna race without a horse?"

"Why not Stimteema?"

"She's too old," I say. "Tell me about the horse. What's his name?"

"Why? Face it, you're not going to get him."

"You've ridden him." I place him on speaker phone and braid my hair.

He chuckles. "My bad. His name's War Cry. He's surefooted, smart, fast, full of heart. All the ingredients that make a great suicide horse. They used to think a tall, big boned horse was the best. But quarter horses come off the hill easier."

I take him off speaker and lean over the couch, peering outside at the sound of a rig passing by. Its lights fade. "I thought this horse was thoroughbred."

"Nope. But he has been on the race track a few times and whatnot. Mostly at fairs where they race that breed. He started out roping, but wasn't as cow savvy as the owner's hoped. I thought Hagan told you more about him."

"No, not really. Just that he raced. So I assumed."

"You didn't make it easy for him, did you?"

I slap my leg. "Why should I?"

"You're right. You shouldn't."

I fetch a drink of water and sink back in the couch. "When did you ride him?" I twirl a loose strand of hair around my finger.

"Mostly as a colt. About five years ago or so. I think he's eight or nine?"

"I thought he was older." I switch ears. *Tell him about the note.* I shudder.

"Nope. Does that scare you?"

"*Scare* me?" I give the phone an angry look.

His laugh rings through the line. "My bad. Wrong choice of words. But did I throw you off? Worry you?" He pauses. "No, nothing worries Charnaye Toulou. Lady racer, expert archer. Ayyyz! " His voice is lathered with mischievousness.

"Aren't you funny," I say. I'm glad I called him. He's got a knack for putting me at ease. I notice the time. 9:08. I open the fridge door.

"Did you eat yet?" he says.

"Not yet. I'm starving."

"Well, I'm going to let you go for now. Get something to eat. I'll call you tomorrow and check on you."

The phone lingers against my ear after the line clicks. I press the off button. After making a peanut butter and jam sandwich for myself, I go to the living room window and pull back the curtains. Nothing out there but pitch black. A branch's top makes me flinch. I whip the curtain closed. *Get a grip!*

I toss the rest of the sandwich on the kitchen table and pull out my precalc book. Finishing today's assignment would be a bonus since I've promised Mrs. Seymour it will be in tomorrow. She must have been in a good mood today because normally the answer to out of class work is a firm no. By the time I finish my math and history homework, the clock glows 11:30. I take a quick shower and fall into bed. My eyes struggle to stay open. I don't fight it.

The last thing I remember is hearing a car pull into the drive, tires crunching on the gravel.

CHAPTER 14

"Charnaye, rise and shine. The bus'll roll in soon," Dad hollers. "Your mother had to go in early for a parent conference. Time to feed."

I roll over and scrape hair out of my face.

"You awake?" His voice sounds impatient.

I wet my lips. "I'm up."

I roll out of bed and pull on clean clothes. I drag each foot to the living room. "Where's Sshapa?"

My father rolls over to me. His brown eyes look weary and cast shadows below thick, black lashes. "He's still in the hospital. Looks like he's had a mild heart attack. I think all they'll do is put him on medication."

I look down at the wheels of my dad's chair. I can't look him in the eyes or I'll cry. I need to be strong. For him. For everyone. Our world's falling apart and I don't know how to fix it. Baling twine won't help this mess.

"He's gonna be okay, Char."

I clear my throat. "Best go feed."

I wheel around and stride to the door, hearing my father say he'll make toast for me. "I'll hurry."

I run to the chickens, throw feed on the ground, and check their water. It's frozen. I look at the heater and see it's been unplugged. It was dark last night when I fed so I didn't notice. I plug it back in and feed the pigs. I hate trekking back to the house in three feet of snow for water, especially when I'm running late. A layer of ice needs to be cracked before I can fill their buckets. This is another reason to win the suicide race. A new spigot down at the barn would be a plus. At least the cows have a creek.

I toss a flake of hay to the last horse. A deep, guttural growl catches my attention and I stiffen. A huge, gray and brown wolf is crouched in the doorway. How did he get in here? Where did he come from? I hold his gaze for a minute. He bares his teeth. Prickles race up my neck and stop at the top of my head. I grab a pitch fork and jab it at him. The horses paw and whinny. He comes closer, slinking low to the ground.

"Dad!" I yell, knowing he can't hear me. Even if he could, I'd still be alone. For some reason I yell for him again. The wolf skulks closer. An ax leans against a stall door. With slow movements, I reach for it. The handle is cold and a toothpick-sized sliver pierces my skin. I wince, eyes trained on the dog. Another step closer, the growl gets louder. "Dad!" I yell again. My body trembles and I wonder if my grip will hold the ax handle. I curl my fingers tightly around it. My heart pounds the inside of my ribcage. My knees threaten to buckle. But my brain tells me to throw the ax. I squint my eyes, focus on brown hair between his golden eyes. The hair on his neck and back stands on end. I lift my arm and heave the ax. The blunt end whacks him on the head. He drops to the ground, yelps, and scrambles out of the barn.

I slump to the ground, breathing heavy. The fires have brought animals close to many of our homes. Yet I never figured a wolf would venture into our barn. I wonder if he's visited before, bedded down in the hay. I hope he's not hiding a deer carcass in here. I glance around and don't see anything out of place. *The chickens.* There might be one or two missing. I'm not sure. Mom will know how many. I count them so we can keep track.

I race to the house and shove the door open.

Dad wheels around from watching the news. "What took you so long?" He points to the table. "You're food's cold."

I open my mouth, shut it, open it again, but nothing comes out. Words stick to the back of my throat.

My father makes his way to me. "What's going on?"

"Yeah. I just had a conversation with a wolf. In the barn." I stretch my arms wide. "This big!" My body won't seem to stop shaking. I rub my arms.

"What?" Dad wheels to the kitchen window and leans over, peering outside. He flips the break lever on his chair.

"He's gone, Dad. I was feeding the horses and he walked in the barn like he owned it. Bared his teeth and everything." I shuffle to the sink and wash up. "He's got one deep growl." I take in a few deep breaths, hoping he doesn't show back up. If he got a taste of a chicken it's likely he will try and creep back.

My father wheels his chair around to face me. "Deep growl? Bared teeth? How'd you get him out of the barn? Are there any chickens missing?"

"Threw an ax at him." I stand tall even though I'm still trembling. "I don't know how many chickens we had, but there are fifteen left. I'll ask Mom."

My father frowns. He wheels into his room without saying a word. I sit down and eat my tepid toast and drink a glass of room-temperature milk. Once done I pluck a can of chicken and rice soup off the cupboard shelf and set it on the countertop for his lunch. I watch him wheel back into the kitchen, rifle over his lap and a box of bullets between his knees. He thrust the rifle into my hands. "We practice shooting once you get back from school today. I want you to get Kari and come straight home."

From out the front window I watch the bus stop at the end of our driveway.

"But I have archery practice—"

Red-faced, he says, "Not today." He slams the box of bullets on the kitchen table. The bus pulls away and heads back down the road. "Now get going." He holds out Sshapa's truck keys and jingles them.

I lay the rifle on the table, grab the keys and backpack, and give my father a kiss on the top of his head. "Can I go see Sshapa first?"

"No, he'll be home soon enough. We have to make sure this wolf leaves our chickens alone. I don't think he'll mess with anything else, but he's got to be pretty hungry to come here."

"You gonna be okay?"

"Yeah. I'll call Walt to come over and help keep watch. He'll feed the cows."

I hold my father's gaze, eyebrows arched. "You sure? I can stay home." I plant my bottom in a chair, hoping to change his mind.

"No, you can't. Now do as you're told, child! Get out of here."

I tilt my head.

He sighs, eyes pleading. "Please, Char. I'll be okay. When you leave I'll call Walt."

I hand him the phone. "Chase should have stayed to help this morning."

Dad sighs. "We needed his help last night."

"When will Sshapa be home?"

"In a day or two. He's dehydrated and they want him to get some rest. Watch his heart." He waves his hand, motioning for me to scoot out the door.

I nod again. "All right. I'm going."

I march out the door and to the truck. My father searches out the window with his binoculars, scanning for the visiting predator. I take one last glance around. The animals seem calm.

I speed to school, watching for slick spots, my foot on the pedal for straight stretches and braking for curves. I scan my rearview mirror for cops, not that we ever see any. I'm tempted to visit Sshapa before school. What will it hurt? I'm already late. Instead of driving straight ahead, I pull into the school parking lot. I can check in with Mom during her prep period.

Five feet or taller berms of snow surround the parking lot. When I turn to park, the truck slides to the right. I turn the wheel to the left, tap on the breaks a few times, turn to the right. I eventually straighten out, just missing someone's mud-covered Subaru. I jump out and slip on the ground. My head bangs hard against the running board. I lie there, dizzy and cold. What else can go wrong? After a few moments of groaning, I sit up and rub the knot on my head.

"You okay?"

I glance up to see Hagan hovering over me. "Yeah."

He grabs me by the coat and heaves me to my feet. "Nice shiner."

"Yeah." He looks away.

"So, you owe me a horse." I stare at him. He glances down, shaking his head.

"Dumbest thing I've ever done."

"What, bet on a girl or lose a horse to one?"

He shifts his weight. "Both. You'll get your horse, don't worry." His Adam's apple bobs.

"I hope so. Stinkin' horse of mine, just not fast enough. Right?"

"Right." Hagan stomps off. "Last time I help you," he says over his shoulder, spouting off a string of cuss words.

I guess I should've been nicer, but I recently learned if you give a nasty, mean bronc rider a rope, he'll form a noose and hang you with it. I brush myself off, snatch my pack out of the truck, and head for class. My feet walk toward the high school building, but my mind is on one particular fifth grade teacher. So I swing around and open the elementary building door.

"Hello, Charnaye," says Mr. Boles, the elementary principal. "Your mother…"

I keep walking. My parents taught me better than that, but my heart can't take not knowing how Sshapa is. I round the corner and step into her classroom. A sub is standing before the class, modeling the math assignment on a projected screen.

"Can I help you?" she says.

Twenty heads turn in my direction. A few wave and say hello. I give a small smile, shake my head, and wave back. I turn and bump into Mr. Boles.

"Like I was saying, Charnaye. Your mother took the morning off to tend to your grandfather. I take it you haven't seen her yet?"

"No. I haven't," I say. "Sorry about ignoring you. I just…" For a minute I think about pulling Kari out of class to make sure she's all right. But then again she may want to come with me. At this point I'm not sure if my mom would be delighted or slap me.

He nods. "You're checked out to go to the hospital and see them," he pauses, "before you come back to class this afternoon."

"Thank you!"

"You're welcome. Don't…"

I turn and run down the hall. "Sorry…" I shout back at him, not wanting to waste time.

The bite of heavy snow pricks my face as I rush out to the truck. It feels to be around five degrees outside. Large flakes resemble shards of glass falling from the sky. I jump in and turn the key. Nothing happens. I try again. The motor ticks. I pound the steering wheel and try again. The motor chugs and spits until it finally turns over. I'm off to the hospital.

Country music blares as I pull out onto the highway. A cop passes in front of me, lights twirling. I slam on the brakes. After looking both ways, I creep onto the slick pavement, nerves rattled. Blake Shelton and I sing. I hit the words I know and hum to the ones I don't. My muscles relax, but my mind stays alert.

The hospital sign comes into view and I pull in, creeping to a stop. Instead of jumping out of the truck, I test the surface with the toe of my cowboy boot. Once on the ground, I slip the truck keys and my red, chapped hands into my coat pockets. I shove them in deep, pull up my coat collar, and shuffle into the hospital. Dime-sized flakes blind my vision. My lids blink to keep my eyes clear.

Warmth envelopes me as I step into the foyer. The front desk is abandoned. "Hello?" My voice echoes down the hallway. I peek around the corner, glance both ways, and turn toward low chatter. Rooms line the right side of the hall, the first one labeled administration and the next numbered one. A hallway to the left is branded emergency and exits outside. A middle-aged woman leans against the nurse's station, thumbing through a patient's chart. She squints my direction, exposing sapphire eyes that match the color of her uniform.

Her expression brightens. "You must be Charnaye."

I give her a questioning look.

She chuckles and says, "Your mother suggested I keep an eye out for a petite, spit-fire of a teenager." She looks me over. "You seem to fit the profile."

The stethoscope around her neck makes her seem official, but the playfulness in her tone puts me at ease. "Yes, ma'am."

"We shorties have to stick together. Your grandfather's much better. He's a strong man. And what a gentleman. I promised him a coffee date once he's out. He's a kick." She giggles, eyes shining. "Your mother's a sweetheart. You're lucky to belong to such a lovely family." A dozen steps takes us to room number six. "Well now, let's go in and see them, shall we?"

She's got to be about five-foot tall with feet the size of a small child's. Her short, curly brown hair is as bouncy as her personality. She leads me by the elbow to Sshapa's room. "Hear ya go. Enjoy your visit." Turning to my mom, she says, "Nice daughter you have here, Mrs. Toulou. Manners go a long way." She winks and shuffles off.

Sshapa's frail appearance leaves me speechless.

"You come to break me out of here?" Sshapa smiles. His eyes reflect pee and vinegar.

I walk into the room and give him a gentle hug, exhaling my worry. His smirk ignites my wit. "Yep. Get away car's outside." I nod to the door.

Mom stands, shaking her head. "You two probably would pull some kind of shenanigans if we weren't all here to spy on you." She rolls her copy of the Tribal Tribune and smacks Sshapa's toes that stick out of a blue and red Native print fleece blanket.

"Where'd you get that?" I point to the blanket.

"Mr. Miller brought it in this morning. Thought I needed something better than the hospital napkins they offer." He winks.

"Maybe I should fake a heart attack and get one too."

Mom wacks me on the shoulder with the same Tribune. Me and Sshapa laugh. I sit on the bed next to him. "How long you in for?"

He waves me off. "Over night. That cute nurse wants a coffee date, but needs to make sure my ticker's going to last long enough to pay the bill." He pats my hand. "I'm fine, Char. Creator plans on keeping me around. He's got plans."

A tall, fit man in a white coat saunters in, clipboard in hand. He looks to be in his late thirties. Maybe older. Hair the color of pine bark and just as coarse.

"How are you feeling this morning, Mr. Toulou?"

"Couldn't be better, Dr. Jones." Sshapa looks hopeful. "Ready for our morning *smimmy*?"

"Sure am. Sorry I'm running late, I helped an elderly couple dig themselves out of a snowbank on my way here." He flips through Sshapa's chart.

I run my fingers over the knot on my head and wince. Ease back on the window ledge. Mom gives me a curious look. I shrug. Out of the corner of my eye, I can still see her staring at me. I pretend I'm concentrating on the doctor's words. What I'm absorbed with is his dark eyes and square jaw. His expression makes his soft face look younger. Not knowing he's a physician, I'd peg him for a rancher.

He explains the stress test and Sshapa's heart condition. His words are simple. His tone patient.

Sshapa plays down his situation, telling the doctor he's fit as a fiddle. Mom tells him if he wants to keep playing music, he'd better do what the charming doctor says.

Dr. Jones shakes our hands, instructs Grandfather to rest, and leaves.

"You two need to go back to school so I can get some shut-eye. You heard the man." Sshapa closes his eyes. "Turn the light off on your way out." He pulls the blanket up to his chin.

"I'll go find a cup of coffee, but I'm not leaving you, ya old coot!"

After hugging my mom, I find my way to the truck. *He's fine. Yeah, right.* He looks to be in good spirits, but the seriousness of the doctor's voice and butterflies in my belly seem to warn me otherwise.

CHAPTER 15

Low murmurs float down the hall of the elementary building. Guilt leads me to check on Kari before going to class. I stroll to the fourth-grade classroom and see Kari reading a book out loud at her desk. Her teacher has a group of students who are choral reading at a u-shaped table in the back of the room. I thread my way to my sister's desk and tap her shoulder.

Wide eyes blink up and fix their gaze on me. Kari's teacher nods. Her gaze shifts to the door. I take Kari's hand and lead her to the hall.

"How's Sshapa?" Round eyes stare at me.

"Ornery as ever," I say. She smiles and wraps her arms around my waist, squeezing tight as her body trembles. I rub her back, leaning against the wall and let her hold on. My head throbs so I rest it against the cool wall. Close my eyes.

"When's he coming home?" Her voice is low and soft.

"In a day or two. Don't worry, Swaskee, he'll be all right." I stroke her hair. "I have to go check in. Want me to eat lunch with you?"

She shakes her head. "Becky is. We're gonna read to each other at recess instead of go outside. Teacher said it's okay."

I give her one last hug before leaving. She goes and sits at her desk, turning to wave goodbye. My fingers wave back.

I swivel around to mom watching us, tears pooled in her eyes. She must have decided to come to work after all. She smiles and walks into her classroom. I smile, but it's too late. She's already gone. The happiness she displayed at the Okanogan Fair has disappeared. Somehow, she has to find that place again. Wipe away the bags under her eyes. Claim joy.

Images of Sshapa lying in the hospital bed reel through my mind. They stop at the one of my hand clasped between his. "Creator, heal his heart, please." I whisper the words as I walk. "I can't lose him." A lump wells in my throat. After checking in at the office, I breeze to the library. Class has already begun and not wanting to interrupt, I check in with Mrs. McMillan.

I sigh, slide into a chair, and pull out my history book. Maybe if I study for today's quiz my mind will simmer down. It doesn't. I close my book and lean back in my chair, tossing my pencil on the table. It rolls off.

After a few minutes, I crack my book open and try again. I'm studying the Knights of Labor and its secret Philadelphia society when footsteps squeak down the hall and stop in front of the library. I lift my chin to find Hagan staring at me. I purse my lips and shake my head. Can't deal with him right now. He walks away. With a heavy heart I go back to reading. My eyes scan the words, but nothing sticks. I read three paragraphs, re-read them, and still have no idea what they say.

I close my book and wander to the art room. My eyes swing to the easel. Someone's project is on it. It's a scenic piece. A winter wonderland. Birds perch on trees heavy with snow. Smoke swirls out of a rustic cabin chimney. Blues create a haunting yet soothing aura. Makes me want to climb into the cabin and sleep.

Jill bounds in the room. "There you are! I've been looking everywhere for you." She points to the counter.

"I was at the hospital." I hesitate to tell her more.

"At the hospital?" Her eyes examine every inch of me.

"I'm fine. My grandfather had a mild heart attack."

"Is he okay?"

"Yeah." *I hope so.*

"Oh, good. I'll add him to my prayer list. Not sure how much more your family can take."

"Thanks. Why did you rush in like your pants are on fire?"

"Oh, that. Well, I…oh, boy." Her gaze drops.

I swallow hard, cross my arms in front of my chest. The look on her face tells me the news is bad. "What's going on?"

She sighs. "I'm just going to tell ya."

"That'd be nice."

Her eyes fill with moisture. She stares at her gray boots while a tear slips down her cheek. I hold her arm. "What?"

Heavy feet take her to the counter. She shoves our art project into my hands. My mouth falls open to black marks covering the canvas as if a toddler found a Sharpe and decided to decorate our picture with helping hands. I gasp and find a chair to sink into. I lean down and put my head between my legs. What else can go wrong?

"Found it this morning. I wanted to add finishing touches. Don't know who did this, but I hope to find out." She wipes her cheeks.

"Has to be Hagan," I say from between my knees.

A *click-click* of woman's heels approach us from behind. I wish her away. A gentle hand rubs my back. I lift my head to see Mrs. Larson leaning over me, her eyes soft and caring.

"I'm so sorry about your project, Charnaye. Like I told Jill, I don't know who has done this, but I did turn it in to the principal and they will look into it."

"Thank you. We worked so hard on it." A groan escapes my lips.

"You did, and it won't affect your grade. Vandalism is taken seriously in my class. I plan to get to the bottom of this." She places her hands on her hips.

"I know you will, Mrs. Larson. Thanks."

She leaves us staring at one another. "Do we start over?" I say.

"It's not like we can erase the marks." Jill rubs a finger over the black ink. She glances around and leans close, slipping a piece of paper out of her jacket pocket. "This was taped to the back." She hands it to me.

I warned you to back off. It's not your rite. Watch your back!

I rub my forehead.

"Is the note you're keeping from me like that one?"

I nod. "I don't want to make a big deal of this, so don't say anything, okay?"

"Don't say anything? Are you crazy? I'm gonna show Mrs. L." She stands.

I grab her arm. "No! I don't want to give the creep any more leverage. I think if we ignore him, he'll go away."

"I doubt that, Char."

"Sit down, please."

Jill slinks back into her chair. "I won't say anything for now, but if you get another one, I will."

"Fair enough." I hand her a purple pencil. "Can we work on this now? Please?"

"Fine, but I still think we should hand the note over to Mrs. L. This entire theme is strength and courage. We have to show whoever did this they can't get away with it," Jill says. "Mainly you. This attack is against you."

"That's how I feel. But it's our project. It's against us both." I rub my head. Scrunch my face.

"You have a headache?"

I wince. "Yeah. This morning I slipped getting out of my grandfather's truck. Hit my head on the running board." I'm still surprised Hagan tried to help me, since he's the one threatening me.

Jill runs her finger across my scalp. "Dang, Char. You have a nice bump. The nurse is here, maybe you need to have her look at it."

"Nah, I'm okay. I'll go get some Tylenol from my mom." The lunch bell rings. "Can I keep this? I can start retracing it tonight at home."

"Sure. I'll fill it in when you're done," Jill says. "At least let me grab you a bag of ice."

I let her, wishing we had Native studies for an elective like Inchelium does. If I had a different project, maybe this one wouldn't be ruined. I'd love to learn to bead. A smaller project could be locked in a cupboard. Better yet in my bag. With me. I would be learning the language and know more than I do. Which isn't much.

Tribal history is taught and I bet I could have more information about the Suicide Race. Which reminds me I have more research to dig up. I need to find a woman who has actually raced down the hill. That would be better than one of Sshapa's friends.

I pull out a second canvas from the cupboard and put it in the truck before I eat. Although it's warmer outside than it was this morning, the snow is coming down hard and thick. Several inches have accumulated on the truck's hood. While walking back to the elementary building, I hear male voices talking and snickering. Hagan and his culled predators watch me. They huddle beside Hagan's truck, forming snow balls. I pin him with a look that would send any snake back to its hole. He shrugs his shoulders, lifting his hands into the air. They laugh.

What animals. Not one kind bone in their bodies. Someday they'll get what they deserve.

I somehow make it through the rest of the day. A day squandered that I could have stayed home and helped my father. Shooting wolves would have been way better. And constructive. After archery practice, I fetch Kari from Mom's classroom and Chase from basketball practice, and head home. Mom's going to check on Sshapa. I wish they'd let Chase drive. If only we had another car so I can stay with Mom. I'm scared for her to drive home alone in this weather as tired as she's been.

It's dark and windy outside, and the snow is raging straight at the windshield. I dread the long drive home going thirty-five miles an hour. Silence hangs heavy in the truck as I concentrate on the road and Chase concentrates on my driving.

"Watch for deer," he says.

"No kidding, genius." I'd give him a dirty look, but don't dare take my eyes off the road. "Most are bedded down by now. Especially in this storm. You should know that by now…"

Kari sits between us, crowded next to Chase. My eyes scan the road from side to side. I won't admit it, but deer may not be bedded down, not all of them. I don't quite get that thought out as one jumps in front of the truck.

I slam on the breaks the same time Chase yells, "Deer!"

Kari screams.

We swerve in S curves all while I pump the brakes until I'm able to stabilize the truck and get back on our side of the road. Chase slams both hands on the dash. He's smart enough to keep his mouth shut.

Until he just can't stand it any longer. "Told you to watch the road!"

"I am," I say through gritted teeth. A quiet sniff comes from beside me. "It's okay, Kari. We'll be home soon." She nods as she leans closer to Chase, tears streaming down her face.

Chase puts an arm around Kari. "Didn't see you in school."

"Because I wasn't there."

"Why not?" Chase's voice is a mix of snotty and whiney.

I squint against the snow, foot hovering over the brake. Something appears to be hiding in the brush, but the closer we get, I realize it's a stump or fence post. I lean closer to the window, wiping off the fog with the sleeve of my coat. We drive past and nothing jumps out. I put my foot back on the gas pedal. "I was with Sshapa."

"How come you got to go?"

"Because I needed to see him."

"You aren't the only one who needs to see Sshapa. You get to do everything, I swear."

"Holy, cry baby. For one thing, I'm older…" I struggle to focus on the road.

"Can't wait to hear more." He grunts.

"Listen. I don't want to fight." I pin my gaze to the snow blinding road.

The only sound on the way home is the flogging of the wipers to window. Fog rolls in and covers our already cloggy visibility. I grip the steering wheel, clenching my jaws.

CHAPTER 16

I jerk awake.

The glow of the alarm clock reads 2:45. My pajama shirt sticks to my sweat-covered body. I search my room, blinking toward the Pendleton blanket that covers the window. Shadows from the clock cast an eerie light on my bed. I hug my knees. Hold tight. Bury my head deep against the pain. *He can't die.* I pull at the quilt nestled in my fingers and curl its edges around my head.

It was too real. Grandfather in his tribal issued pine casket, lying on a brown and green Pendleton blanket with a gray hue to his face. A new brown suit covered his scrawny body. He looked peaceful. Stone dead, but peaceful. A beaded eagle feather rested in his hands that lay clasped over his chest. A huge bouquet of flowers and his black cowboy hat adorned the closed half of the casket.

Mom wiped tears with an embroidered hanky, smiling and nodding as if her gesture could comfort me. Kari curled herself on Dad's lap, a trembling bundle. I search the darkness for Chase. Couldn't find him. Asked Mom where he was. She continued to smile, her eyes the usual dark and puffy.

Tree branches bang on my window and jerk me to the present. I lean against the wall, creeped out, and think. Listen. "Creator, why Sshapa? What does my dream mean? Am I just worried? We can't lose him. Moisture gathers in my eyes. Mom's got nothing left." Tears roll down my cheeks, and I hug a pillow.

Think about our early morning talks in the barn. His gentle touch. The low tone of his voice when we share about life and legends. It all swirls around me as if his spirit is giving me comfort and reassurance.

The wind outside breaks my trance. It's not a gentle tap, but more like someone's fist pounding the glass, vying for my attention. I lie on my back and pull the covers over my head. A taunting fear enters my mind and so does Hagan's voice telling me I'm not good enough. *Life never works out for people like you.* My minds flashes images of him laughing and pointing at me in the school hallway. In the parking lot. His little cowboy gang joins in. Carla's wicked laugh bounces off the walls and chills spritz through me from head to toe.

I imagine Sshapa watching me, smiling. "Focus on the Creator," he says. I shake my head. The clock reads 3:10. I'm exhausted and wish my mind would surrender. If only I could smoother my fear and awake fresh. And know this is all a bad dream.

But it's real.

Grandfather's in the hospital and looks like death warmed over. I roll onto my side and bring my knees to my chest. *Knock. Knock. Knock.* The sound gets louder with every beat. I jump against the last bang, kink my neck from twisting it too fast. *Don't race. You'll regret it.* Regret what? Becoming a woman? After I rub the knot for a few minutes, the pain eases. My mind seems to cling to fear no matter how hard I fight it off. Fear of insults and threats. Fear of loneliness. Fear of losing Sshapa to the ancestors. A tear trickles down my cheek. I wipe my eyes with my sheet.

The disappointment on my father's face due to the weather when we got home last night jabs my conscious. But there was nothing we could do. Just trust. A wolf howls in the distance. I shiver. The sound is faint as the wind carries the cry. *Knock. Knock. I warned you.* My eyes dart to the window. *Knock. Knock.* It's not the window. "Who's there?" My bedroom door creaks open and little footfalls scramble to my bedside. A small shadow stands before me, little whimpers coming from it.

I hold out my quivering hand and help my sister into bed.

"I'm scared. Can I sleep with you?" Kari says, barely a whisper.

I pull the covers over her shoulders and tuck blankets around her as she curls up against me. *Knock. Knock. Knock.* Her body shakes like leaves in a breeze. The clock glows 3:47.

"Don't worry, Kari. It's just the tree branches outside. That old aspen just likes to dance in the wind. Its long arms stretch out like a ballerina, twirling and singing to the Creator." I stroke her long, ebony hair. Its softness soothes me. She relaxes in my arms and nestles close. It's not the most comfortable angle for me, but the back pain is worth her security and peace.

It's not your rite. How does Hagan know about the race being a rite of passage? I shake my head. Or did he just misspell 'right'?

An old Okanogan lullaby comes to me and I sing, trying to dissolve the pit in my stomach. I peer at the clock. The red flickers 4:10. My heavy eyes close, but my mind spins like a child's top.

My sister sighs. Her body relaxes more and her body sinks against mine. I hum now, a quiet, easy sound. My fingers comb her soft, coffee-colored locks. A wave of peace washes over me. I close my eyes and an image of Tone Highwater drifts in. With his deep voice he's telling me everything will work out. I'll be safe. Hagan's harmless. That he'll always be there for me because that's what friends do.

Kari's breaths are shallow now, so I will myself to sleep.

I'm almost out when footsteps clamber to the bathroom. A stream of what I assume is urine makes me cringe. The footfalls are heavy and lazy like a boy made of rock shuffling down the hallway. Those same footsteps come to my door and halt. My eyelids fight their way up. The knob turns and a squeak shrills from the hinges. I quietly hum as Kari wiggles under the blankets. I think she's having one of her nightmares.

"You awake?" Chase peeks his head in.

"Yeah. Hurry up, get in here. Don't wake her up." I hum and rub my sister's back as she stirs. I whisper, "Sshhh."

"Who's in here with you?"

"Kari. Who do ya think?" I wish I had something to throw at him.

Chase tiptoes over to the bed, hands out in front of him. He fumbles for the edge and eases down. Kari's body stills. I continue rubbing her back, humming the lullaby.

"For a minute I thought maybe Mom, but…" Chase lets out a frustrated breath. "I'm not here to fight. I'm… I'm just…"

"I know. Me, too." I go back to humming.

"When did she come in?"

"Just before you did. I think she had a nightmare."

"How do you know?"

"She came in crying and shaking."

The bed bounces as Chase flips onto this side. "Is she ever gonna be normal?"

"Holy, she is normal, idiot. She's been through hell and back. Things like this take time. Especially at her age. She doesn't understand. Not like we do."

His voice hitches as he says, "I know." I fumble for a blanket next to my bed and throw it at him.

"Do you think Sshapa's gonna die?"

I shake my head as if he can see me. "No. I don't." I keep the dream to myself. I swallow the lump in my throat. "He's strong. And ornery. He'll come home."

Chase chuckles. "He never gives up, does he?"

"Never." I go back to humming as I close my eyes.

The wind sounds like it's dying down. The *tap, tap* of the branches against the window is like a drum that keeps time to my song. Not much time has passed when his breathing steadies. My mind wanders into the darkness. *It's not your rite. I warned you to back off?* Why warn me? Why do I have to back off? Who does he think he is?

If only my mind would turn off.

You'll regret it.

I try and focus on my siblings, being together is comforting. Sshapa tells us blood is thicker than water, even during the hard times. The clock reads 4:55. I close my eyes and listen to the sounds of the night. They get slower. Fainter.

CHAPTER 17

The alarm blares and I jolt upright. I reach over Kari to push the snooze button, but can't find it. My fingers fumble around the nightstand, but find nothing. I lean on one elbow and try to open my eyes. They stick together. I blink them open. A slit of vision tells me the clock reads a fuzzy 6:30. I groan.

"Ouch!" Kari pushes me.

"I'm trying to turn off this stinking noise." I stretch further and slam my hand against the clock and it tumbles to the floor, still squawking.

"I thought you had it set to music," Chase says.

"I thought so, too."

He rolls off the bed and shuts off the alarm.

I roll over Kari and push myself to my feet.

Kari rubs her eyes and looks at Chase, at the bed, and back at her brother. "When did you come in?"

He shrugs. "Late last night. You were out cold."

Kari sniffs. "Like Sshapa?"

I throw Chase a twisted look and mouth *nice one* to him. He jerks his hands out, palms up.

I sit back down beside Kari. "I know you're scared, Swaskee, but Sshapa's gonna be fine. They'll give him some medicine and he'll be home before you know it. Old people visit the hospital a lot, but always come home."

"Not always." Chase snaps a hand to his mouth.

I shake my head and point to the door.

He leaves.

Kari's sniff turns into a sob and I wrap my arms around her. "He'll come back. Chase is just big and stupid. Boys say dumb stuff. They don't know what they're talking about."

"Is Sshapa gonna die?" She wipes her shirtsleeve under her nose.

I tighten my hold on her. "No. He's strong. Like you." I rock her until her trembling stills.

"Come on. Let's get ready for school. I'll go feed and make Chase cook us breakfast. We'll let Dad sleep in."

Big, licorice eyes stare back at me. "Where's Mom?"

"At school."

She nods and pads out the door.

In less than an hour, we manage to feed the animals, have breakfast and get dressed—braids, bows, and all—grab three days of mail from the mailbox, and careen down Highway 21.

"Slow down!" Chase puts one hand on the window and the other one the dash.

My eyes drop to the speedometer. My heart flutters when I read 55. I gently pump the brake and slow us down to 40, watching for looming patches of black ice. Kari's reflection shows big, round eyes in the rearview mirror. I sip my coffee.

Chase sits back and thumbs through the mail. "Mom, Dad, Mom, Mom." A pause. "Mmmm…"

He chuckles, holding up a large white envelope. "Lookee what we got here."

I roll my eyes. "Humor me."

"Oh, yeah. You got some kind of package." He turns the heavy envelope from front to back and presses it against the windshield.

"What are you doing? You can't see through it Knock it off." I reach over and slap his chest. "Open it!"

"Ooww! Just for that, you'll have to wait."

I slap him again. Harder. Hot coffee splatters on my leg. "Ouch!" I squirm, rubbing my jeans.

He grabs his chest and lets out a high-pitched laugh. "You hit like a girl. Ayyyz!"

"I am a girl, stupid."

Giggles come from the backseat.

"I mean a weak girl." He laughs more, rubbing his chest.

"What's in the envelope? Tell me or I'll pull over and tear it out of your cocky, little hands."

He laughs harder.

More giggles bubble up from behind me.

"Hold on, grumpy." He turns the envelope in his hands and reads, "Gates Millennium Scholarship. Seattle Washington."

"Give me that." I rip it out of his grasp and hold it to my chest. My fingers tremble. I thrust it in his belly, making him wince. "You open it."

He tears open the envelope and pulls out several sheets of paper. "Oh, snap!" He grins and sets the letter in his lap.

I glance over at him. Irritation rolls up my back and out my mouth. "Stop it! What does it say?"

"Looks like…well I…I don't know…" He shrugs.

"Knock it off! Tell me…" I can hardly stand to keep my fingers on the wheel. I'm about to slam on the brakes and read the darn thing myself when he pipes up.

"You…well…seems you've been awarded the honorable Gates Millennium

Scholarship." He chuckles. "I really didn't think you'd get it done, as distracted as you've been." He shakes his head. "Nice going, sis."

"What do you mean distracted?" I take a cautious sip of coffee and place it back between my knees.

"What's the Gates Mill…millin…what you got?" Kari says.

Chase and I look at each other and laugh. Kari laughs with us. "It's money to help me go to college."

"Oh, yeah. Nice going, Char." She claps a hand against the seat.

"Thank you." I glance in the rearview mirror and smile at her.

Thoughts scramble in my head. We are on a straight stretch of the road so I brake. I get out, dance around the truck, and shout at the top of my lungs. I get back in the truck and turn the radio up. We all sing, and Kari claps to the song, wiggling in the backseat.

We pull into school and I let Kari out in front of the elementary building before parking. Chase reaches for the door handle.

"Wait," I say. "What do you mean I've been distracted?" I give him a sideways glance.

"I'm not blind. Horses. Fancy archery shots. Hagan's horse deal. Rumors. Tone. The way he looks at you and how you flirt back with him." He rolls his eyes.

"What are you talking about? Tone and I are just friends. He's like a big brother. Besides, how did you know about the horse deal?"

He throws his hands in the air. "This is a small town. We go to a small school."

"Who told you?"

The tension in the rig thickens. Finally, he admits it. "Jill."

"Ha. I should have known. Best friend goes rogue. Tells brother everything."

Chase grunts. "You never tell me anything. I have to find out from someone else. All the time. But who cares, you're only gonna be home for a few more months, and you're out of here. Forever." He motions to the back. "It'll just be me and her." He turns his head away. "Then we're done. The fun ends, right?"

I lean back. "Holy, I'm sorry. Didn't think you cared."

He opens the door. "I don't!"

"Why are you mad?"

He closes the door.

I can't see his face, but I'm sure he's got a stone cold glare going on.

"I'm not." His voice sounds sad.

"Come on. Talk to me."

"Yeah, right. If you don't get it by now..." Chase shrugs, jumps out, and jogs to the high school.

The bell has already rung, but we're not that late. I walk to class and see Mrs. McMillan standing in the hallway, talking to the vice principal. She sees me and comes over.

"Hey there, Charnaye. How are you?"

I settle on a bench. She sits across from me. "I'm good." My eyes drop to the table.

"Not buying it. But, listen, I spoke with your mom this morning. She figured you'd find me sometime today." She tucks a few strands of hair behind an ear.

"She says your grandfather is doing much better. He'll be home in day or so. She'll meet you later and fill you in. She's going to take your sister to see your grandfather while you're at practice."

"Really? She's taking her there?"

"Yes. I guess your grandfather is asking to see her. Misses her pretty badly."

"She normally doesn't go to the hospital. Not after the accident. She hates them." I cross my arms.

"I guess your mom thinks it time she moves forward." Mrs. McMillan leans in. "Perhaps Kari's stronger than you think."

I shrug. "Maybe." Mrs. McMillan shared with me once about her rotten childhood. Her dad left when she was nine. They had no money. Her mom worked odd jobs to make ends meet. She's a true survivor, and I believe she gets what I'm going through.

"How's your senior paper coming along?"

"Haven't really started."

"Oh? That's not like you."

"I've been busy. Precalc and AP History take a lot of my time. That and biology. I hate biology." I tap my pencil on the table.

"Really? As much as you love animals, I thought you'd like it."

I snort. "Yeah if it was just dealing with animals and not humans."

We laugh.

Mrs. McMillan studies me for a long moment. "What help do you need with your paper?"

An image of Sshapa pins to my mind. "I thought I needed to talk more with my grandfather. And interview his friends. But what I really need is to find a woman who's actually raced down the hill. She'd give me firsthand knowledge."

"Wesley'll be home soon. I bet he could suggest such a woman. Or one of his friends can. I encourage you to talk with a couple of them. Especially if he offered. He'll need something to focus on. It'll be good for him."

"You think?" I want to tell her my grandmother was one of the first woman to come down the original Keller hill. For some reason I hesitate.

She nods. "Of course. Don't worry, you'll come up with someone. Do you know any of the male racers? Start there."

Benton's face comes to mind. I head to my next class, wondering if I should've told her about the notes. Not paying attention, I ram into Jill as I round a corner. "Hey!" I rub my head.

"Ouch!" Jill holds her forehead, her face scrunched.

I finger my scalp. Great. Another lump. "You okay?"

She nods. "How come you're so distracted?"

There's that word again. I sigh and come clean. "Sshapa's in the hospital. He had a mild heart attack."

The space between Jill's eyes bunches. "Sorry. Is he going to be all right?"

"Yeah." Should I tell her about the dream? "But hey, crap, I forgot to tell Mrs. McMillan."

"Tell her what?"

I flash her a smile. "I landed the Gates Scholarship!" Then hold up a hand.

"No way! That's awesome. I'm so happy for you." She high-fives me.

"Found out this morning when Chase checked the mail."

Jill leans against the wall, her arms hugging her books. "What did she say? Does she know yet?"

"Not yet. Don't even know if she's in her room or at the hospital. I'll see her after school."

Jill nods. "Hey, listen, about our art project and the threats. Maybe you should tell Mrs. M. She listens and would know what to do without making a scene."

"I don't know…"

Jill brightens. "I have another idea for the art project."

"I like how it is." The words blurt out and I immediately regret them. I lean against the wall.

Jill frowns.

Maybe it was the hurt on her face or my selfish reaction that makes me drop my shoulders. "What do you have in mind?"

"Thought it would be nice to actually get it framed is all."

"Great idea!" I feel like a heel. "Sorry for my snide remark. Guess I'm more worried about my grandfather than I'm willing to admit. What kind of frame?"

"I told my dad about it and he wants to build a frame out of old barn wood for us."

It would add a touch of nostalgia. Especially with the old, gray barn wood. "That's perfect."

"I'll tell him." She bounces down the hall.

The bell rings and I'm relieved to have avoided biology. The rest of the day, I manage to get my class work done with minimal distractions. A few times my attention flits from my nightmare about Sshapa to the scholarship award and back to the dream.

The last bell rings and Mrs. McMillan strolls over to me. "I hear you forgot to tell me something this morning."

I gasp. Big mouth, Jill. Or was it Chase? He would have mentioned the scholarship just to get his point across. However, Jill is the only one I told about the threats. Did she tell Chase about the notes? I just saw her. She didn't have time to say a word. It had to be Chase. I'll kill him. I can't believe he blurted out my news. I wanted to tell her myself. I hang my head. "Sorry. Guess Sshapa's on my mind."

"Don't be sorry. I'm happy for you." She leans over and gives me a hug. "I'm so proud of you."

"Thanks." I smile and relax. "I'm pretty excited. Can't wait to tell my parents."

"I bet. They could use some good news about now." She glances back as another student approaches, calling her name. "Better go."

I spin around, take a step, and bump into Hagan. His glare send shivers down my arms. I lift my chin and walk around him.

CHAPTER 18

I skulk down the hall, footsteps stomping behind me. I turn around, slam into one of Chase's teammates, and apologize. When I look up, my gaze locks with Hagan's. He averts his attention to a conversation others are seeming to have without him. Something snaps inside and I march over to him. Get nose to nose. The others notice and slink off, leaving him hanging. I smirk. "Your threats don't scare me."

"What do you mean?" His voice is deeper than usual.

My fists clench. "Don't deny it." Sshapa tells me patience is the key to life. Never be in a hurry and look fear straight on. That's the only way to conquer it. So I stand and glower at Hagan and his small, pig eyes.

"Oh, you're still mad about the horse. The bet you won," he says it as if I lost. "You'll get him when I'm ready to give him to you." His cackle sounds fake.

I spot a crack of weakness. "Have you had the guts to tell your dad about your loss yet?" My chin gestures to the yellow-blue shadow under his left eye.

His face twists and his gaze flicks to the side.

I grunt. "Haven't have you?" I take a step closer. Close enough I can smell his rotten breath. "I don't think you have the guts to tell your daddy. What would he do if he knew you'd blown three-hundred bucks on some Indian girl and a bow shoot? He'd whip you good, that's what. You can threaten me all you want. I'm not the coward you are."

He shoves me against the wall and my head hits the concrete like a bowling ball to the lane. He holds his hands around my neck. Squeezes tight. Panic snares me like a rabbit in a noose. *Help* forms in my mind, but I can't get enough air in my lungs to make the sound. I try to pry his meaty hands loose, but his grip is crazy tight. Claw his hands and face. Attempt to kick his groin, but can't lift my knee more than a centimeter high. He's got me pinned to the wall, his body heavy against mine.

White spots dangle in my shadowy vision and I go limp against the wall. I open my mouth to scream again. Nothing comes out. Hagan's deep red face is inches from mine, his mouth pursed and eyes squeezed shut as if he's fighting some kind of demon. Out of nowhere I find relief. Someone tackles Hagan and they are on the floor. I slide to the cold tiles and gasp for air, holding my neck as tears tumble down my cheeks. I cough, struggling to catch a breath.

Teachers rush out of their classes and pull the boys apart. So far I haven't seen who my knight in shining armor is. Once I'm able to lift my lids, Chase comes into view. One teacher holds onto a bloody Hagan and the other clutches my still-lunging brother. He's fisting the air, screeching verbal threats. Another male teacher steps in front of him and they walk my brother backward. Not a mark on him, just a smear of Hagan's blood on his gray shirt. His face is flushed and his hair sticks out in all directions. His eyes look like they've come out of a monster flick.

And all to protect me.

Hagan got a cracked lip and blood oozes out of his nose. Red smears his shirt and hands. Pink lines cover his face where my nails dug in. They haul him off.

Chase breaks loose and drops beside me. "You okay?" He leans close. "I'm gonna kill him."

"What's going on here?" The teacher holding Chase releases his grip.

"Hagan attacked me," I say, my voice raspy. I press my head into my hands. The lights hurt. Sound hurts. My throat burns when I swallow.

"Chase, what's your story?" the other teacher says.

Sharp footsteps crack down the hall. "What's going on here?" It's the vice principal's voice.

I massage my throat. Chase stretches a hand toward me.

I use my shoulder to block him. "I'm fine."

The teacher again says, "Chase, your story?"

Without looking at him, Chase answers. "I was going to the bathroom and turned the corner to find Hagan pinning my sister to the wall. He was choking her, what was I supposed to do?"

One of the teachers kneels beside me.

"Look at her neck," Chase tells him.

He inspects my neck, eyes, and head with a gentle touch. "She needs medical attention."

"That matches Hagan's story," the vice says. "Now we just have to find out why. You want to add anything, Charnaye?"

Chase jumps to his feet and gets in the vice's face. "And what are you gonna do about it? He was choking her!"

The principal rests a hand on Chase's shoulder. "Calm down, son. We'll take care of it."

"I ain't your son." Chase slaps the hand away.

I cringe. "Don't be a punk." I doubt he'll listen to me, but it's worth a try.

"Take care of him, or I will. I'm tired of Hurst talking crap about my sister. Us being Native." Chase's jaw flexes.

I reach for him and try to stand, falling into the teacher who's beside me.

"Look at her," Chase says. He raises an arm as if to strike the vice.

"Come with me, I think you need a few days to cool off." The vice motions for Chase to follow him.

"That's freakin' crap! I get kicked out for defending my sister?" Chase balls his fist and strikes the wall. Blood trickles to the floor.

One of the teachers grabs him by the arm. "That's enough!"

"Take him to my office." The vice turns to me and holds out a hand. I take it and stand, legs wobbly. "Take your time."

My head throbs and I'm dizzy. My knees are about to buckle when Chase grabs me and lets me lean against him.

"I'm staying with my sister."

More steps click down the hall. Fast, short steps. I squeeze my eyes shut.

"Crap! It's mom," Chase whispers.

My gut roils and I hug myself. Bile rises and burns my throat. I cover my mouth and breathe deeply through my nose. The pounding in my head quickly becomes unbearable and I lean over, puking all over the floor.

"What on earth is going on here?" Mom's nostrils flare.

I wipe my mouth. My breaths come quickly, and my mouth waters. I reach for my mom, wanting her to remain calm. She thrusts her hands on her hips. Looks from one man to the other and lands her focus on Chase.

He gives her a hard glare.

"I just saw a bloody Hagan Hurst being escorted into the office by Mr. Rustle." It wasn't a question. "Both of your names were mentioned."

"I'm sure you did—" Chase stands tall.

Mom raises her brows and takes a step toward Chase. I silently applaud him for opening the bull's gate and elbow his ribs. He jerks away and throws me a nasty scowl.

"Are you daring to backtalk me after the night I've had? Sass at a time like this?" The pitch of her voice drops to a low drone. Eyes narrow, she takes another step forward. The vein on her neck is as thick as a night crawlers.

"No." Red-faced, Chase backs down and steps back. But it's too late. The bull's out of the corral and has been slapped on the butt. I shake my head and nudge him forward. No way is he getting out of this. Even after defending me. He's won the wrath of Arlie Toulou. If it wasn't for her looking like she'd been to hell and back, I'd let her come unglued on him. But in her defense, I step in destruction's path.

"Mom." I reach out to her, trying to pull her attention off the idiot and on to me. I try and focus on her, but things are a little fuzzy. I put a hand up to my eyes.

A custodian mops the floor with sudsy water. We move to the side and watch him for a minute as we all seem to gather our thoughts. At least I do. Mom crosses her arms. By the look on the vice's face, he appears to be forming a way to calm the bull.

I turn back to Mom, weaving back and forth. She places her arm around my shoulder.

"Hagan and I got into an argument, he pinned me to the wall and choked me. Chase came to my rescue and pulled him off before I passed out. No big deal. It's over." I hunch over and hold my belly. The smell of vomit makes my mouth water. So I cover it, willing myself to hold any remaining contents in my stomach down.

"Hagan did what?" Mom turns to the vice principal as if he's holding a red flag and back at me. "Did anyone call the police?" She presses my head with her fingers, lingers over the bumps, and turns to the vice, upper lip curled. "Why do you allow these students to behave in this manner?" She spins back to me. "Why would Hagan choke you?"

"Because he's a lying, cheating, coward." The words come out of my mouth before I had time to spit out the poison. I glance at Chase. Now he's shaking his head.

Mom points a finger at the vice. "I'd prefer to handle this myself. It's a family matter. I think I need to get Charnaye to the hospital, and Chase, I'll deal with you later." She points a finger at him. "Our family is under a lot of pressure at the moment, and I think..." She bites her lower lip.

The vice nods. "You can handle things however you want, Arlie. But Chase will be staying home for three days for fighting. I think he needs to cool off. He can go around to his classes now and get his work. Maybe take the time and help his father at home while Wesley's in the hospital. I think Charnaye should go home, and if the doctor agrees, she can return tomorrow. I'll take care of Hagan, trust me." He probes her with his eyes.

"Very well. I assume you'll take care of this incident in the *appropriate* manner. I'll let you know if we decide to press charges."

"You may." His gazed pins on Mom for a brief moment.

She turns to me and slides her arm into mine and walks me to the bathroom. She doesn't say one word while I rinse my mouth out with cold water. Just stands there, tapping her foot, taking deep breaths. She hands me a piece of gum. "We'll talk about this tonight. I want all the details."

I wince at the pain. The mirror reflects redness under my eyes and purple fingerprints around my neck. Jill pops her head in. Mom glares at her. Jill gives me a puzzled look. I shake my head. She backs out the door. Once I finish wiping my face with a damp towel, I follow Mom out of the bathroom.

The hall is cleared out. Mom watches me. "Is your head hurting?"

"Yeah. I should have grabbed a cool towel and brought it with me."

"I'll get one for her," Mrs. McMillan says. "Mrs. Larson is covering your class."

Mom searches my pupils. "Let's take you to the school nurse." She takes my hand is if I'm a toddler and marches me to the office. The nurse is gone. I'm glad because Mom's in mother mode and I rather her not baby me right now. She sits me down in a chair and goes into the principal's office. Mrs. McMillan brings me a cool, damp towel and leaves. I lay it over the back of my head. They're in there for what feels like an hour. When Mom does come out, she rests in the chair next to me. Red rims her eyes. I reach out to comfort her, but my hand ends up back on my lap.

"Sorry, Mom. You didn't need this." I pause. "I started the fight with Hagan…I'm—"

"I don't care who started what. He had no right to lay his hands on you." Her voice low but forceful. "Mr. Aspen will handle it. He's going to talk to Mr. Morris. I'll take you to the hospital to get your head and throat checked, peek in on Sshapa, and come back for Kari and your father. We'll go home and sort this all out. I'm taking a few days off. We need to get our family back in order." Her mouth sags. "The sooner the better."

"What about Chase?"

She thinks a moment. "I suppose he'll have to come with us."

"Speaking of." I point to him.

We walk out to Mom's car and get in. The afternoon chill and cloudy sky matches my mood.

"Your Sshapa needs a medication change and he'll be home in a couple days. They want to make sure the right meds keep him in rhythm." She cranks the motor and eases out of the parking lot. "I took your father to Mr. Anderson's for the day. We'll pick him up after we get Char's head checked."

The doctor finds a slight concussion, gives me pain meds, and discharges me. We check on Sshapa and tell some jokes. When Mom leaves to get him some juice from the vending machine, he praises Chase for protecting me.

"Fighting with words is best, but sometimes, you have to use a swift right hook." His eyes shimmer as he speaks. "I think you did the right thing."

Chase takes in the tributes with a deep laughter and puffed out chest. May as well let him enjoy it. The real sparks will fly tonight.

I desperately want to tell Sshapa about the threatening notes. I need to talk to someone. Then again, I don't want to upset him. Not sure his heart could take it. What if it's not Hagan? Who would it be? His cronies? I'm not sure they're that smart. Evil, yes, but smart? Sshapa would understand. He'd tell me what to do. But looking at him, small and frail like a dried up prune, I can't bring myself to open up to him. If I told Chase to leave, he'd know something was up.

I can't take that risk.

CHAPTER 19

Dad's eyes narrow as he struggles to roll his wheelchair to the car through the roughly plowed snow. Mom and Chase push from behind. Lips tight, it looks like he's waiting for more private moments to let loose on my brother. I'm kind of nervous. He's not the only one in trouble. I'm sure I'll get hit with "watch your mouth" and "don't pick fights with fools" when we get home. Kari's in the car which may be our saving grace. I hope so. But won't bet on it. With two of three kids making trouble in school, even though I didn't really get into trouble, I'm sure Dad's blood is reaching the boiling point.

I jump out of the car and open the door for him. He scoots in, eyes averted. There has to be an easier way for him to get around. Dad settles in the car while Chase wipes off muddy snow, lifts his chair into the trunk, and ties it down with baling twine. Mom backs out of the Andersons' driveway using her side mirrors.

"Mom, want me to get out and guide you back?" Chase twists around.

"I got it," she says, her tone sharp and weary. Her lips tighten as she glances from mirror to mirror, creeping back.

We need a decent van. I've seen ones in Spokane with lifts on them. Another reason to win the suicide race. It would take a lot of bake sales to purchase one of those. On the other hand, the race winnings would bring in a hefty down payment. We turn down Highway 21 and head for the ranch. Tension is thick in the car. So thick it's hard to breathe. Chase and I exchange worried glances.

"Dad, can you turn on the radio?" Chase glances at Mom.

Brave move on his part. Dad neither answers nor turns on any music. I think he enjoys knowing we're squirming in the backseat.

I give Chase a snarly look. Kari sits between us, stone still. I don't know what Mom told her. Maybe nothing yet. You think she'd act happier being pulled out of school for half a day. Her stomach growls and she hugs herself. The ride home feels like it's taking a whole lot longer than normal.

"Mom, we left the truck at school," I say, worried it may get broken into. I'm surprised she didn't have one of her friends pick it up as much as she and Dad fret about this era of high crime. They can't afford to get it fixed if it's vandalized and what a burden to have one less rig.

She nods. "The doctor suggests you not drive for a day or two. We had to leave it behind."

I'm not sure what the look on her face is, but her tone says she's had enough talking. I rest my head against the seat and close my eyes. Hagan's bloody face agitates the already dark spaces in my mind, so I watch trees heavy with snow race by and hum.

Back at home we eat a quick meal of tuna sandwiches. No one says a word. Mom sends Chase and me to our rooms. Kari gets to watch a movie. Dad's eyes are drooping when I walk past. I guess that's our punishment for now. Silence. Steel, cold silence. It's working. Why can't we get the punishment over with now and not have to drag it out?

I drop to my bed and bounce a few times until my body settles into the ragged mattress. Music rebounds from Chase's room. I pound the wall with my fist, hoping he'll turn it down. He doesn't. I reach for my bag and remember it's at school. So much for homework. I close my eyes instead, hands cupped over my ears, eager to drift off to sleep for an hour or so. Mom bangs on Chase's door and tells him to turn the music down. He does.

Thoughts thump around in my head, reliving Hagan's hands around my throat. Me gasping for air. His eyes bulging with rage. I feel for swelling and go to the mirror above my dresser. Deeper bruises have formed. Claw marks appear that I didn't see earlier. I plop down on my bed. Tears pool in my eyes. I blink them away and stare at our ruined art project that looms from the top of my desk. I grab it. After contemplating the fine details, I retrieve the clean canvas and dig a pencil out of my desk. The only thing that will quiet my mind at this point is to sketch a new copy.

After a couple hours, I put down the canvas for a break. The pain meds make me feel loopy. I have most of the artwork transferred: Native woman, horse, bow and quill with arrows. Jill can touch it up and paint tomorrow. Her detail work will make it good as new. I carefully lay both canvases back on my desk. Chase's country music drifts from his room. I stretch stiff muscles, open my bedroom door, and turn the corner. As I get closer to my parents room, I hear muffled voices. Talk of homeschooling me filters through the door.

No way!

They can't keep me home. I'll suffocate. The voices stop as if they know I'm just outside their door. I can handle Hagan. Hiding out will only make things worse. I'm sure he won't touch me again after the beating Chase gave him. Not to mention the one his Dad gave him. Forget the stupid horse. He was never mine in the first place.

In a rush of panic, I pull on coat, hat, and gloves and run out the door, letting it slam behind me. I won't let them keep me home. I'll beg Mrs. McMillan to make them understand I need this last year. They can't keep me away now. They can't keep Chase home either. It's ridiculous. I won't let it happen.

I grab Stimteema's bridle and open her stall door. She stands there all warm and cozy, eyes half-mast. Until I blast in with the cold air and startle her. I slow down. "Easy, girl." I stroke her neck. Eyes wide, she snorts. "I'm sorry. Didn't mean to frighten you." I put my thumb in her mouth, insert the bit, and slip my new headband over her ears.

We walk out into a light snow fall, and I hop on bareback. Her body is warm against my legs. I rein her west and head down the old logging road. Even with her long thoroughbred legs, it's a slow crawl in two feet of snow. I concentrate on my surroundings. At how quiet the woods are when it snows. I pray my parents' change their mind as I soak in the last minutes of daylight.

Even though the crisp air and smell of my horse has offered peace and calm, a dull pain in my head resurfaces.

Coyotes yip in the distance. Stimteema's ears twirl. A shiver runs down me so I rein her around and head back. Trees look like shadows against the snow-covered ground. My toes are cold and so is my nose. The last trace of light now fades at a faster pace as the muddled sun drops behind the mountains.

Once back, I do my chores, looking forward to a hot cup of cocoa and my next pain pill. I toss an extra handful of grain into Stimteema's bucket and press my face to her neck. Inhale her scent. I take a minute to form a battle plan before tackling the trenches, my tummy in knots.

I brush off snow and stomp my boots before entering the kitchen. The smell of homemade chicken noodle soup and fresh-baked biscuits waft through the room. Mom pulls out a pan from the oven while Kari sets the table. As Dad watches the news, Chase is on the couch tackling homework. I do a double take. He lifts his chin and smiles.

I shake my head. "Homework? Really?" I toss him a smirk and mouth *suck-up* to him.

He gives me a lopsided grin and turns his attention back to his studies.

A calm sifts through the house. I'm not sure what took place with my family while I was out riding. Things seem awfully strange. Perhaps this is the fattening before the slaughter.

Mom twists around. "Go wash for dinner. It's ready."

"What the heck?" I drag past Chase. He offers nothing. Once in dry clothes, I enter the kitchen. Everyone is already around the table. I settle in my hard, wooden chair next to Chase and across from Mom. Dad is on the end to my right. Kari is next to Mom. Everyone stares as if I'm a sacrificial lamb.

We pray over the meal and dig in. I lean back in my chair, arms folded across my chest, and inspect my parents' faces. I'm not sure how to decipher the meaning. Will they give us our tongue-lashing during dinner? After? Surely not after Kari goes to sleep. Would they make us wait that long? The thoughts itch my mind.

My father sees me staring at him as he's lifting his spoon to his mouth and pauses before sucking the juice. He butters his biscuit, glancing at me. I fidget and scowl at Chase. He chews with a smile on his haughty face, making me want to smack it off his lips. Why is he not squirming? I unfold my arms and lift one to smack him.

"Is there something you want to say, Char?" My father says. "You've hardly taken a bite of your food. Is there something wrong with your mother's cooking?"

Kari snickers.

I drop my arm to my lap. "Mom's cooking is fine. I'm…I'm…" I shake my head and collect my thoughts. If I tell them about the threats it'd take the pressure off me. But add more on them. I groan. They don't need the extra drama. No one does. I shift in my chair, throwing caution to the wind, and blurt out, "What's going on? Earlier you were ready to strangle us both"— I glance at Chase—"and now everyone's acting as if nothing's happened. Like I didn't almost die today!"

Dad takes of bit of biscuit and chews, his compassionate gaze pinned on me.

I grip my spoon, assuming he's assembling his own thoughts and allowing me time to calm down, but it only agitates me more. "Chase gets kicked out of school and I'm almost choked to death by a psycho kid. I'm expecting you guys to crack the whip and you're all sitting here calm, like some happy little family." I pause to catch my breath. "We're not happy. We're the most broken family I know." Tears well in my eyes.

Dad takes another bite of his biscuit, glances at Mom, and stares at the table.

I jig my leg and wait and allow curiosity to hold me in my seat.

Chase opens his mouth to say something. Mom arches her eyebrow at him, and he closes it. Slouches in his chair.

"We seem like a happy little family because we are one," Dad says. "We have much to be thankful for. I've never been more proud of my son for saving his sister, let's see now, how did you say it, from some *psycho kid* at school." He gives me a wide smile and shoves another bite in his mouth.

"So that's it? We live happily ever after? What's wrong with you people?" I snap my hand over my mouth. "I'm sorry. I didn't mean that." I twirl my spoon in my soup.

Mom sips her coffee. "Here's the thing, Charnaye. I know Hagan has been after you for a while. I work at the school, remember? I know about…" She pauses and looks at Dad.

Oh crap. They know.

"We know about the horse bet." She takes a few bites of soup.

Panic sets in. What else do they know? I bet Jill told Chase about the threats. I give Chase a scrutinizing glare.

He lifts his hands in the air. "It wasn't me."

Mom gives Chase a look of admiration, making me want to puke.

"It's a small school. People talk and they love to tell me all about you kids' life. Great times for me, as you can imagine." She lifts her eyebrows. "We know Hagan got beat pretty badly. It's sad really. But what you don't know is his father found out about the bet and worked Hagan over pretty good, giving him bruises you can see…and ones you can't. It was after he called us." She places a hand on Dad's. "I hope there's no serious damage."

I slump in my chair. "Serious damage? You really care about him? He cost me a horse!"

Dad slams his fist on the table. "There will be no horse deal. And Char, look at me," he says, his voice low and stern.

Kari jumps.

I face him, my gut roiling.

"You will not race down that hill." He seizes his biscuit and tears off a bite. "Arlie, this is the best meal. I could eat your homemade noodle soup and bread every day." His breaths come hard and fast.

I swallow. "What do you mean? It's just my senior paper?" *Can I lie worse than that?* Who'd they hear it from? I've told no one. It was my secret. I'm coming on eighteen, I can do whatever I want. I study my parents' faces. They resemble two bulls with sharp eyes and pointy horns. I wait for them to charge. "It's just a paper," I say softer. I take a few bites of soup for good measure. Choke down the food, praying it doesn't come back up.

"That better be the truth, missy." Mom points her spoon at me.

Heat rises from my curled toes to the top of my head. Searing heat, the kind they brand cattle with. The truth is, they'll thank me later. When I win and things are fixed around here and dad has a nice down payment for a new van with an electric lift. If I take it all, I could potentially hand over ten grand.

Everyone eats and pretends we're fine.

"Your mother and I were talking," Dad says after dishes are cleared from the table. He folds his hands.

Chase pushes away from the table to stand, but Mom motions for him to scoot back over. He does.

I give him a sideways glance. I'm the one in trouble and the prodigal just had his feast. My mind wanders back to Hagan's hands around my neck. I finger the bruises. He must be scared in his own home. But I don't care. I'm scared to go back to school and face everyone's judgment. Three years ago we were a happy family. And now the house feels more than strained.

"We're worried about your safety at school," he continues. "We were thinking"—he glances at mother who nods—"that maybe you should homeschool for a spell until you get back on your feet. When the time is right and things are settled we can talk about you finishing at the high school and in time to graduate."

"What? Why?" I can't believe what I'm hearing. It's true. It's got to be a mistake. "Homeschool? Who would teach me? Dad? Sshapa? No way. I can't agree to this. I'll suffocate."

"It would just be for a month or two," Mom says. "I've already cleared it with the principal—"

"You've already decided? Without me?" I shove away from the table and run to my room. I slam the door shut, turn on the radio, and let the music shut out those words. *Homeschool. Never!*

I grab the canvas and drop to my bed. My head pounds. I fumble for pain pills and pop one in my mouth. The clock reads 6:45. It's gonna be a long night. I survey my work with blurred vision. I set my canvas aside and lie back. My eyes close, leaking.

I roll over. The clock reads 8:30. Knots across my shoulders and back and down my legs feel as though I've been run over by the same log truck that crashed into Dad and Kari. My throat aches. From Chase's room drifts Carrie Underwood singing her newest hit. I groan and face the wall. A sharp corner pricks me in the thigh. My fingers fumble around on top of my quilt and come into contact with the corner of the canvas frame. I roll onto my back and drag my art project out of the covers. There's a hint of smearing, but nothing Jill can't smooth over with her magic touch.

After placing the canvas on my desk, I hit the shower. The hot water running over me clears my head. I breathe deep a few times, letting the steam cleanse my lungs. Being homeschooled may not be a bad gig. I would have more time to research my project and possibly stay with Aunt Jamison in Omak for spring break. I'll bring Kari if needed. Jamison's my dad's sister. She and Uncle Buck have race horses. She'd have information and resources to fill in the cracks concerning the suicide race, or would know someone who can, so I can finish my paper.

I flip on my radio and get dressed. Hum along as I think about the upcoming archery shoot in Ellensburg. I have one week to get ready. Two weeks later is spring break. I can hold on until then. Take a hiatus and come back fresh. Hopefully after the break, I can go back to school. Shake off senioritis. I want to be done with high school and start my life. The adult life my parents and Sshapa have prepared me for since birth.

I drag a brush out of my backpack and the notes spill out. I sit on my bed and read them again. Who wants to stop me? It's got to be Hagan. No one else has a reason to hate me. No one else gives me that hard of a time. Now that he's out of school for a while, they should stop. *Get a grip!* I crumple up the notes and toss them in the trash. Pull them back out, smoothing out the wrinkles, fold them all into one bunch, and slip them into my desk drawer. *No one can see them. Ever.*

All I need to do is get through school and graduation. Forget boys—they're too big of a distraction—and zero in on training. I still need a horse. My heart sinks. I plop down on my bed and drop my head into my hands. "Creator, I need something to ride in this race. Help me find that perfect horse. One with heart. One that will take me into womanhood. Open the door for more female jockeys. I'm tired being shoved to the back, like I'm weaker. Bring me the people who have a horse that will get the job done…" I stand, remembering the vow to act like an adult. And trust.

CHAPTER 20

I shuffle into breakfast, still rubbing my eyes. The hot shower seemed to help me relax. A misty fog casts eerie shadows out the window. "Now I know why I'm so sluggish." I stand by the fire and take a moment to will myself to do chores. Chase plods down the hall and appears, hair spiking out in all directions, eyes half-mast. I raise my eyebrows. "You look worse than I feel."

"It took forever to fall asleep last night. I woke up all sweaty from a dream I had about you." He combs his hair with his fingers, takes out the milk carton from the fridge, and guzzles some.

I cringe. "You disgust me." I'll wait and get milk from the next carton. The one I'll ask Mom to buy today. "What was your dream about?"

Chase puts the carton on the table and closes the fridge door. "I saw Hagan choking you again." Anger flashes in his eyes.

I keep my mouth shut. I never thought he cared that much about anything but football and cheerleaders. Someday he may actually talk to one. "I still feel his hands squeezing my neck. Especially at night." A shiver ripples down my back. "It's hard to sleep."

"Yeah, but this time I'm stabbing him with a knife. Blood shoots everywhere…" His voice chokes.

"No wonder you didn't sleep." My tummy flip-flops as I relive yesterday in my mind.

"If I see him again, I'm afraid I'll lose it." He shakes his head. "He won't ever hurt you like that again..." He looks down the hall as if searching for self-control. "Dad can't defend you. Sshapa's too old. It's on me now." He grabs his coat off the hook and narrows his eyes. "And I'm up for the challenge. No one hurts my sisters." A red web covers the whites of his eyes.

I've never seen the veins on his neck bulge like they are now. I'm glad to know he's got my back, but dang, I don't want him to go after Hagan. "Hey, listen. Thanks for standing up for me. Love you, too." I smile at him.

With a blank look on his face he says, "Don't joke about it."

I sigh. "Don't go looking for trouble. Hagan'll find his own easy enough. Sounds like he's got it pretty hard at home. I never knew that. Did you?"

Chase shakes his head.

"Anyways, he's kicked out of school for a while from the sounds of it."

Chase flexes his jaw. "Let's go feed." He slips on his boots, hat, and gloves, and stomps out the door.

Looks like I'm going to have to keep an eye on Chase from now on. Maybe he needs to come with me to Aunt Jamison's, not Kari. Hothead mixed with revenge makes for a dangerous combo. We rush around and feed in record time. When we come back into the house, Mom and Kari are dressed and sitting at the table with toast and peaches. The carton is still on the table.

"We need fresh milk." I scowl at Chase.

He flashes me a playful grin. Feeding must have allowed him time to blow off some steam. Unless he's putting a show on for Mom. I'm not sure, but if so, he needs to become an actor.

Bread pops out of the toaster. "That's yours, Charnaye. Why don't you get it and come sit with us." Her tone tells me that's an order, not a question.

I swallow as fits of nervousness churn inside me. "Coming." I pluck out my toast and slink over to the table.

Mom takes a sip of her coffee and holds it to her chest. There is a twinkle in her eye. "You didn't let me finish last night." She fingers her cup.

I lift my eyes to her. "Oh?" I sink in my chair. "I'm sorry…" I don't know what to say. I should have listened. It would have saved me a heartache, I'm sure.

"We are *not* going to make you homeschool." She takes another sip of coffee.

Who's the fool now? Assuming the worse doesn't normally work for me, but for some odd reason, I just keep doing it. Like the *tap, tap, tap* on the window from a tree branch not long ago. The branch doesn't want in. But it keeps tapping in the wind. No rhyme or reason for it. Assuming things just keeps tapping my head. Maybe I should open that window. Let some savvy in. "Wow. Should have stayed in my chair, huh."

Kari chuckles. "Yeah."

I pop her on the head with a napkin.

I finger our old, worn pine table. It was a wedding present to my mom years ago. Dad had made the entire table with his hands, no nails, just some kind of spline joint he'd learned from his dad. Grandpa used to be quite the craftsman before he died of a stroke at the tender age of thirty-five. Dad asked his shop teacher if he knew how to make this type of furniture. He did. Together, they built a couple small pieces during his last two years of high school. He'd spent a lot of time during class and after school learning the craft.

Eating crow off it tastes bad. Like kerosene. And it burns just as hot going down.

"We simply wanted to offer the option if you felt you needed it." Mom finishes her coffee. Time for school. At least for me and Kari. The bus will be here soon. I want to ask Mom about going to Aunt Jamison's place. I've got to get out of here, but the timing stinks. I'll talk to her in a few days. When things are back to normal. For now, another day in the trenches.

When I arrive at school, everyone gawks at me, like they do at the movie star tabloids. The air around my head feels warmer and heavier even though the hallway is frigid. I finger the back of my neck by my hairline. I've already eaten breakfast so I meander to the library, ignoring the stares. I search for Mrs. McMillan, but don't see her. She's probably in a staff meeting.

Sally's crumpled on the floor, hugging her knees, in the corner of the library between bookshelves. Her lips release muffled sobs. Eyes red and watery, she holds a tissue to her nose, tears streaking down her face. I ease to the floor beside her. "You okay?"

She blows her nose and shakes her head. Throws the tissue on the floor. Plucks another one out of the box and presses it against her red nose. "Sam dumped me last night. I saw him in the hall. It's…I can't…" Fresh tears stream down her face. She squeezes her knees and buries her face inside her arms. Her shoulders lurch with each moan.

My first instinct is to jump and shout for joy. My second keeps me beside her. "I'm sorry." I pat her back. "He'll come around." Part of me hopes he doesn't. I'd at least have a morsel of a chance.

"No, he won't," she lifts her head. "He told me he's applied to Montana State and has been accepted." Balled tissue covers the carpet.

"Oh…" I can't seem to manage anything more than a lame sound out of my mouth. My heart leaps, twists, and falls.

"I thought we had our lives mapped out. Both attending Central. I love Ellensburg. What does Bozeman have that offers more? There is nothing there!"

"I don't—"

"We had a plan, Charnaye. What went wrong?" Fresh tears roll down her soft, white cheeks.

I drum my fingers on my leg. "Maybe that's the problem." What I really want to say is *run. Find someone who will appreciate you.* I keep my thoughts to myself.

She wipes her nose with a fresh tissue. "What do you mean?"

I clear my throat, voice still hoarse. "Think about it, what boy wants his life all mapped out? Especially a senior. I mean, he's ready to fly on out of here and experience the world."

"I…he said…" She extends her legs and folds her hands in her lap.

I sigh. This is exactly why I avoid guys. "They are a thriving, exploring, shambled mess full of testosterone mixed with arrogance." Except Sam. He's gentle, kind, compassionate. Why on earth did the dip-stick break her heart? That I'll never understand.

Sally cocks her head. "What do I do?" She daps her eyes.

"Tell him he can go to Montana State, take the pressure off, and you can see if he circles back to you, tension free. Besides, lots of people do the long distance thing and it seems to work out. I hate to say it, but if you two are meant to be together, it'll happen."

Sam shuffles in and finds us. "Hey. Can I talk with Sally?" He fidgets.

She nods.

I push myself off the carpet, bump Sam on the shoulder with a fist, and amble out. I honestly hope they get back together because in reality, they fit like a hand in glove.

The bell rings and I head to class. One of Hagan's cow pie friends runs into me as I try to trample through the herd of kids rushing to first period. He pins me to the wall. "Hagan may be out, but we aren't. There will be hell to pay. Watch for it!" He rushes off with the rest of the students.

My body trembles. Usually, none of them make a move without their fearless leader. Is he egging them on from home? Mrs. McMillan joins me. I shake my head and hold up a hand to stop her from speaking. Carla's behind her watching us, a smirk on her face.

Later in art class, I hand the canvas to Jill.

She brushes the smudge with a finger. "I like your outline, Char. Nice job!"

"Thanks. It's now in the hands of an expert."

She giggles and playfully shoves my shoulder. "Ooh, sorry. How's your head?"

"Still hurts."

She frowns, her gaze dropping to my neck. "Your throat? Your voice sounds raspy."

"It'll heal." I shrug.

"I talked with Mrs. Larson. She said I can take the project home to finish it so no one else messes with it."

"Holy! Mrs. L never lets anyone take projects home."

"Yeah, she told me she knows how important it is to us and is going to let us work on another project in class." Jill claps her hands.

"That's awesome!"

I catch a glimpse of a guy walking by. *You'll regret it.* I bite my lip. *It can't be.* I peer around the door and sure enough, it's Hagan. I shudder. My legs wobble like one of those painted wooden egg-shaped dolls. I can't think of what they are called. But inside the first one is four or five smaller dolls. I catch myself and take a chair, head between my legs.

CHAPTER 21

It's good to have Sshapa home. His face is back to its darker color, though he's still weak. Most importantly, his smile once again lights the room.

We seem happy around the dinner table, catching up. Until I say, "I saw Hagan at school today."

"What?" Dad's mouth creaks open. His gaze drifts to Mom. "Arlie?"

"He's suspended for a week and came for his books. His father made him sign a document stating he would stay away from Charnaye," Mom says. "I was just as surprised as administration, but apparently his father made him get his own assignments. Maybe he wants the boy to feel the shame of walking back in and getting snide remarks thrown in his face by his peers. Who knows?"

Chase smiles and twirls his fork in the air, a chunk of elk meat stabbed on the end. A haughty laugh escapes his throat.

Sshapa eyes him, brows raised. He takes a bite of steak, appearing to savor the flavor.

Chase turns to me, eyes sparkling. "Yeah, I saw him, too."

I drop my chin, eyes on my plate.

"What's going on with you two?" Distrust lathers Dad's tone.

"Nothing." Chase shoves the meat in his mouth and stabs another.

"There better not be," Dad says. "Vengeance is *not* yours."

I glare at Chase. "When did you see him?"

"Went and picked Sshapa up from the hospital this morning with Mom," he said. His upper lip curls. "We stopped at school."

My gaze darts around the table and falls on Chase. I will him to shut his cocky mouth. I weave my fingers together so I don't punch him. Chase keeps his eyes forward, eating his meal as if forming a plan.

"Whatever you two are drumming up, it stops now," Dad says, his voice low.

Kari pushes back from the table and flips on the television. She curls up on the couch, arranging a blanket around her as if to protect against thick tension.

"Nothing going on with us, Dad." Chase wipes his plate clean with a biscuit and pushes away from the table. "Great dinner, Mom. Time for homework."

"Hang on, homework?" I've never seen him play this game so well.

"Kari, do you have any school work to finish?" Dad says.

"Reading." Her head pops up. "I get to sketch a picture for Miss Best. Can I do it now?"

For two years my sister has hidden in a dark internal cave. For a while I was scared she wasn't going to immerge. A counselor that sees her at school once a week seems to be leading her back to the living. That and Mom's prayers she says every night for Sshapa, Dad, money problems, me, and college. But mostly she prays for Kari. She doesn't know we listen. We hear her pray for Creator to intervene, heal little Swaskee's broken heart. I guess He is.

"We leave for Ellensburg tomorrow morning bright and early," I say to Mom. "Can I get a ride or borrow a rig?" I finish off my glass of water.

"I'll drive you to your competition. You know I don't miss them," Sshapa says.

Mom glares at him. "You will not!"

"Oh now, Arlie. I'm just fine. You heard the doctor say I can resume normal activities."

"Yes, normal activities. That includes fiddling with the animals and tack and blending in long afternoon naps." The look on her face tells him he'd better listen or else.

I let out a snicker. "Maybe I can borrow your truck, Sshapa and drive myself."

He shakes his head. "I'll drive."

"No way, Pops. You won't be driving anytime soon." Dad pushes away from the table and opens his arms, seeming to invite Kari on his lap. She finds a couple of books, climbs up, and wraps her arms around his neck, kissing him on the cheek.

I glance around the table, "Well?"

Mom taps her mug. "Here's what we're going to do. Since I've been gone from work more than usual, I'll take Charnaye to school so she can catch the bus with the team, make lesson plans, pick everyone up, and we'll make the trip to Ellensburg. As a family."

"Yay!" Kari says. "We're gonna watch Charnaye."

I slump in my chair. It's a six hour ride on stiff seats. Hopefully Mom will sign me off. I can at least ride home with them. My hand drifts to my neck. I sigh, relieved Hagan won't be with us. At least I can concentrate on my shots and have a chance at nationals. The only problem is, if I make it to Louisville, Kentucky, it will disrupt the middle of training. Can I afford to take a week off?

"Sounds like a plan," Dad says.

Sshapa winks. "Guess I get to go after all." A sinister expression forms on his face and he leans close to me. "I'll drive next time," he whispers.

But there won't be a next time. My heart sinks to my toes, knowing it is my last local competition. Might be my last one period if I keep Hagan in my head.

The alarm goes off early. It's 5:00. The bus leaves at 6:30.

I hurry and dress, rush down the hall, and slam into Chase as I make the corner to the fridge.

"Ouch!" he says. "Watch it."

"Sorry. Got to go feed before we leave. I only have a few minutes." I roll the length of my hair, twist in on top of my head, and snap in a clip.

"I fed." He stands there with his hands on his hips. The look on his face suggests he's waiting for me to throw a smart remark in his face.

"Really?" I can't believe what I'm hearing. "Thanks." I stand there like a confused school girl.

"You hungry?" Chase opens the fridge door. "We got bacon, eggs, toast, milk—"

"That better be fresh." I cringe at the thought of his germs in my food.

He grins. "It's fresh."

I don't believe him. "Why are you so happy this morning?" I slug him in the arm.

"Part of my punishment for slamming Hagan to the ground is having to make Saturday morning breakfast. For a month. So while you go beautify yourself for the shoot, I'll cook." He pulls out bacon and eggs. He points to my hair with a spatula. "You might want to do something with that."

I sneer at him, looking at the food in his hands. "Enjoy your punishment?"

"I hate to cook," he says. "Besides, it's woman's work." He opens and shuts cupboards.

I watch him for a minute, not sure I want to offer any help after his snide. "What are you looking for?"

"Don't worry. I'll figure it out."

I grunt and head to my room. Voices drift out from behind Mom's bedroom door. I don't hear anything coming from Kari's room. They'll let her sleep longer to keep the grumpies at bay. The sound of a flushing toilet alerts me—Sshapa's awake.

The cold truck chugs to life. I slide out to get Mom and meet her at the back door. She holds out a steaming cup of cocoa for me and I take it. "Ready?"

I nod. "Yep. Just let me grab my stuff." I take of sip of cocoa, hand it back to her, and run into the house for my bag. I rush back to the truck. Mom's in the passenger's seat. I slide under the wheel and back out.

Even though it's the middle of March and the roads are bare, patches of snow stick along shaded banks. We chug along at a snail's pace.

"What does the doctor really say about Sshapa?" I give her a quick glance.

"In time he'll be back to normal." Her head turns toward the window and she stares outside.

I don't believe her.

It doesn't take long before we pull into the school's parking lot. Instinctively, my eyes search for Hagan. They land on Jill, who's waving her hands over her head. Sam is by his truck, Sally in his arms. She must not be coming.

Six hours later we drive into the parking lot at Central. Buses line the pavement like sardines in a can. We all have on matching orange shirts with a black tiger in the middle of a target. My nerves kick sparks throughout my body. My muscles constrict. My breaths come out in ragged spurts.

"Wow, I've never seen you this nervous, Char," Jill says. "What's going on?"

I shake my head. "I don't know. I've never felt this way before. Not racing, not..." My mind whirls back to being in front of the school board as I lie my way into their trust. My knees were knocking that day. So yes, I've felt this way before. I glance up and see the back of a guy with red hair. I drop my gaze. *No!* What am I thinking? He can't be here. Who am I trying to fool? I felt this way when Mom rushed into the house with the news of Dad and Kari being in a rig that was wrapped around a pine tree. When Dad hit his head because I was late. At my stimteema's funeral. Seeing Sshapa in the hospital, looking like a pale prune under a blanket.

"Char?" Jill puts an arm around my shoulder. "You look like you've seen the walking dead."

I stare at her, eyes blurry. "I think I have. I need to pull it together." I sway for a second and hold onto her shoulder. Am I coming down with some sort of flu bug? My eyes scan the crowd. The guy is gone. My nerves light up like fireworks. Once inside I'll settle down. It's just like before a race.

"You've been through a lot lately, Char. Maybe things are just catching up to you."

"Yeah, you're probably right." I drop to my knees and Jill grabs my arm to keep me from falling over. "I'll be all right. Maybe I need a snack and some water." I rummage through my bag and pull out my water bottle and a protein bar. I half expect another note to fall out. Thankfully, none do. So, it's got to be Hagan who's writing them. I can't imagine who else it could be.

"He's not coming," Jill says. "He's not allowed."

We grab our bags, bows, a box of arrows, and follow the other kids into the college gym. The quarter-mile walk is a relief after the long, harsh bus ride. One break in Ephrata was not enough. We enter the hallway of the building and run into a river of people checking in each bow for inspection. Chatter bounces off the walls as kids and coaches wait at each table.

I place my bow on the inspection rack, strings up, and as I slide my fingers off, they glide across a paper that's taped to the inside of the bow grip, right where the crook of my thumb and forefinger rest. I bite my lip. He knew I'd find it, and I bet he was counting on me finding it just as I was about to shoot. I rip the paper off the bow. Jill grabs my arm and gasps. I race to the bathroom. Between a bout of fear and a bottle of Gatorade near Vantage, my bladder's chaos.

I sit on the toilet and pull the note out of my jeans pocket, reading as I pee.

You can't run. You can't hide. Something bad will happen to someone you love unless you announce you won't be coming off the hill. This race is for men, not girls who have something to prove. Not you, not any girl!

After zipping up my pants, I fold the paper and shove it in my back pocket. It's all I can do to not scream. I stomp out and wash my hands. Other girls watch me as if I'm some kind of freak. I flash them a snarky smile and reappear in the hall, fighting the human current and finding my orange island of T-shirts sitting in the bleachers. I plunk down on the wooden seat, blocking the noise with my hands over my ears. Dizziness slinks back.

White National Archery in the Schools posters are plastered everywhere. The gym floor is covered with gray tarps and blue painter's tape, forming a line behind the bow racks, a line in front of the bow racks, and a line stopping us before we are allowed to retrieve our arrows from the targets.

"Another note?" Jill arches a brow.

I wipe my face with a towel and shake my head.

CHAPTER 22

It's my turn.

I make my way to the south end of the bleachers, my head spinning. That initial feeling of panic in the parking lot is back. I cover my mouth and search for the nearest garbage can, but don't see one, so I wrap my arms around my gut, sucking in deep breaths. *I can do this.* Maybe Jill's right. Stress is getting a hold of me. And now I'm sick. That's why my muscles ache. But I'm never sick.

We are herded in like cattle and the announcer tells the crowd where we are from. I search the crowd for Tone, but don't see him. I do see Benton. He's talking with friends.

People shout, pounding their feet on the bleachers. The booming noise would normally spike my adrenaline. Not today. Instead a spirit of fear engulfs me. I try and shake it off, but to no avail. Sshapa stands tall and claps in the stands. He raises a fist as if to calm my nerves. Calm my spirit. I take a moment to connect with him, take his confidence and transfer it to me.

Three blasts of the whistle ring through the gym and we snatch our bows off the racks, line up behind the tape, and put the tip of the bows on our toes. I peer down at the wooden gym floor, adjust my stance. I think about the elders in the forest in the old days with bow and arrow, hunting for nourishment. It snaps my focus into place. I envision one of them is me. Imagine the cool breeze of a fall morning at dawn in the San Poil mountain range brushing against my face.

Benton shouts, "You got this, now, Char. Come on!"

A renewed self-assurance swirls around me like a hedge of protection. My gaze glues to the floor until my head clears of all distractions. The whistle sounds a single shrill and I pull an arrow out of the orange quiver. The crowd drags to a quiet murmur.

The paper target mounted onto the square block stands ten yards away. I lift the bow and draw, resting my thumb on my jaw. I pull back my shoulders, chest out. Hand relaxed, I release the arrow and watch it stick a hair to the right of the ten mark but inside the ten point circle. At the same time 120 arrows *thwack* sixty square targets. I let out a sigh as the edges of my mouth tilt up. *No room for error.* Giddiness bubbles inside. My stomach feels settled. I have five more tries.

This competition is tight. Most of the girls' arrows in my division have hit within the ten point range, others in the nine. We all shoot our remaining arrows and return the bows to the racks.

After three whistles sound, we walk down the gym to retrieve our arrows. Round bunches of fletch form tight circles. Most of the arrows are inside the ten point marks. Very few are in the eight and nine. How will they break a tie if one occurs? A shoot off? Maybe I can pull another Robin Hood out of my quiver. Sshapa tells me not to leave all my arrows in one quiver, but in this instance, it may be what gains me this state title.

After recording my lane teammate's scores, I tug my arrows out of the targets and stroll back to the line. I soak in the crowd's cheers. The rules here are strict. We have to stand behind one of the blue lines that are behind the bow racks until the range master gives the signal. Murmurs run wild throughout the bleachers. Benton surveys me with a wide grin. My tummy flutters as our eyes lock. His sense of calm glides over and encloses me like a cocoon. He nods. The desire for Sam slips away.

After a couple of hours, the second round starts. Again we record scores, retrieve our arrows, and place them in a white PVC pipe attached to a wooden stand by our spots. I find Benton by the wall, standing with a bottle of water. I wave him over and take a drink. Its coolness splashes down my throat, reviving me. "Keep it up, Char. You're looking good."

I hand him the bottle and say, "I hope so. It's my final year."

"Take your time," he says. "Go get 'em." He turns and claims his spot against the wall. A tall, dark, wallflower full of dazzling hues and smells that entice me.

The double whistle blows. I grab my bow for the last time. That thought sinks in. My hands tremble. I concentrate on a vision of my ancestors in the woods. The deep green of the grass, leaves fluttering in a light breeze. I try to replace the smell of greasy burgers with clean mountain air. A single tweet from the whistle echoes through the gym.

I wet my lips, my mouth cotton dry. Palms sweaty. I take a moment and stare at the center of the target and envision a clean shot before I raise my bow, aim, pull back, and release. My arrow swooshes, striking the target right in the center. The next few arrows slide in with a snap. I sigh. An image of Hagan flashes through my mind and I quickly thrust it out.

The last arrow. I lift my bow and aim. Let it dangle from the crook of my thumb and forefinger. I aim low and to the right, release, and watch my arrow snap into the target. It sinks straight in, edging up to my previous one.

Once everyone is finished shooting, the range manager instructs us to meet in front of the target line. It's hard to tell how I did. These are tough competitors and they want the trophy just as badly as I do. We all want to move on to nationals. It's also hard to know how I did considering I'm mixed in with high school, middle school, and fourth-grade kids.

Benton's not at his usual post. Unknown arms wrap tightly around my shoulders. I'm lifted off the floor and twirled around. The grip feels familiar. Just as quickly as I'm set on the floor, I whirl around and gasp. Tone stands before me, hands lifted in the air, waiting for me to high five him. I do.

He wraps his arms around me and squeezes. "Proud of you." His lips brush my ear.

"That's my girl!" Benton stalks toward me, acting like he's going to mark his territory, and hands me a bottle of water.

I roll my eyes. *That's my girl?* When did I become someone's property? I take a sip.

The boys nod at each other and Tone turns to walk away, but not before adding, "I knew you'd nail it." He eyes Benton.

Jill comes at me like a wild beast, flailing arms, bouncing down the bleachers. Chase grabs me in a choke hold, screaming how great I am in my ear.

"Holy! Calm down. I haven't won anything. Yet."

Benton and I visit the rest of the day, taking the time to get to know one another. I can't help but think he's someone I'd be willing to take a chance on. His caring manner. Respectful touch. He gives me faith in guys again. I guess we'll see where this journey takes us.

CHAPTER 23

Chase and I are on our way to Aunt Jamison's in Omak. I can't believe we talked our parents into letting us come for the week. A flat valley back splashed with rocky benches comes into view as we soar down the hill into Omak. I roll down my window and breathe in the dry, desert air. The Okanogan River snakes its way through town and down the valley toward Okanogan. Its smell twists in the air as it combines with the scent of sagebrush, giving off a clean, sharp aroma.

Chase and I glance at each other and grin. He winds down his window, leans out, and bellows out a war whoop. My first place archery trophy sits between us. It's a new Genesis bow for girls' highpoint score. I brought it to show our auntie. My heart races as we close in on the ranch.

I wish I could have brought Stimteema, but one of the horse trailer tires is flat and no one had time to fix it. The hills near Aunt Jamison's place would have been a great spring workout for her. Circling sage brush and galloping on sandy soil, a perfect leg and lung regimen.

We drive through Omak and wind around the hill heading west, tip south toward Okanogan bringing us past homes and fields and small hobby farms, finally reaching our relatives' place—160 acres of sage, hills, and salmon creek off Spring Coulee Road.

We approach the log archway of auntie's ranch and roll under her sign that reads "Twisted Arrow Racing Stables." She named the stable the Twisted Arrow for the way one of her favorite colts came out of the gate for the first time, body twisted and fumbling for his footing. But once he got his balance, he gusted straight ahead with the speed of an arrow shot by the ancestors.

"Man, it's good to be here," I say.

Chase nods, a wide grin on his face. "Yeah. Sure is. But I hate the drive. Two mountain passes and windy roads. Not my idea of fun."

"Quit whining, you wuss. We're here. Free for a week. It's all good."

I pull up to the house and kill the engine. Aunt Jamison bounds out of the house, waving her hands high in the air. Her black shoulder-length curls bounce with each perky step. She rubs her hands on her apron, a bright smile on her face. She's always smiling—until someone crosses her or a family member and she comes out fighting like a wolverine bit by a mangy dog.

We slide out of the truck and into her arms. "Soup's on the stove and rolls are fresh out of the oven. Hope you two are hungry." She's not much taller than me. Short enough to need a step stool to mount a horse. Her heart is as big as her grace. The chipped tooth in her straight line of coffee-stained teeth is from a barrel racing accident. It was slick from rain down at Pendleton. Her horse went down and when Auntie stood and smiled, she exposed a tooth that had a dip in it.

Shiner, their Australian shepherd, greets us, wagging his white and blue tail. I rub his ears and wipe his slobber off my cheek. "Missed you, boy."

"I'm always hungry, Auntie," Chase says. "Where's Craig and Timmy?" His gaze hunts the ranch for our cousins.

"They'll be in with your Uncle Buck soon enough." Aunt Jamison gives me one last squeeze before heading into their rustic log house.

I hang my coat on a horseshoe hook in the mud room and enter the kitchen. "Need any help?" The place looks the same. It's clean, with the smell of food on the stove and Native art on the walls. Running horse curtains drapes each window. Rays of sunshine burst through a skylight.

"Sure," Aunt Jamison says. "Set the table and fill glasses with water." She turns to Chase. "Go ahead and dump your bag in Timmy's room and your sister's bag in the loft."

Chase sniffs a pot on the stove before settling in. "Smells good. I'm starving."

Aunt Jamison snaps him with the towel. She turns to me, eyebrows arched, ladle in hand. "My brother says you've changed your senior-paper topic." She gives me a sly grin.

I shrink like a child being reprimanded for sneaking a ride on a pony without asking. Which did happen when I was five. No one could find me for hours. Me and Sugar Cube were out back, and I guess up the road a ways. It was spring and we meant no harm. We just wanted to follow the wild spring flowers and a rabbit. Then a doe and fawn. It's easy for a little girl to lose track of time on the back of her pony.

Right now I feel that small again. I'm here all of five minutes and already my fanny's pinned to the wall. Dad wasted no time.

Auntie clears her throat.

I open my mouth to defend myself and hesitate for a moment. "I did. I've had enough conversations with lawyers. I want to do something different that has a traditional twist." I pull a pitcher from the cupboard and fill it with water. Goosebumps rise on the back of my neck. I know it's the right thing to do. When I win—

"What's the real reason?" Aunt Jamison stirs the soup.

"Huh?" I fill six glasses with water. "I told you. I want to share our traditions. There aren't many of us Natives in school and no one else, at least that I know of, is presenting any type of historical accounts."

"That is a good reason. And I'm proud of you for choosing it. But is there an ulterior motive?"

The spirit of lies wraps its arms around my neck, its grip tightening. "No," I say.

For a long, uncomfortable moment, Aunt Jamison searches my face, I'm guessing for sign of a fib. When seemingly satisfied, she takes the pot of soup off the stove and moves it to the fabric horse hot pot on the cedar table. Either that or she can see right through the horse poop and is pondering her next move.

Chase bounds into the kitchen, waving my bow in the air. "Look at this!"

"What is this?" She reaches for it, eyes round and fingering the bowstrings.

"Char won girls' highpoint at the shoot in E-burg," Chase says.

"Char, this is incredible." She comes in for a hug. "I'm so proud of you."

"Thanks. I worked hard for it. For a minute, I didn't think I had a chance. The girls I shot against were better than good, but somehow, I nailed the high score."

"Not by chance, you know that." She arches a brow. "I can't wait to show your uncle." She sets my bow on the table where Uncle generally sits. "I wish I could have been there. You know we had the funeral."

"I understand. I really do, Auntie." I give her a gentle gaze.

"They're here." Chase motions outside and shoots out the door.

Ten minutes later Uncle Buck hangs his sweatshirt on a hook as do my cousins. The boys are look-alikes, resembling the chiseled face of their father. The only difference is one is two feet taller. Both Timmy's body and brown hair is long and gangly, where Craig is more filled out and refined with short black hair. All three wear wranglers and long-sleeved western shirts over T-shirts.

A round of hugs and high fives fill the room. Aunt Jamison hands the bow over to our uncle, telling him about my victory. He hugs me and my cousins all punch my shoulder. I hate that. Someday, I'm gonna punch them back so hard it's gonna knock them over. We settle around the table and Uncle Buck says a quick prayer of thanks. We dig in, catching up on everyone's endeavors.

"So, Char, you're gonna take on the hill this year, huh?" Timmy says. He butters a roll and shoves a hunk in his mouth.

I choke down a mouthful of soup, nearly dropping my spoon on the floor. "Where'd you hear that?"

Timmy glances at his mother. "Am I wrong? I thought that's what you said."

"You are!" The words pop out of my mouth before I think them through. I squint at Chase. He shakes his head. "I'm doing my senior paper on the hill, where it started, when and why, and what it means to the people today."

"Where did it start?" Craig stares at me with narrow eyes.

I know he's testing me. "Keller." I take a drink of water, wanting to pour it over my flushed face. Aunt Jamison stares at me. I fidget, wishing my peripheral vision wasn't so sharp.

Uncle Buck stirs his soup. "We have lots to do this week. I'm glad your folks let you come over."

I nod. "Yeah, our neighbors came over for dinner and offered to help with calving and whatnot, so we were able to come over and lend a hand. I needed to get away."

"That's what my brother-in-law said. Something about some kid bothering you?" Uncle says.

I swallow the boulder lodged in my throat. The last thing I want to do is say Hagan's name while on vacation. I fold my hands in my lap. Gaze down at my food. Chase must have zeroed in on my reluctance because he went ahead and relayed the story, blow by blow.

"Way to get him!" Timmy says to Chase. "You need help, call us. No one messes with family."

"I'm sure the school and proper authorities are handling it, son," Uncle Buck says.

Craig skims the faces of his parents. "He touches you again, I'll nail the—"

"Okay, that's enough. I'm sure Charnaye hasn't come here to beat that bush to death." Auntie waves everyone off. "Let's talk about what we're doing this week."

"Yeah, we've got a horse for you to try out, Char. He's fast, strong, has loads of heart and a great pick for the—"

"We call him Rooster," Aunt Jamison tosses Timmy a searing gaze. "His registered name is Grass Dancer."

"Why'd you name him Grass Dancer?" I say. The name has a traditional ring to it. Like the men who compete in their colorful grass dance regalia at powwows.

Everyone looks at each other, seeking answers.

Aunt Jamison shrugs. "It just sounded good…"

We all laugh.

Timmy pushes from the table and clears his plate. He plucks the cookie jar from the counter and plops it on the table, pushing it toward me. He watches me, confusion across his face.

I scrape the sides of my soup bowl with my roll.

"Do you know Hope Bradeen?" Aunt Jamison wipes her fingers on a napkin.

"I know of some Bradeen kids from sports," I say. "But not Hope. Who is she?"

"She came down the hill in the '90s. I talked to her and she's agreed to meet with us."

My spoon hangs in mid-air as thoughts careen inside my brain.

She smiles. "Want to meet her?"

I swallow the soup and set my spoon on the table. Wipe my mouth with a napkin. "I'd love to. When?" I smooth my jeans.

Aunt Jamison pours herself and Uncle Buck a cup of coffee. She sits back down and studies me. "It's more than a paper, isn't it?"

I think she, like my dad, gets a kick out of watching us kids squirm under pressure. "Why do you think that?" Anxiety claws at my chest as they wear me down. I refill my glass with ice from the fridge door. Anything to get everyone's eyes off me.

"For starters, I visited with your grandfather over the phone while he was in the hospital. He used your mom's cell phone to call me—"

"Was she with him?"

"No. She left the phone with him so they could rustle up more help for the ranch. Your family has helped so many people out over the years. Those same folks are coming in droves to pay them back. There's a lot of love in your parts, Char. A lot of love and support." She reaches for a cookie.

People's faces who've helped us with food, chores, and repairs flash through my mind. Along with the teachers who've been there for us. Their love wraps long arms around us. "Yeah, there are." I glance over at Chase, his face somber-looking.

"Your grandfather thinks you're as set on the hill as the old ones were set on keeping the salmon swimming upstream. He knows it's not just a paper. He sees the same look in your eyes as was in your grandmother's. He's convinced that same urge runs through your veins."

"What do my parents think?" I hold my breath.

"They've decided to support you, Char," Chase says. "Dad says he knows you're bull-headed enough to do what you want and since you'll be on your own and freshly eighteen by the time stampede rolls around, our family better get on board and support you instead of fighting you."

I wait for one of them to inform me this is nothing but a bad joke. Maybe this is some kind of reverse psychology tactic to get me to stand down. For my parents to hope I'll get a taste of fear and drop the whole thing. But Sshapa's right, it's thick in my blood and I'm going to follow through. Smiles, concern, worry, and encouragement all balled to form a net of protection stare at me.

"Wow. I don't know what to say. When was this decided?" The knot in my stomach unwinds a smidgen.

"Just before we came. I overheard Dad and Mom talking about that bet you made with Hagan over the horse. They knew you'd do anything behind their backs to get what you want," Chase says. "They'd rather work with you to make sure you do things right, not sneak around. That's when I told them they were right." He lifts his chin like it was all his doing.

I smirk at him.

"They're right, ya know," Aunt Jamison says. "Why don't you finish school then come back here the following day and start training Rooster?"

"Yeah, training that beast will get you the win. Show them boys it's not just a man's race." Timmy bites into his second cookie.

"Why do you want to do it?" Craig stares at me with a harsh expression.

I shrug, heat rising up my neck. "Just have to."

Craig shakes his head. "That's not why and you know it. You may not 'fess up now, but you will," he says. "I support you, Char. But you have to ride for the right reason or you're gonna get hurt." He pushes from the table and stomps outside.

"There's truth in that." Uncle Buck dunks a cookie into his coffee. "If you ride just to say you can because you're a girl, it'll come back on you. I don't need to tell you this is a dangerous sport. You won't be focused. The horse'll feel your distraction. They can't be fooled. I know you are a talented jockey, but this race, it's different. It's special. It's about honor. It gives our men another way to become warriors. Anything else, well, it's just not good enough."

I reach for a cookie, finger the chocolate chips before taking a bite. "And women." I wash the cookie down with milk. "When do we meet Hope, Auntie?"

"Tomorrow at lunch. She works for Enrollment in Nespelem but took a few days off for spring break to play with her grandbabies. She lives in North Omak," Aunt Jamison says. "She's the president of the Owners and Jockey Association and can give you lots of info from different angles. For your paper, that is." She winks.

Chase laughs. "Yeah, for your *paper.*"

I groan. "I haven't even started it yet. With what I've got from Sshapa and what I'll get from Hope, it should be a good one."

"She'll give you insight and tools you need to compete as a woman." Uncle Buck arches his shaggy brows. He breaks out into a smile. "You are determined, aren't you?"

I nod and eat the rest of my cookie. "I know it's going to be rough. I'm sure the guys are *not* going to want me there. More so than on the tracks."

"Hope mentioned that, but not all the men are against girls racing. Some even encourage it," Aunt Jamison says. "She'll teach you how to handle it, especially when you come back in June.

I bite my lip. "Is there any way Rooster can come stay with me so I can ride every day? I don't think riding him three weeks in June and two in July is going to be enough. I need to get a good feel for him. I need to learn to trust him…him trust me."

Uncle Buck winks at his wife. "We've already discussed that with your folks. Craig'll follow you back with Rooster. We'll take this week to help you work with him, break the ice."

"Your grandfather is making a place for him this week," Aunt Jamison says. "He's tired of sitting around and doing nothing. His words."

Chase and I exchange a look and laugh.

"When are we going to ride?" Timmy says. "I want Scooter."

"Well, I think it's about time." Uncle Buck puts his cup on his plate and takes them to the sink.

We clear the table, pull on our boots, and beeline to the barn.

A mix of anticipation and nervousness swirls inside of me as I approach the horses. For the first time I've said it out loud—I'm racing. No one's going to stop me. I have a horse and the backing of my family. I think I'm in shock because my legs feel as if they are filled with lead.

"Here he is," Craig says, stopping in front of a stall door.

Rooster is in good shape for a ten-year-old quarter horse. He's got that thick chest and rump most stock horses have. "We picked him up a few years ago from a woman who had to relocate and couldn't take him, or her other five head," Craig says as he halters him.

Underneath the muddy coat, I'm sure his chestnut hair shines and his three socks are white. Most of the horses on the ranch are thoroughbreds they race across the country and in Canada, and enter in Indian Relays across the nation. Their saddle horses are used for riding herd on cattle, branding—typical ranch work. Some of the finest bloodlines run through their race horses, including Seattle Slew and Native Dancer. Taking in the barn, it's plain to see my aunt and uncle have worked years to get the desired breeding. It's paid off this year.

Craig hands me Rooster's lead rope. I take it as though he's mine, closing my fingers around the cotton rope. I remind myself he's not. I reach up and stroke his forehead. His large, ebony eyes blink as he sniffs my open palm.

"His tack's over there." Craig points to a western saddle, pad, and bridle set on a wooden rack under the eaves.

"Just so you know, I'm riding to honor the people," I say in a low voice.

He nods, tossing me a brush and taking one for himself.

We work to shed off mud and winter hair from their coats and by the time I'm done, my light blue sweatshirt has a dark brown tinge to it. I pick Rooster's hair out of my mouth and from my nose. Loose hair covers the dirt floor, and everything else it can touch.

"I thought we'd all just take a nice ride up the road and check on some cows. There are some low hills we can tackle. Nothing fancy today," Uncle Buck says. He turns to me. "Char, you and Craig can get a training program outlined tonight and start tomorrow when you get back from visiting Hope. We'll take the morning and go to Big R for supplies."

Craig stares beyond the back of his horse as if he's dreading the whole thing. "Sounds good." His feet seem snug in freshly oiled cowboy boots. Mine are tattered and cracking. Saddles here are conditioned and tack and tools have their place. Even the barn floor is raked. Back home, tools and tack are scrambled and worn. I can't help but feel out of place. I don't think Craig has an inkling as to what life is like with mounting hospital bills and one less person to help out on the ranch because that man sits in a wheelchair with a brave face, a strained sense of humor, and a worn out wife.

We ride together the rest of the day, making small talk here and there. After a couple hours, I zip my black fleece jacket to my chin and pull the hood over my head with stiff, red fingers. Not only is the cold getting to me, but so is Craig's silence. How will I ever prove myself to him if he doesn't give me a chance? Which makes me wonder why he even agreed to train me.

That night, Craig and I line out a racing schedule. He records it in a notebook. His demeanor has softened. I can tell because he's starting me out with one or two hours a day of light workouts. Which may be beneficial because Rooster needs to get back into shape after a long loafing winter. Earlier he showed me his kind and gentle manner. I thought Stimteema had heart. Today I learned its true meaning.

"Just keep to the schedule until you come back. The work'll get harder and faster once you return. I'll call you Sunday nights for updates and we can always change things around."

"I want to take him down to Keller and work him on the beach. The sand in the inlet should strengthen his legs," I say.

"Good idea. Maybe I can meet you there and we can ride together. That would be good for a couple of our racehorses," Craig says. "I know the hills over there on the east side will give them a great workout. By May he should be ready for that." He pauses, studying me like a professor. "Take your time though. We can't have injuries or all our hard work is in the toilet. Got it?"

I nod. "Got it."

He stares at me, eyes narrow. "You know what comes before the fall, don't you?"

I fan my hands out in frustration.

"Pride." He shoves the notebook toward me.

"I want this more than anything, Craig. I'm not gonna do anything to screw it up." I finger the photo of Rooster Auntie gave me. "He's a special horse."

"Real special." Craig shoves away from the table. "Remember that."

CHAPTER 24

I stretch and moan. My muscles are so tight it's hard to touch my fingertips to my toes. But my insides twirl like a girl waiting for my first date to arrive. I think. I don't really know because I've never been on a real date. Benton and I've seen each other a few times now, and though we are getting closer, I still feel awkward. Maybe I just need to jump in the puddle and commit to a boyfriend. It can't hurt. Besides, we live in different towns. It's not like we'll consume every minute together, wasting precious riding time.

We do have things in common like archery, horses, food. And clothes. Speaking of clothing, mine are pathetic. Comfortable but pathetic. Jeans and T-shirts aren't my first choice for a lunch date with Hope. Right or wrong Mom has always allowed me to wear what I want, never pushing me to dress fancy. The only time I've worn skirts and bows was as a little girl. I wore dresses heavy with lace and tights for occasional church outings.

I pad down the hall in my sweats, hair twisted in a scrunchy and hanging loosely to one side at the nape of my neck, in search of Aunt Jamison. All I have to do is follow the smell of eggs and bacon. She's in the kitchen whipping pancake batter.

"Good morning, Char," she says. "How do you feel?"

My body feels like the bowl she's beating. "Tired and sore," I stretch my back. I retrieve a glass from the cupboard and fill it with tap water. "Rooster and I are gonna get along just fine. I love riding him! Just need to get back into shape."

"I bet you are a bit stiff." She flips pancakes, shoves bacon around the skillet, and pours me a cup of coffee. "What can I get for ya?"

"Um…well…you know I normally wear jeans and T-shirts." I lean against the window and peer outside. The boys are feeding the horses, Chase and Timmy goofing off as usual. Shiner runs around, barking, and wagging her tail. I'm thankful for a few minutes of quiet girl time before they plod in and take over.

"Ah, you're worried about looking nice for Hope." Aunt Jamison smiles. "I think I have the perfect blouse for you."

"Not that I'm worried. I just didn't know we would be meeting her and I'd like to look nice. Not so…so…"

"Tomboyish?" Aunt Jamison laughs. "Finish here and I'll go get the shirt."

I grab a spatula, place the remaining hotcakes on the plate, and fork the bacon on the dish covered with a paper towel. I put the food on the table and sip my coffee, wincing at the bitter flavor. A container on the counter entices me. *Toffee creamer.* I shrug and pour some in my black drink. It turns brown and smells like

Thanksgiving in a cup. I take another sip and the sweetness runs down my throat, playing with my taste buds.

"Here you go." Auntie hands me a light green blouse. "Figured I'd break ya in easy. When we go to town for dinner tomorrow night, I'll loan you a shirt with flowers. If you think you're that brave."

We laugh. The boys plow in, ripping off boots and flinging coats on hangers, hoping they stick. Shiner sneaks through the whirlwind of testosterone and inches over to me, sniffing the air. I rub her head. "Hide under the table and I bet you'll slide under the radar," I say quietly. She licks my hand.

"Timmy, put Shiner outside," Uncle Buck's voice booms through the kitchen.

"Sorry, girl." I run my fingers over the top of her head before draping the shirt over the back of a chair.

She drags herself to the door like a wounded bird at Timmy's command.

"Can't stand a begging dog," Uncle Buck says. "It's disrespectful."

After breakfast, I change into the green shirt and observe myself in the mirror. "Not bad." It slims my already trim figure and slight curves. I braid my hair and glance in the mirror one last time. Tug at the bottom of the shirt to straighten out a few kinks. Run a finger over faint freckles around my nose and under my eyes. For a brief moment I consider eyeliner and mascara. Would it be too much? I shrug. "Good enough." I trot down the stairs and stop on the last step, fingers clutching the iron rail. The guys halt their chatter and examine me, mouths open and eyes wide. I avert my gaze as my cheeks warm.

"I saw the shirt on the back of your chair at breakfast. Had to see with my own eyes if you were gonna really wear it. Must be meeting Benton today, on the sly. Ayyyz!" Chase laughs and high fives Timmy. Uncle Buck whistles. Even Craig checks out the new look with a broad smile on his face.

"Come on, you guys, leave her alone." Aunt Jamison grabs me by the arm and escorts me out the door. "You do wear that blouse well. That shade of green looks good on you. Don't wear it much anymore. It's yours. Fits you better anyways."

"Thanks. I do like it. The clothes in my closet won't know what to think with this kind of style moving in." We giggle and slide into her truck.

Auntie pulls up to the curb on the south side of the street in front of The Corner Bistro. "Have you eaten here before?" She kills the engine.

"No, but it looks fun."

"Best burgers in town. And you'll love the photography on the walls."

I open the cafe door for my aunt and we slip inside the small but quaint restaurant. She's right. Beautifully framed photos of ranch life and horses hang on the walls. The colors in some are vivid while a couple of black and whites offer a mysterious mood.

"Looks like we beat her here," Aunt Jamison says. "Let's grab a booth before they fill up."

Five minutes later a woman with dark, shoulder length hair and a big smile enters the bistro wearing a deep red blouse, beaded earrings and necklace to match, and black square-tipped cowboy boots. She finds us and waves. She strolls over and scoots into the seat across from us.

"Aw, this must be your niece," Hope says.

I extend my hand. She greets me with a firm but womanly grip.

"It's nice to meet you," I say.

The waitress hands us menus and glasses full of ice water. "Can I get you coffee?"

Aunt Jamison and Hope take her up on the offer. I choose hot cocoa topped with whipped cream. After a few minutes of scrutinizing the menu, we order. I heed my aunt's advice and order the best cheeseburger in town.

I wring my hands in my lap, trying to convince my tummy to stop twirling and study the only woman I've met who qualified for the race. I lean forward, eager to hear her experience. How did she place? Why did she quit? What was it like? My gaze drops to the stretched out horse head tattoo on her forearm. Letters naturally drift out of the mane and read "Only the strong conquer fear."

Hope and Aunt Jamison catch up before Hope turns to me and says, "So, you're writing a paper on the Suicide Race?" She reaches into her purse and drags out a few photos and a newspaper article. "Check these out."

The first picture sends chills up my arms. It looks as if one horse is about to stumble. What if I come off the hill and have a terrible spill? What if I'm caught underwater, trampled by hooves? The riders' faces show their passion as they tear down the hill at breakneck speeds. My thoughts gallop as I flip to the next photo. A young Hope stands at the top of the hill next to a gray horse. She's wearing an old cowboy hat and life vest, a deep look of concentration on her face.

The angle suggests the photo was taken from the side of the hill, close to the ledge. Her expression could not have been captured from anywhere else. How amazing it would be to have the rush of air from the horses brush against ones face as the horses barreled past.

I place the photos on the table and read the article. Part of the text is highlighted. It mentions Hope as being one of the few women to ever qualify. Not much more is mentioned. "Figures." I shake my head. If the article was mine, I'd crumple it and toss it in the garbage.

"What does it say?" Aunt Jamison leans over and peers at the article.

"It hardly mentions Hope, but sure loves to boost the male riders and their egos. Isn't that how it always goes?" I slap the article on the table and go back to the photos.

"I know," Hope says. "I suppose they could have chosen not to mention me at all." She pauses, taps her fingers on the table.

The waitress brings our food. My nerves dissolve my appetite.

Hope picks out the pickles from her burger. She lifts her gaze to me. "We have to win the battle of the sexes one clip at a time. Small steps and persistence will eventually get us there." She takes a bite of her cheeseburger and motions for me to do the same.

I pick at my fries.

Aunt Jamison digs into her burger. "I think it's hard for my niece right now. She's had a boy harassing her at school."

I shoot her a snarly sideways glance and sigh when she doesn't elaborate.

"There'll be plenty of trash-talk during the first round of trials," Hope says. "Heck, that stinkin' thinkin' attitude will pick at you from the minute you step onto the horse all the way to the arena. And beyond. Just like life, there are people in this world who irritate us to death. But it's how we handle it that defines our character."

"I've been racing long enough to know what comes out of their mouth and why. I get a lot of crap slung my way on the tracks, especially when I win. You think they'd accept me by now." Her encouragement settles my tummy enough to take a stab at my food. I take a huge bite of my burger, its juice rolling down my chin. "Mmm." I nod and point to the food in my hand.

"I think you're gonna be just fine, Charnaye," Hope says.

"Yeah, my niece isn't afraid to throw it right back in their faces." Auntie pats my arm, her face beaming with pride.

We finish our meal. Hope has thirty minutes before she has to meet her son and grandchild.

"So, Charnaye. How do you want me to help you?" Hope fingers her cup.

"Any way you can," I say. "Sshapa told me how the race began. I know simple facts like that. But head knowledge isn't enough. I want to know how it feels to speed down the embankment and plunge into the water. What sound does that make? What do you see in the dark? What noises do you hear in the staging area? What is the wait like before the gun goes off?" I tap the photo of her coming off the hill. "I want a woman's point of view. Especially because I'm going to enter. It's not just a man's game anymore. Times have changed and I want to be a part of those changes." I stop my rant for a sip of cocoa.

"Those questions haunted me at first too," Hope says.

"Why did you try out?" I wipe the moisture from my glass and rub it on my forehead.

Hope chuckles. "I see this means a lot to you—"

"It does." I feel as though my heart will burst. The desire to get up and move, pace or something, nags me but I sit like a lady, respectful of what Hope has to offer. I jig the heel of my foot instead.

"At the time, I was in my late twenties and already winning races in Wellpinit, Kartar, at the fairs, and whatnot. I figured the suicide hill would be just a small step up. I was nervous and all, but like I said, I'd already been winning most of the races. Figured it wouldn't be much different. Many of the jockeys I'd been up against also rode down the suicide hill." Hope motioned to the pictures. "As you can see, I came in the middle, but at least I went for it."

"That's you right, number three?" I point to a figure in the middle.

"Sure is." She taps her image.

"Why did you stop racing?" I say, not sure it's any of my business.

"Life. I had a couple kids and my family pressured me to stop," Hope says. "I knew if something happened, I'd be cheating them out of something special. Me." She hands me a family portrait. "After a while, I let guilt take over."

"Some would call that responsibility and a good move on your part," Aunt Jamison says. She covers her friend's hand with hers for a brief moment.

Hope looks down, her face glows a shade of crimson.

In the print Hope stands in a field, surrounded by her adult kids and grandkids. Everyone is smiling and their faces display admiration. "Did something bad happen?" The words slip out before I can stop them. For sure I've crossed the boundaries.

"Yes. It did. I don't want to scare you, but at the same time, you need to know the risks," Hope says, her voice soft. Serious.

I lean back against the bench seat and close my eyes. *I knew this was coming. My family's way of shoving fear inside of me. A way to stop the madness. This was all too good to be true.*

"Three years in a row I qualified." Hope rests her elbow on the table and taps her fingers together. "The first year was when the papers mentioned my name. It's been awhile since a woman qualified. It was the third and final year that I got hurt."

"How? Did someone come after you?" The painful memories etched in her face gave me caution.

"Not really. They all seemed to hate me equally. They made it clear I wasn't welcome and would do whatever it took to make sure I didn't come off that hill." She took a sip of water. "I figured they were idle threats. The guys tossed them around freely, but no one intentionally tried to harm each other. They were only head games."

The waitress refills the coffee and lays the bill on the table. "No hurry to leave, ladies."

Aunt Jamison thanks her and reaches for the bill.

After ten minutes of Q and A, Hope gives me a fixed look and says, "I'll be praying as you train. Know your surroundings and always, I mean always, watch your back. I thought I had."

CHAPTER 25

"When we hit the river I was boxed in and felt someone tugging the back of my shirt. I was in the middle of the pack, not a good place to come off a horse. I heard the rush of water and muddled voices. Felt hooves pounding my back and legs into the bottom of the river. I knew I was going to drown. All I could think about were my babies. About the time I thought I'd surface, a horse hoof nicked the back of my head. All I could do was pray I'd make it out alive to see my kids grow up. Thankfully it was over in a matter of seconds." Hope stares out the window. "It felt a whole lot longer."

I rub a fry around my ketchup-smeared plate. Every tingling nerve orders me to pull out. The paper's sufficient. As I sit in the stiff booth and question my motives, I wonder if pride is the driving force.

The waitress clears our dishes. "More coffee?"

Hope and Aunt Jamison decline. Auntie hands the waitress her credit card.

I pick up the picture of the young Hope. "Is that when you decided to quit?"

"It is. I broke a couple ribs and my femur. Was out of work long enough to let the consequences sink in." Hope looks at her watch. "I have to meet my son, but we can talk more anytime." She scribbles her phone number on a napkin and hands it to me. "Listen, I'm not trying to talk you out of anything. This is your journey. Just make sure you consider all the angles." She thanks Aunt Jamison for the meal. "When are you coming this way again?"

"When school's out for the summer."

"Great. We'll hook up then. In the meantime, you have my number." She motions to the napkin with a short, round finger.

"Thanks, Hope." I nod. "For everything." *I think*. Even though Hope's account spooked me, a deep burn inside tells me the race is still on. It feels like two dogs fighting inside my soul. They'll tear me apart if I don't get a grip.

"Later." Hope scoots out from her seat and taps the table with a single finger. "Take care of this one," she says to Aunt Jamison. "She's special." She winks at me.

I give her a small, confused smile. My eyes drift to her finger on the table, leaving my emotions in her wake, open and raw.

We head back to the ranch, country music the only sound in the truck. Houses and desert terrain speed past, draining any morsel of courage I had left. It could easily be me pinned under the water. I suck in several deep breaths and angle the AC vent toward my face.

I focus on Rooster's daily routine. What will I do with him today? Herd cattle? Check fence? Tend calves? My mind sticks to images of the babies. I try and fix them with names. Spunky. Sugar. Bear. How lame. Butch. Cassidy. Daisy. I can't even think of good ones. I lean my head against the window and close my eyes, hoping to fall asleep.

My head jerks and bangs against the window. Auntie glances at me, brows furrowed. I wipe my mouth, look out the window, and close my eyes. In my dream it wasn't Hope at the bottom of the Okanogan, it was me. Horse's hooves bashed my head against the bottom of the rocky riverbed. I rub my forehead.

"You okay there?" Aunt Jamison's shifts the stick into park.

"Yeah." I give her a fake chuckle.

"Go get changed. Craig's gonna take you out to check cow and calf pairs." The look on her face makes me think she is uncertain if lending her brother's daughter a horse to ride down a steep grade with a bunch of kamikazes is a grand idea.

"I need to work on my paper tonight. Can I use your computer?"

"Yeah, no problem." Aunt Jamison turns the key and climbs out of the truck. "I can help you edit if you want."

"That'd be great." I scramble inside to change.

When I reach the barn, Rooster is in the corner of his stall, eyes drooping, bottom lip hanging loose. "Catch you napping, big guy?" His ears perk forward, and he walks to the door, nosing for an apple. I give him one. "At least one of us is relaxed." I shove the door open, and halter him before he tries to sneak into the hay just outside his stall. His warm muzzle brushes my cheek. I inhale his scent and allow a shard of courage to seep in.

"Keep that up and he'll be in your back pocket." Uncle's voice booms from behind me.

"He's gonna give me the ride of my life," I rub Rooster's neck, and he lowers his head, eye's droopy.

"He sure will." Uncle gives Rooster a handful of hay.

"Keep that up and he'll follow you around like a big, overgrown dog."

Uncle Buck pats my back. "Too late. He already does."

I lead Rooster out and tie him to the hitching post. "This makes me feel like I'm in an old western." I motion to the post with my head.

"It's the real deal here." He winks. "Just like at your place."

"We don't have a fancy hitching post like this one." I tap the wood with the end of the lead rope and give Uncle a sassy grin.

His chinks, Hoss-like cowboy hat, and round belly make him appear as though he's stepped out of an episode of Bonanza. Don't see that get up around our barn.

I brush Rooster and saddle him. I pull a bridle with a snaffle bit off its hook and show Uncle.

"Not that one." He hands me a different bit. "Use the curb on cows. You'll need the bigger stops. Save that one for the hill."

I switch out the bits.

"Craig's waiting for you at the east gate." He points in the direction I'm to travel.

"On my way." I swing into the saddle and guide Rooster toward the gate. I sink down into my saddle and urge my big, brown friend into a canter. His easy swing sends my thoughts to the hill and I imagine us barreling down the steep grade, into the river, up the dike. I see us riding together as a team, never leaving the other behind.

I find Craig fixing a section of loose barbed wire and offer to help. With Chase around, I don't usually get to work the fence line. A job I tend to enjoy.

"I've got this." He gives the fence stretcher one more click to tighten the wire. The tone of his voice suggests I leave the heavy work to the men. He makes a loop on one end, pulls the tail of the other wire through, and wraps it tight. He sweeps a gloved hand over his brow. "Let's take those cow and calf pairs through the gate and push them into the other pasture. It has more grass."

"Got it." I don't like this tension between us. The scowl he seems to hide digs deep. I fiddle with Rooster while I wait, making him back in circles, side pass, two track.

We spend the afternoon herding cattle between gates, Shiner working the strays. One calf breaks away and the Aussie nips its heel, playing Ring Around the Rosie until the darn thing catches up with its mom. With each hour that passes, Rooster responds to me with the slightest pressure of rein and leg. His movements are quick, attention sharp, and he's not afraid to throw his weight around the bulls—signs of a decent cow horse. Signs of a magnificent suicide horse.

A slight drizzle spills from dark clouds as suppertime draws near. My sweatshirt is dotted with raindrops, the green deepening at a rather fast rate. I blink back rain and tug my hood over damp hair, wishing I'd worn my cowboy hat.

Craig sits tall in the saddle, eyes narrow to the trail.

"If it's a pain for you to train me, I'm sure I can find someone who'll work with me. Hate to put you out." When he doesn't answer, I fix my gaze between Rooster's ears.

After a long moment, Craig says, "You still haven't told me the truth of why you want to enter?"

At his words I nearly topple to the ground. If I had a rock in my hand I'd hurl it at him. "Can't you see how badly we need the money?"

Craig's head snaps toward me, his eyes big and round. "What? That's your reason? You may land a good chunk of change, but it'll never be enough."

"What's wrong with that? I know I can win. It will at least take the edge off." He's got to realize every dollar counts. He's used to living with money. He doesn't understand. How can he?

"There are better and safer ways to get money. We can hold a benefit auction, raffle off a log load of wood, a cow, both."

"We've done all that and it's not enough. It's never enough. We don't have money like you guys do. There's a lot to be made from the race, and I know I can win!" I kick Rooster into a canter as my throat tightens.

I make my way back to the barn and untack him. After brushing him down, we walk around the pasture until his coat dries. I fight back tears, refusing to let the boys see me cry. Shiner follows me around as if we are on some cow-herding journey. Nose to the ground, she meanders and sniffs. "You understand, don't ya, girl?" I call her over and scratch the back of her ears.

The fall of horse hooves approach, but I turn the other direction, knowing it's Craig. I'm afraid if we speak, I'll break down, proving in his eyes I can't handle the pressure. Do I really need to prove myself to my cousin? I kick the ground. I at least need him on my side.

Aunt Jamison hollers to come in for supper. I take a deep breath, hoping a snap of courage will ride in on its current. Craig is no where to be found, so I put Rooster in his stall. He waits for a treat before heading to his water tank. I take a few extra minutes to put the tack away in its spot.

After washing, I take my seat at the table. Uncle says grace and we dig in. That is everyone but Craig. Timmy and Chase talk about their hiking adventure. I keep to myself, listening to the clink of fork to plate as everyone eats their fried chicken and mashed potatoes. Auntie and Uncle exchange worried glances.

Five minutes later, Craig walks in, fills a plate, and goes back outside.

I choke down a spoonful of potatoes. The guys push back from the table at once and put their dishes in the sink. Aunt Jamison stays.

"What's going on between you and Craig?" she says.

I stuff more potato in my mouth and slowly chew. Take a long swig of sweet tea. "Why do I have to prove myself?" I stab my chicken like it's Craig's head.

"How do you mean?"

"Never thought he'd go against me. Figured that wrong. Thought he'd be my biggest supporter…you the biggest opposition." I twirl my fork.

"Craig's not against you. It's the opposite. You two have always been close. He's trying to protect you. Can't you see that?"

"Is that why he gives me the cold shoulder and hardly says two words to me that aren't filled with venom? I thought when we made a plan, things would run smoothly. That's not the case." I drop my fork and cross my arms.

Aunt Jamison sips her coffee. "Come on, Char. Craig has your best interest in mind. Which is your safety."

"Worried about my safety?" I grunt. "He acts like I'm in his way."

"What's the real issue here?" She tips her head back toward the door.

I swirl my salad around the bowl.

"I know your family's low on cash. We're committed to make sure your dad has everything he needs for however long he needs it. You know that, right?"

I stare out the window, wanting to agree. It's hard to have faith when my family seems to be treading water on a daily basis, ready to sink. When will it all end? Will it end?

"Charnaye, this isn't your burden. Creator will provide the money. Let it go. Craig loves you so much he wants you to be safe. That's his goal. He's always been your protector, right?"

I shrug. "I don't think he understands how bad I want this. Need it."

"Doesn't he? You don't think there are things in life he's wanted so badly he'd do whatever it took to get it?"

"He probably has. But he doesn't understand what it's like to have nothing." Hot tears pool in my eyes. I wipe my face before they leak out.

"Oh?" Aunt Jamison leaves and comes back with a scrap book with a torn spine. "Look at these."

I take the book, open its pages, and study a yellowed three-by-five print. "Where's this?"

"The ranch."

"This ranch?" I run a finger over an old single wide trailer, a lean two with a few horses in a pasture with a broken down fence that looks to be mended with wire and baling twine.

"Yep." Auntie smiles. "As you can see, this place wasn't always pretty. Over the years we built a house and barn, added trees and spigots, better horses and cows. It's taken years to get this place like it is now. Your dad had big plans for his ranch until the accident. His herd was growing and he had money in the bank. But it all went to medical bills."

I swallow the rock in my throat.

"Life was tough when the boys were young. Craig knows more about hard times than you think. He was old enough to remember them. Especially the Christmases with only one gift under the tree for each boy."

"And here I thought Craig just had a holier-than-thou attitude."

Auntie chuckles. "Yeah, sometimes he thinks that way, idnit? Must be the oldest child syndrome. I'll leave it to you to knock down his sainthood a few notches."

I roll my eyes, stab at my chicken breast a few more times. "So?"

"I think you need to pray about it. Sweat with Craig tonight and let the Creator speak to you. He'll show you the way."

"It's been a while since I've had a good sweat. Feels like Creator's spirit talks to me in those quiet times." Sshapa always tells me that if we commit everything to Him, trust Him, He'll give us our heart's desires."

"I'm not so sure."

CHAPTER 26

When it is time to leave, Chase and I load Rooster and his tack into Uncle's horse trailer and say our goodbyes.

"Holy, that was the best week I've had in a long time. Chasing and roping cows, what a blast. I miss those days on our place." Chase stares out the window a moment before adding, "Where'd you and Craig go last night?"

"Took a sweat."

"Did it work?"

"Yeah, I guess. Seems Creator's showing me how to honor Him by keeping our traditions. We're warriors, well, maybe not you, ayyyz!" I laugh. "If you think about it, even after generations on this reservation, we're still going strong. I just got to remember, He's the one who needs to be glorified. Not me."

"Idnit! That's hard for you."

"Whatever!"

"Face it, things come easy for you and you know it. I'm glad you've finally figured out you're not some big, important saint," he says in a teasing tone.

I laugh and quickly grow serious. "That goes for all of us. Especially Dad. Just cuz he's stuck in a wheelchair doesn't make him less of a man. In fact, it makes him more of one. He's got a voice people listen to."

"Yeah, guess they do," Chase says.

We turn into our driveway. Sshapa's outside by the barn, waving us in. I honk to let Mom and Dad know we're home. We roll to a stop and shoot out the door. I land in Sshapa's embrace. It's good to see him up and around, even if he does look frail. His steps are slow and steady. A good sign.

"I've missed you, Char."

I squeeze harder. "I've missed you, too."

After he gives Chase a fist bump, I motion to Craig where to park Uncle's rig.

"I have a spot all ready for your new ride. What's his name again? Your mother told me but I can't recall it. Grass Eater or…?" He watches Chase walk behind the trailer before saying, "Rooster. Like Cogburn?"

I chuckle. "No, as in he struts around like a rooster in the winner's circle." I pat my grandfather's shoulder. "Kind of like how you were back in the day." I walk off before he has time to deny anything.

Craig meets us at the back of the trailer. Chase has already opened the door. Craig steps over and unties the chestnut. Rooster seems to methodically back out of the horse trailer and snorts, head high, eyes scanning the ranch.

Craig hands the lead rope to me. "He's all yours, cousin."

I take hold of the rope like it's a lifeline. "I'll take good care of him."

"I know you will," Craig says. "Just keep with his schedule and get him in shape. When you get back to our place, we'll start training fast and hard."

I hug him and whisper, "Thanks."

Craig hugs me a little tighter before stepping back.

"You want to come in and say hello to your family, get a cup of coffee and a bite to eat before heading back?" Sshapa says.

"Yes. Of course." Craig extends his hand, allowing Sshapa to lead the way. Chase follows behind.

I take Rooster to the barn and put him in a stall. The exterior door leading out to his turnout pasture is open. Fresh straw covers the floor and a flake of hay is in his feeder. A bucket of fresh water stands in the corner of the stall and is tied to a wall hook with orange baling twine. I think Sshapa must be as excited as me. I sing an old country song, one of my father's favorites, and sway from side to side as I run my hands over Rooster's back. He turns his nose my way and noses for a treat.

I dig a slice of apple out of my pocket.

"I snuck this from Auntie's fridge before I left. Just for you, big man." I step out of the stall and slide the door shut. He leans his head over the top of the half-door and roots for another. I give him a handful of grain and walk away. He trots into his run outside of his stall and whinnies. Stimteema answers. I stroll out of the barn, smiling.

Then rush to the house, realizing how much I've missed my family. Everyone is settled around the table, chatting about the week. Chase talks with his hands about his adventures with Timmy, and Craig shares how he thinks we are coming along. Mom nods, worry in her eyes.

Kari jumps out of her chair and rushes to me. She throws her arms around my waist. I squeeze her back. Her eyes dance as she tells me how much she missed me and about her time with our mother, riding horses and playing games. Mom hands me a plate. I take a big bite of turkey sandwich and chew, savoring its flavor. There is something about Mom's cooking that says home.

"Your trip was good?" Father says.

I glance at Craig and grin. "Rough start, but we came to an agreement. I learned a lot." I turn to Sshapa and say, "Craig and I had a good sweat last night." I take a gulp of water.

Craig nods.

"I learned I took on a burden that's not mine. Auntie helped me see that. But I flubbed that up." I glance at my father as my gut twists. "Now I know it's up to Creator to take care of us…and you. Our needs." I drop my gaze to my plate.

"Is that why you wanted to race? For the money? Thinking we don't have enough?" Father says.

My tummy roils at the honesty and tone of his voice. "Yeah." My voice is soft, not like any warrior I know. Why can I be so tough on the track, and so unsure and weak in the knees around my family?

Dad peers at Mom, the corners of his mouth turned down.

She nods. "We wondered if that was the reason behind all of this. The way you've acted in school, at the hospital, at home. Why you were bent on getting out of here so fast last week." She runs a finger over the brim of her mug. "I've kept our financial strains away from you so you wouldn't worry." She glances over at Chase as if to include him. "Guess you two are old enough to know what's going on."

"We are, Mom. We're not little anymore," I say.

She folds her hands and rests them on the table. "I realize that. And I'm sorry. The tribe is picking up all the medical bills the insurance doesn't pay."

"They are?" Chase leans forward in his chair.

"That's good news," Craig says.

Sshapa nods. "They're covering all of my medical expenses, too."

"We are having a benefit to get repairs on the house and barn, which your aunt and uncle and Craig have offered to set up and run. The funds should also help us get a van for Dad." Mom gives Craig a small smile.

"Our family and friends have really pulled through for us," Sshapa says, his voice shaky.

I let out a heavy sigh and breathe without the feeling of my chest being crushed. We finish our meal and send Craig on his way with extra snacks and a thermos full of coffee.

I head to my room and finish my paper. When I finally stop, hand cramped, I've written fifteen pages in my notebook. I thought the required six would be a stretch. After editing for two hours and cutting my words down to eight tight pages, my essay reads like smooth country two-step.

My stomach gurgles. I stroll to the kitchen and find a bowl and plate wrapped in tinfoil and a note on top.

I know you are busy with your paper. I'm happy to have you home. We fully support whatever you decide to do, Char. I am filled with pride at the woman you've become. I hope you can be at ease knowing Creator really is taking care of us. Mom

I pop my potato soup in the microwave and grill a cheese sandwich. After wolfing down my dinner, I reach by the kitchen door to turn off the light. On the shelf where keys are hung, there is a letter addressed to me. No return address. I open it and gasp. *It's just begun.* When will it ever end?

CHAPTER 27

The roar of the bus's diesel engine rolling away from the house jars me awake. I jump out of bed. The TV blares from the living room. I rush out of my room, bumping my hip against the corner of the hallway. I groan and rub the tender spot. My father's watching the morning news and turns to me when I trip into his space.

"Why didn't anyone wake me up?" I say.

He turns around in his wheelchair. "Because you were sleeping."

"But I've missed the bus."

"I know."

"Ugh." I stand in front of my father, hands on hips, brushing hair out of my face.

"You going to comb that mess before going to school?" He smiles.

"How am I gonna get there?"

The door slams shut as Sshapa stomps mud off his boots, his eyes dancing. "I like that Rooster horse."

I shift my gaze from Sshapa to Father and lift my eyebrows.

"She wondering why the bus left her?" Sshapa says.

"Yep." Dad grins.

"She wondering how she's gonna get to school?"

"Yep." Dad motions me to move out of his way. He goes back to viewing the news.

I bend over and lean closer to my father, about to ask him again. Keys jingle from the kitchen, and then drop on the table.

"Here, I'm not supposed to drive yet. Doctor's orders. Remember the young, cute one? He says to tell you hello." Sshapa shuffles to the cupboard and opens a door with gnarly fingers. "Chase and Kari made the bus." He digs through canned and boxed food. "Looks like sleeping beauty had a hard time shaking herself out from under the covers this morning." He pulls down a can of pears and sets them on the table.

"You two are pretty proud of yourselves, aren't you?" I shuffle over and snatch the keys off the counter. Sshapa kisses my cheek.

"Better get going or you'll be late," Dad says.

Sshapa pops bread into the toaster. "Horses have already been taken care of."

"You owe your brother," Dad turns up the TV volume.

"I don't owe him anything." I traipse down the hall and into the bathroom. But really I do. I'm just not gonna admit it to those two clowns. Dad's and Sshapa's laughter breezes through the closed door. "Bunch of coyotes." I shake my head.

I shove open the school's heavy glass doors just as the bell rings and walk down the hall with a bounce in my step. I'm on my way to AP History, when I realize my book is in my locker. I get there, turn the dial, and pull the lock down. One last test and I'm done. Never to take this subjective class again. My fingers open the door and a paper shoots out, gliding on the linoleum. My gut drops like a carnival ride. I scramble to get it. I'm about to unfold the slip of paper when I get bumped from behind. Hagan's cronies circle me, sneers on their faces. I clench my fists.

"Guess who's coming back to school…soon?" one of them says.

"Guess who's gonna come after you?" another says as he steps close to me.

"Guess who's gonna get the beating of a lifetime if you lay one hand on her?" Chase says. "I don't want you even looking at her crossways or we'll come after you." He raises a fist.

I twirl around and see my brother and seven of his biggest friends standing behind me. Got to love the football linemen. Hagan's friends slink away. The team follows them while Chase walks me to class, looking around as if to make sure no one else is a threat.

"Holy, good timing," I say. "What were you guys doing?"

"We have a football meeting for summer camp." He glances at the note I'm clutching. "What's that?"

I shake my head and for a second I consider handing the note to Chase, but decide it's not his battle.

He reaches for it. "I saw how you scrambled for it."

I shove it in my pocket. "Nothing. Class notes from Jill." The lie squeezes my throat. I sigh. "I wish Mom and Dad would have pressed charges." A shudder rips through me.

"Yeah, me, too. They feel sorry for him, since his dad beat the crap out of him and all. I heard Aspen made him get some kind of counseling before he's allowed back in. He needs to be shipped off to Martin Hall."

"No kidding. Before we left that day, Mom was in his office for a long time. I bet she was making sure he gets some kind of help. You know Mom." I sigh. "I don't know. Maybe she's right. Better to reform than shove him in juvie to have him back, making the same stupid choices. The only thing is, I don't think spring break was enough time…"

The second bell rings.

"Got to go. Let me know if they give you any more crap." Chase darts off to his meeting. I watch him round the corner.

Butterflies keep me outside the door for a few more seconds. Hagan and I have this class together. I take a deep breath, stand straight, and enter the room. My eyes scan every head. I don't see him. I find my seat next to Jill. I wish I was back at my auntie's. At least I wouldn't have to put up with this drama. I reach into my pocket to show Jill the note. I've got to tell her before I burst.

She leans close. "Did you hear the news?"

I release the note. "What news?"

"Somehow, Hagan broke two ribs and a leg. He'll be out longer."

I swallow. A smile forms on my lips then turns down, thinking about his dad. "How'd it happen?"

"Not sure. But rumor has it he fell out of the barn loft." Jill glances at the teacher and turns back to me. With a low voice she says, "I think his dad may have had something to do with it. An argument or something." She lowers her voice. "He could have been pushed off the loft in a fit of rage."

I lean against the seatback. "You watch too much TV." My mind wanders to images of Hagan's dad beating him. "It must be tough growing up with a dad like that." A shudder hops down my arms. I tap my pencil on the desk and try to concentrate on my lesson, but my thoughts keep skipping back to a beaten and bruised Hagan. My leg jigs.

I lean over toward Jill. "I got another note."

Her eyes grow big. "Lemme see." Her hand reaches toward me.

The bell rings and we head to art. I pull our canvas out of my bag and set it on the easel.

"What did the note say?"

"I haven't opened it yet."

"What? Why not? Where is it?" Her gaze drops to my backpack.

I pat my front pocket. She opens her hand for it. I shake my head and gesture to the teacher.

"How's your project looking?" Mrs. Larson peers over our shoulders, a big smile on her face. "It looks lovely, girls. I can't even tell it was vandalized."

Jill scrutinizes the project with a hint of sarcasm saying, "Hmm" and "Aha". She grabs colored pencils and watercolors from the cupboard and gets to work. Mrs. Larson sashays off.

"Lemme see the note." Jill reaches out her hand.

"No. Not here."

Jill frowns. "When?"

"I don't know. Lunch. Maybe I should just ignore them. It's got to be Hagan sending them, even through his friends."

Jill deepens the brown on the saddle. "Can't see them being that smart."

"Idnit!" We laugh.

By the end of class, half the sketch is in color. Only fine details are left. "I'll have this done by tomorrow and we can finally turn it in and move on to our final project."

"Your idea is next," I say.

"No, reading the note is next. This is killing me, I can't wait anymore." She sets her brush down.

"Later," I whisper.

I flutter aimlessly through the rest of the day, anxious to get home and on Rooster. After lunch, I type my final senior paper, print it out, and turn it in. All I have left for my senior duties is a few job applications and trudging through AP History and Precalc.

Graduation day can't come quick enough.

CHAPTER 28

I pull my gown over dress slacks and my new green blouse, slip into the new cowboy boots Aunt Jamison and Uncle Buck gave me for graduation, and glance in the mirror. The note lies unopened on my desk. I reach for it then retract my hand. This is stupid. Jill's right. I should have read it two weeks ago. I shouldn't let Hagan get to me. But what if it's not Hagan? Maybe they mean business. A knock sounds on the door. I slip the paper under a book. Mom enters and settles my graduation cap on my head. It's adorned with an orange and black beaded eagle feather that hangs off the side. Her hands rest on my shoulders.

"I'm so proud of you," she says softly, a hitch in her voice.

"Thanks." I peer into the mirror and see her soft, ebony eyes fixed on me. She appears younger-looking and rested. Her dark green dress with white flowers blends into her dark brown skin. Her dress hugs her petite frame in a lady-like fashion. I run a finger over the edged beadwork. "Angel did a great job."

"She sure did." She leans her head against mine. "You've become the woman I've prayed for."

I drag in a deep breath and smooth wrinkles from the arms of the gown. "Thanks for being my mom. You've taught me to be strong. Determined." I place a hand on one of hers. We stand still a moment as she whispers a prayer over me, asking Creator to watch over and protect me. She reminds me He's made a promise to not harm me, but to give me a future and a hope. Our heads link a moment longer before she releases me.

"Let's get some pictures, shall we?" She smooths my hair.

I nod and follow her lead, stopping at the door for one last glance at the note. "I'll be there in a minute."

"Hurry," Mom says as she rounds the corner.

I close my door and unfold the note. At first, I avoid the words scrawled on the lined paper. I drop to my bed, tell myself I have nothing to fear, and read.

I bet you thought I'd forgotten about our deal. I haven't.

You have until Friday to announce your change in plans.

I hear you have a new horse…

I crumple up the note and throw it in the garbage. Friday has come and gone. Nothing's happened. This has to be Hagan and his empty threats. I laugh. *What a punk.*

"Char, pictures." Mom's voice floats down the hall.

"Coming." For the first time in months, a light and somewhat giddy tingle comes over me. I'm ready to get graduation over with, get out of here, away from the threats, and begin training.

Kari slides off the couch when I enter the kitchen and shoves a framed drawing in my hands. "I made something for you," she says, eyes downcast. "For graduation." Her voice trails off.

I study the paper. A dark brown girl with long black hair sits on a tall bay horse. She's wearing a purple T-shirt with a horse and squiggly lines across the front. I'm guessing those lines read: *Life is better on the back of a horse*. She signed and dated the bottom right corner.

I gather her in my arms and hold her tight. "I love it! Thanks."

Her eyes brighten. "It's you on Stimteema and you're wearing the shirt I got you."

"This is the best gift ever. I'll bring it with me to college and hang it on my wall."

She attempts a smile.

"It's okay, Swaskee. I'll be back to visit." I rustle her hair.

Graduation is a simple affair. To celebrate us Native students, one of my dad's cousins drums an honor song. My mind lingers on the threats. With each beat of the drum the words pound at me—*regret, warning, deal, harm, broke down, horse, stop!* I rub the back of my neck. Squirm through a speaker, listen to what the valedictorian and salutatorian have to say, and watch a slide show of a few growing-up years. Most of mine were on the back of a horse. *Heard you have a new horse…* Is he going to hurt Rooster? Poison him? Kill Him? Should I warn my family?

Sam's valedictorian this year. His speech is short, but with words like future and drive and vision, it packs a powerful punch. Before we are handed our diplomas, scholarships are awarded. They go in alphabetical order so I sit and wait for the T's. My mind won't let up. It churns each threat: *It's not your rite. Don't race. I warned you. You can't hide. I'm watching.* I find myself picking through people I know that would want to hurt me. Or Rooster.

Finally, they call my name.

I make my way on stage and stand next to Principal Aspen. Mr. Peterson, the school board president, joins us. I search the crowd for anyone who looks guilty. They award me the Gates Scholarship, announce I will be attending the University of Washington in the fall, and talk about how I changed my senior project to my cultural passion. As he talks, my mind wanders to the race. Is all this worth it? Would it be easier to go into the mountains for a few days on a spirit quest? Any rite of passage is supposed to be a challenge. Never a threat.

I stiffen at Hagan's glare. A couple of his buddies sneer.

They call Jill to the stage and she bounces up the stairs, eyes glimmering.

"It is my honor to announce this year's Lilac City Junior Arts Contest winners." Mr. Peterson hands Jill our canvas. A huge, blue rosette is attached to it. Mr. Aspen taps his hand with an envelope, smiling at us. He turns to the audience. "The girls' journey did begin in my art class with Mrs. Larson." He waves her on stage and hands her the mic.

Jill and I exchange surprised glances.

Mrs. Larson saunters to the mic, florescent pink heals clicking the stage. Her dress looks like it was soaked in Pepto-Bismol. A pink plastic flower peeks out of her blond curls. She waves everyone to silence. "Yes. This did begin in art class. But I think the idea, the vision if you will, began with a young woman who dug into the depth of her heart and stirred a storm of pride in her heritage. Her Okanogan heritage." She talks about how the project was ruined and how we didn't give up, but began again. "After the girls turned in their final project, I immediately called the contest director. I explained the girls' situation to her and was able to drive the piece to Spokane that Saturday and enter it into the Lilac City Junior Art Contest." She giggles, clutching the mic like she's making an acceptance speech.

Benton leans against the wall in the back of the gym, holding a bouquet of flowers. A smile stretches across his face as he listens to Mrs. Larson, staring straight at me as though I were his prize. Our gazes lock. How wonderful it will be to live in the same town as him this summer.

"And now," Mrs. Larson turns to the principal with an extended hand. He flops the envelope in her palms, "I would like to present Miss Toulou and Miss Lamore with an award." She opens the envelope and tugs out two checks. She hands one to each of us.

Benton gives me a thumbs up. Jill places an arm on my shoulder and leans over, looking at the amount. She lets loose a ear-piercing squeal.

The crowd bursts into laughter. My family belts out high-pitched, staccato sounds of honor.

Mrs. Larson again waves the crowd to a hush. "Well, ladies, I believe you've each won a monetary award of one thousand dollars."

I finger the check and wonder if its enough to buy lumber for a new ramp for Dad. Jill and I hug each other as the audience applauds.

"I've decided to take your advice," she says quietly.

"What advice?"

"To go to college for art. Miss Larson and I've been talking about it."

"Where?"

"I'm still deciding."

Someone makes a throat-clearing sound. Miss Larson stares at us, tapping her foot, eyebrows raised.

I give her a small wave, shrug at Jill. We exchange embarrassed looks. Hagan sneers at me as if his beatings are my fault. My belly clenches. The wall Benton held up is empty. I find him in the bleachers, still in the back of the gym and still smiling. I smile back.

"I'm so proud of these two ladies," Miss Larson says. "Let's give them another round of applause."

I exit the stage and find my seat among my peers. I wiggle through the rest of graduation, thinking about tomorrow, while the principal gives his final proclamations. Craig and I will drive back to their ranch and train. I reflect on our time riding horses on the sandy beaches near Keller Park. We were able to meet twice in the last couple of months. My fingers curl in my lap as if holding Stimteema's reins. I close my eyes, see us racing over hills, galloping along the river, swimming the horses out a ways before circling back. I recall the smell of the air swirling off the Columbia River inlet. How cold the water felt. An image of Hagan's bloody face comes to mind. Chase's rage. Mom's worried expression. Not sure I want this anymore. Hanging this up is looking good.

The sound of clapping hands jerks me out of my daydream. We rise, receive our diplomas, and find our parents.

Once home, Benton and I visit with family and have some cake before he has to head back to Omak. When he's ready to leave, I walk him outside.

We hold hands, leaning against his Toyota pickup.

"I know you'll be busy training, and so will I, but we have to remember we are on the same team. I won't let any of the other guys mess with you," Benton says. He strokes my arm and we lock eyes, his forehead wrinkled.

"Thanks, but I can handle myself." I step back.

"I didn't mean it that way. I know how they can get—"

"So do I. This isn't my first race." The fight in me is back.

"No. But it is your first time down this hill and it gets ugly."

I toe the dirt with my boot. "Look, I know you're trying to help, but I have to do this on my own. I don't want people saying anyone favored me or anything. I can handle it."

Benton pulls me into a hug. "I know you can. I'll see you in a few days. Let's try and make time for each other once in a while." Benton's warm lips press against mine. He wraps me in a tight hug. I lay my head on his chest, drawing in his scent. My fingers cling to his blue Wrangler shirt.

"I'll call you in a few days."

I step back and watch his truck bounce down our driveway.

"Keep your head in the game," Craig says.

"I will. Don't worry." I stomp to my room, hang my gown and cap in the closet, and shove jeans and T-shirts in my bags. He's spying on me now?

A soft knock stops me. I finish stuffing a couple shirts in my bag. "Come in."

"Got a minute?" Sshapa peeks his head in.

"Always, for you."

He closes the door. "I found this." He hands me a smoothed out piece of lined paper.

The garbage can is empty. I sink to my bed. "It's nothing."

"It is more than nothing." Sshapa sits on my desk chair. "How long has this been going on?"

I open my palms. "It's the fifth one." No sense in lying.

"True," he says. "Do you know who wrote them?"

"Not for sure. I think it's Hagan."

He nods. "We need to turn these in."

"Why? School's out. They'll stop coming now. It's over. He was just trying to get in my head."

"Did it work?"

I shrug.

Sshapa stares at the note. "We'll keep this between us for now. Where are the other ones?"

I point to the desk drawer. "In there."

He pulls them out. "I'll hang on to these." He shuffles out the door.

Please, keep them between us.

CHAPTER 29

"I think we're ready." I slam the back of the horse trailer shut and slip the lever into place. After giving Dad one last hug, I jump into Craig's pickup and buckle my seatbelt. Half of me wants to turn up the music and dance. The other half feels heavy and hollow. As hollow as an empty culvert.

As we pull out of the driveway, Kari looks sadder than normal. I glance into the rearview mirror and see Chase, head down, kicking the dirt with the toe of his Adidas.

"You ready for this?" Craig says.

"Yep." I smile at him through blurred vision, praying Kari will continue to break out of her shell. Hoping Chase will take up the slack around the ranch. I sniff and wipe my face with the hem of my shirt.

"We can turn back, ya know." He squints against the morning sun, pulling down his visor.

I dig my sunglasses out of my backpack and slip them on. "I'm fine." I choke on the lie.

"It's not too late—"

"Craig. Really."

He lifts a brow.

"Yeah, I feel bad for leaving them. Chase gets all my chores now. Sshapa's been sick and…" I slap my leg. "The thing is, I'll be leaving this fall anyway, right? Can't stay forever."

Craig nods and turns up the volume. Jason Aldean's voice floats through the cab. I listen to the music, watching the road behind us disappear in the side mirror. Tap my finger on my leg. A morsel of guilt still knocks at my chest. I shift my focus to the aspen and pine trees that line the swollen San Poil River. Watch them streak by as I leave my adolescence behind.

We wind down the hill into Nespelem and pull into Jackson's to fill the tank with diesel. I grab a coke from inside and walk over to the memorial site of Chief Joseph. I look at the maps of his journey behind glass that hang on the wall outside the bathrooms. If he can sacrifice for his family and people and fight for what he believes in, so can I. I turn and gaze at the large metal sculpture of the deceased chief. Prickles on my scalp leave me on edge. *Is this the right move?* I sense him telling me yes.

The rattle of a diesel engine pulls my attention away from the memorial. Craig waves me over. I press my hand against the cold metal statue before jogging to the truck. I slide in and Craig hands me a bag of Doritos.

"Enjoy. It's your last bite of junk food for three months," he says.

I swipe the bag out of his hand and start munching. "May as well."

A couple hours pass and we pull under the Twisted Arrow Racing Stables sign. A breeze swings the wood. Horse's ears prick forward, their focus trailing us. Rooster must sense we're back because the truck rocks back and forth as his weight shifts. Horses in the adjoining pasture run alongside the rig, whinnying and kicking. The foals whip around in circles, their small noses in the air, fluffy tails sticking straight up. Laughter escapes my lips. In a way I'm somewhat like them right now, unsteady on long, wobbly legs.

Craig gives me a sideways glance, a smile crowning his lips. "Glad to have you back."

By the brightness in his eyes, I believe him. "Glad to be back."

Craig parks the truck and we jump out. Shiner greets me, wagging her entire backside. Once I've satisfied her itch, I jog to the back of the trailer and open the door. "Easy, boy." Rooster stomps, alternating poking his nose out the windows and eyeing the fence line. He greets his herd mates with a drawn out whinny that shakes the trailer. I lay a hand on his rump and walk to his head, untying the lead rope. I make him stand still for a moment before backing out. I rub him until he quiets. The last horse I helped unload at a fair rushed out and split his head open in the process. I put Rooster in his stall and give him a big scoop of grain, more than normal, knowing the hard work begins this afternoon.

The house is empty. Craig catches me snooping around, note in hand.

I pass the note to him. "This has your name on it."

Craig scans it. "Mom had to go into work. Some business has a tax issue and she's lending a hand." He opens the fridge door. "Here it is." He pulls out leftover meatloaf and potato salad.

"I guess this is what they call working through lunch, huh?"

He gives me a courtesy laugh. "Yeah, I suppose. Guess you'll have to get used to it. We've got a lot to figure out, so why not now?" Craig cuts the meatloaf and sticks a few slices in the microwave, pushing the two minute button and retrieves a pen and notebook.

"Making things official, huh?" I find plates and forks and fill two glasses with water and bring the meatloaf to the table.

Craig sits in front of his plate. "Keeping you focused is all." He forks potato salad onto his plate. "Besides, we never know when Enticing Eyes might show his face and try to sweep you away for the afternoon."

"Holy! Enticing Eyes? Really? Is that the best you can do? Sheesh"—I shake my head and chuckle—"I don't know about you, sometimes. Besides, he works during the day. I wad my napkin into a ball and chuck it at him.

He dodges it. Shiner investigates.

I bring the wall calendar to the table and find June. "We have seven weeks to prepare. The actual race is the second full weekend of August, Thursday through Sunday." I circle today's date with Craig's pen. "What I don't know is the order of qualifications and eliminations." I flip to July.

Craig taps his finger on the calendar. "The third Friday and Saturday are vet checks. If we use their vet it's free."

"I assume we will."

"Yes."

"The fourth weekend we qualify with the swim and hill test. The hill will be open to practice, which you will do. This will be no problem for Rooster. He's done it, has no problems." He looks at me and smiles. "You on the other hand…"

I lift my chin. "Ha, ha. No worries, cousin."

"The fifth week is more qualifications and practices, and entries." He circles the date.

The blue oval stands out. I swallow.

"Starting to feel real, isn't it?"

I nod. "I'll be ready."

"You scared?"

"I ain't scared." *Quit lying.* "A little." I scratch my arm.

Craig tilts his head.

"Okay, a lot. But once I get going, I'll settle in."

He turns the calendar to August and taps the first weekend. "Qualifications and practices will continue on Friday and Saturday. Two heats of eliminations will be on Sunday."

I fill in the calendar and slide it aside. "Now about training."

Craig opens the notebook and scribbles the date and day one. We spend the next hour creating a training schedule, for the horses and us, including working out and lifting weights. We explore ways to make training fun, and talk about what it will take mentally to conquer the hill. "You need to strengthen your thighs and upper body."

I cringe. "It's a bit much, don't you think?"

"You want to win, don't you?"

He stares at me a moment, brows arched, and jots down when and where and what horses he'll swap out. Of course, I get Rooster.

I lean over the table. "You gonna let me in on this plan or are you gonna leave me clues, like a scavenger hunt?" My tone lathers with sarcasm. I push away from the table and fetch the cookie jar. I set it on the table.

Craig flashes me a stern look. He scoots the jar toward himself. "You had your chips. You're done with junk food. I wasn't kidding." He opens the jar, takes one out, and salutes me with it.

"You were serious?"

"Very." He takes a bite and scribbles something in his notebook. Underlines it three times.

I reach for a cookie.

He places the jar on the floor and eats his cookie. I slump back in the chair and glare at him.

"We'll stick to moving cows today because we have a couple hills to pull and water to wade through. Rooster doesn't have water issues, although you still need to swim him so it's a natural everyday occurrence for him. There are two areas on the Okanogan we can hit later. Tomorrow we'll go behind the old CIPP mill and ride down that hill a few times. After that we can trailer them down the road and swim them in Omak Lake. There's a nice sandy spot on the north side. You'll mostly just gallop him every day and sort cows to cool him off. When done you can take him to the creek and let him stand in the water to cool his legs."

"What about feed? I assume he'll be eating more than hay."

"Yep. I've got his vitamins all lined out by his grain. His feeding schedule is by the printer. You can grab it and tack it to his stall."

I retrieve the paper and bring it back to the table. "Wow, cousin, it's even on green paper. Impressive." I sniff it. "Too bad it doesn't smell like fresh spring grass or wildflowers."

"Tease all you want, but you'll find out if you ever own a stable someday, organization saves time." He jots something in his notebook. Once done he shoves it toward me. "Here's what I've got so far."

I clear my throat. "Today cows. Tomorrow morning gallop in east pasture on track, sort cows in south pasture, soak in creek. Afternoon, run one mile, lift at the center"—I look at him and he smiles back—"junk food off limits!" It's underlined three times. There is more written in the book, but I get the gist of his plan and shove it across the table. "Just let me know what we're doing the night before and I'll show up."

"You'll get a copy. I'll expect you to be there on your own." He stands. "Let's go."

I pack my bags to my room, throw on an old T-shirt, quickly braid my hair in two separate braids, and top it off with an old baseball cap. After fetching my sunglasses out of Craig's truck, I meet him in the barn. Rooster's feeding schedule is tacked on his stall door. *Oops. Strike one.*

A barrel racing saddle and lime green pad perch on a stand near Rooster's stall. A new shiny helmet hangs from the saddle horn. "What's this?"

"Your new equipment. That's my mom's old barrel saddle."

I run my fingers over the cantle. "She's letting me use this?"

"Yep. Your saddle's too heavy." Craig fits the helmet on my head. "From now on you wear this. That way it's just part of you and not a distraction."

"You sure have a thing about distractions."

He gets in my face. "The number one thing you need to realize is focusing and knowing your surroundings at all times. It'll save your life. This is a dangerous race. Do you get that at all?" I watch a vein pop out of his neck.

I step back. "I know the risks. Just trying to keep the tone light is all, geez. Sometimes you crack the whip a little to hard. I know what I'm getting' into."

"Do you?"

I move rocks around with the toe of my boot, my face heated. "When you get serious like that, I get afraid. I can't focus with you harping on me."

He sighs. "Point taken."

I gesture to the saddle. "Why is this strap bolted behind the cantle?"

Craig gives it a hard tug. "It's called an 'oh, sh–'… um…darn…well…I won't say the word, but you get it. You can hang onto it when coming down the hill to center yourself."

"I don't think I'll need it," I say. "I've got these new guns forming, ya know?" I curl my arms.

Craig shakes his head. "Whatever. Wait a couple weeks and you can show me some big 'uns." His face crinkles.

"Nice attempt at humor." I playfully shove him.

We saddle our horses and head out. Shiner on our heels.

CHAPTER 30

After two weeks of working out my arms can buck a seventy pound bale of hay as though it's feathers. Well almost. I found muscles on my shoulders I never knew existed. By 8:00, I've already run two miles, moved ten bales from the loft, and stacked them by each stall door. As I set the last one in place, a rig rattles down the driveway. Hope's truck and trailer rumble to a stop. I wave to her from the barn. She unloads her saddled blue roan mare and ties her to the trailer. I finish cinching Rooster's saddle and meet Hope halfway.

She lifts her water bottle into the air and shakes it. "Mind if I get a refill?"

"Help yourself." I motion to the house. "Aunt Jamison's in there somewhere."

I jump on Rooster and trot him in circles. Someone wise once told me that either I will be in control or the horse will. If I get the horse's mind from the beginning, I have his feet and body. Boy, was my dad right. I miss riding with him. Maybe someday in heaven we can ride together again.

The screen door slams shut. "I'm ready," Hope says. She slips her water bottle in her pommel holder and climbs into the saddle.

"I figure we can cross the road and head that way." I point to bald hills behind the ranch. The grass fades with each passing day and temperatures rise by ten in the morning. Back home the meadows are still green and the higher we climb a mountain the greener and fresher everything is. Including the smells.

"Let's go," Hope says.

We take our time winding through brush, rocks, and sage, stopping in a creek to let the horses take a sip.

"How's training coming along?" Hope leans over and soaks a couple bandanas in the water, places one around her neck, the other wrapped around her forehead.

"It's going great. Rooster is strong and sure of himself and I'm focused."

"Good. You need to be. Once you get there, distractions will hit you from every angle. Especially reporters, photographers, and animal rights activists. Especially because you're a woman. Once you head up, you can have up to an hour to kill before you line up. I'll try and check on you before then. I'll be up there making sure things run smoothly."

"That'd be great. I know you'll be super busy. But I'll have Craig and Chase to help me, too." I consider telling her about the notes, but don't. I doubt there'll be more.

"And Benton Marchand I hear."

I smile. "Yeah, him too." Definitely him.

We ride up a hill and follow a ridge overlooking Omak. Hope stops and turns to me. "Those animal rights people can be barracudas, but I want to teach you what to say. I don't want them gettin' under your skin."

"Are they that bad?"

"Since we've made improvements to the hill and because we have stern vet checks, they've backed off somewhat. But those city people keep coming because they just don't understand. They don't get why we race. What's behind it, ya know?"

I nod. "I get it. Some people don't know how strong horses are, they don't see them as athletes. They see them as…little frail butterflies."

Hope laughs. "You got that right. But I work with them, reminding them of all the care we put into our horses. Explaining all the training we do. It's hard to be professional when I just want to haul off and punch them in the face at times. But in reality, I know they really just don't understand. It's ignorance." Hope takes a drink from her bottle. Wipes the sweat from her face with a damp bandana.

"What do I need to do?"

"Stay with the guys and don't talk to anyone. Don't go off by yourself. Ever. Even when they give you a bad time, keep close. Walk Rooster in and go directly to the hill. Do whatever you need to do to focus on the ride and on your horse. Watch out for the other riders. They'll line you up by whatever number you draw, so be on your toes. I can't tell you enough to know your surroundings. At all times."

"Why go stand near the hill?"

"Let Rooster look at it. Not many riders walk their horses to the edge. It will keep him calm but alert. Some of these guys and horses are so amped up, they…it's like a domino effect. Just stay relaxed and keep your cool. See yourself going down the hill. Stay balanced and use that handle on the back of your saddle."

I reach back and finger a rope fit inside a soft, sturdy hose and grip it. "I can do that. I don't want to talk to them anyhow. I'm there to ride, not argue."

"Good attitude," Hope says. "Is that kid still bugging you?"

Maybe I should tell her about the threats. Would it do any good? "No."

"Good." Hope nods behind me. "Let's tackle that hill, shall we?" She spurs her horse into a canter and we wind our horses up the hill, reaching the top and overlooking Omak to the east and the Cascade Mountains to the west. We ride for another hour and turn back. Both horses have sweat running down their legs. Even though it's mid-morning, it feels like it's late afternoon. Once we arrive back at the ranch, we hose off the horses and tie them to the hitching post.

After lunch with Aunt Jamison, Hope heads out. I sneak off to my room and lie down, eager to catch a few minutes of shut-eye before Captain Whip Cracker finds me. Only a couple pass before a knock on the door vibrates the room.

"Let's go work out before the center gets crowded," Craig says.

I groan and roll off the bed. "Fine. Got to change first." Dressed in shorts and a fresh T-shirt, I ramble down the stairs and take the last step. Auntie holds a phone out to me.

"It's your mom." She shrugs her shoulders.

"Hey, Mom." My gut turns over as she explains to me that Sshapa is not regaining his strength and she and Dad have decided to sell the cows this fall. "How many?"

A heavy sigh rolls through the line. "All of them."

No! "What? Why? It's his dream. All he's got left. All he looks forward to. We can't…"

"It's the only way, Char. Your dad in his chair and one old man just can't do the heavy lifting anymore. We can't hire anyone on and don't want to put it all on Chase. We want him to enjoy his last two years of high school. He isn't into the animals like you are. It's the only way…"

I plump down on the couch.

"You there?" A weary voice floats over the line.

"Yeah." How can I earn extra money? Prices are at an all time low. It won't be close to enough. There is one obvious choice to save the ranch. My gut twists. It's the only way.

"I wanted you to hear this from me. Mr. Erickson was at the house when we were discussing cattle prices. He's headed that way and you know what a blabbermouth he is."

"Yep. You know I'll help in whatever way I can." I fake enthusiasm.

"We'll figure something out," Mom says. "How's training going?"

"Good. Craig's running me through the mill, though." I throw a decorative cow pillow at him. He gives me a pouty lip. "We're headed to the center."

"Good. I'm praying for you."

"I'm glad, Mom. Thanks." My voice breaks, and I fight off a tear. After the race is over I'll make the call. Will it really work? *They'll kill me.*

I push the off button and can't seem to move.

"What's up?" Craig says.

"Mom and Dad are selling the cows."

"How many?"

"All of them." I slam the phone in its cradle. "It's gonna be weird. The ranch'll seem deserted." *Unless I make the call.*

Craig throws the pillow at me, and I hold it tight.

"I can see why, though. Can't you?"

"Kind of." I lean back into the overstuffed couch and close my eyes. "It's still gonna be weird. What will Sshapa do?" For now I'll keep it to myself. Play along.

"Heck, he'll still have all the other animals. And as long as he has the horses, he'll keep kickin'. Probably live to be over a hundred."

There are only a few of us at the center. The clink of weights and a Van Halen CD filters through the muggy air. I jump rope for twenty minutes. Attempt curls and squats. I work on my shoulders and core. An hour flies by and Craig insists we stay thirty more minutes before hitting the showers. I'm glad because I refuse to ride back with Craig's stink in a pickup, even with air conditioning.

The girls' bathroom is empty. I drop my bag by the line of lockers. Peel off my clothes and jump in the tepid shower. The water rolls off my back and my muscles relax. Do I really want to give it all up? Can I make it work? Save the ranch? Keep my folks in their house?

I hit my bed for a nap when we get back. It's already nearing ninety degrees. I sleep for a couple hours before Timmy turns up the tunes in his room. Aunt Jamison hollers for him to turn it down. Thankfully he does. Sweat runs down my back, so I open a window and place a fan in front of it, angling it toward the bed. Every room has vents but mine. I roll over, wishing I'd brought my quilt. I miss my family. Miss the squeak of Dad's wheelchair and Sshapa's stories. Chase teasing me. Kari's hugs. Mom's voice. I curl into a ball. A faint bass tempo rolls into my room.

I wish I could pick up a cell phone and call them. But I don't have one. I cover my face with my hands. Fight the heartache trying to burst forth. *It's all for them.*

Where is Benton or Tone when I need them? I drag myself out of bed and pull a chair in front of the fan. Hot air blows on my face. I groan and trot downstairs, making my way to the kitchen. Uncle Buck sits at the table, phone in one hand and mechanical pencil in the other.

"Just nabbed you three sponsors," he says.

"Really? Who?" I get myself a cold drink of water and plop down across from him.

"Aunt Jamison's boss at the law firm, the Ketchpen in Nespelem, and Three Feathers Logging."

I shake my head. "How much?"

"Four hundred." Uncle makes the money sign with his finger.

"You're kiddin' me, right?"

He smiles, flashing coffee stained teeth with Copenhagen grits stuck in between. "Got your entry fee paid."

I lean over and high-five him. "What now?"

"I'll cast more of my charm out. See what we can snag." He reaches for an envelope. "This came for you in today's mail." He hands it to me. "Want a cookie?" He extends one out to me. "It's oatmeal raisin."

I glance behind me for the cookie police. He's not around. I snatch the cookie and envelope out of my uncle's hand, shoving the cookie through open lips, hand covering my mouth. "This must be from Kari." I rip it open.

You think you can run from me? Did you see Kari's sad face when you drove away? She thinks you're gonna die. I told her it was possible. and wiped tears from her eyes. Stay alert. I'm coming for you!

I swallow the bulge in my throat. Was Hagan at the house? Who else could it be?

"That's my girl. Those chocolate chips will give you energy," Uncle Buck says. "And I won't tell Craig." He winks. Watches me. Frowns. "Holy, what's wrong?"

I fold the note and stuff it in my pocket. Take a bite of cookie. Do I fake it? Tell him? How did he find me? *I can't...* I give him a sorry excuse for a smile. "Kari drew me a picture. It made me miss her is all." The notes have to be idle threats. Otherwise something would have already happened by now. Wouldn't it?

After washing down crumbs with a gulp of milk, I rush out the door and search for Aunt Jamison. She's in the garden plucking vegetables for tonight's salad. The tip of her straw hat bobs from around a row of corn. I step between rows of raspberry bushes and run a finger over a couple pink berries. How did he find me? Who is this monster? I inhale the scent of flora and dirt. What normally smells sweet and earthy, stinks. *She thinks you're gonna die.*

"What's up?" Aunt Jamison says.

I bite my lip. "Kind of miss home." I ease down on the wood frame of her raised garden bed and pick a carrot from the soil. Do I show her the note? Did he really get to Kari, or is he lying? What will Auntie do? *It's your burden.*

"I suppose talking to your mom stirred up some feelings, huh?"

"Yeah." I choke on the simple word. "Did she tell you?"

"About what?" Aunt Jamison lays zucchini in a box.

"About them selling off all the cows?"

"She didn't. Want to share your thoughts? You seem pretty far away."

I pluck a tomato off its vine and hand it to her. Clench my jaw. *I wiped tears from her eyes.* Did he really touch her? My mind sorts through everyone who was at the house after graduation. "If I stayed around to help do you think they'd have to sell?"

"Is it your responsibility?"

"Maybe. In part…"

Aunt Jamison peers at the sun with shaded hand. "Even in the shade of this big leaf maple, it's warm." She gulps water from her bottle. "I think the enemy is trying to distract you."

"Probably." I wipe the carrot on my pants and take a bite.

"Char, is there something you're not telling me?"

I take another bite of carrot for show. *Regret. Warning you. New horse. Kari. Die. Stop*! I shake my head, unable to squeeze any sound from my clogged throat.

"Don't you think Creator's taking care of your folks? Do you think they need a break? Seems to me, the ranch is too much for them to handle. I know my brother has lost his dream, but he's alive and will make new ones." She picks a zucchini from the stem. "We've been trying to talk them into selling their stock for two years now."

"You have? Why? It's something Sshapa and Dad have in common. They wake up and have something to look forward to. Have something to talk about."

"Yes, but it's a lot to handle. This way, they can actually enjoy what remains."

I help carry vegetables into the house and go to my room. I reach for a water bottle on the side pocket of my bag. The corner of an envelope sticks up behind the bottle. I freeze. Rush to the window and peer outside. A slight breeze flutters leaves attached to the big oak. *Not again*. I yank it out, sink to the floor, and slip out a photo. On the back it reads:

Happy graduation, Queen of the Hill. Keep in touch. I'll see you at the races. I'm gonna miss you! Jill.

I turn the picture over. Jill and Benton bookend me in the gym, our arms draped around each other. Jill's mom had taken the photo. I rub Benton's face with a finger. How did the photo get in my bag? I find his number and a phone by the couch and head back to my room, taking the stairs two at a time. I punch in the number and get his voice mail. I hug a pillow and squeeze my eyes so hard no tears can fall.

CHAPTER 31

The morning's galloping session is like every other time—circling the same dirt track. An iPod would fix that. This is the one time a distraction would come in handy. Rooster stumbles and drops to his knees. I fly off and hit the ground rolling. My nose lands in the dirt. I jump to my feet and wipe my face. Rooster's a few feet away, looking at me as if he's trying to figure out what just happened. I dust off and grab his reins—a little too rough. With one hand on his neck, I bury my face in his hair and I pray.

I rub his neck and tell him I'm sorry, check his knees for blood, and walk him around, paying attention to his legs.

After making a few more laps, I put Rooster up and plod up the stairs to my room. I dig a piece of paper and pen out of my pack and make a list. I list cell phone as number one. iPod as number two. For kicks I list Queen of the Hill for number three. I cross it out and list it as number one with a smiley face next to it. Satisfied, I set the tablet and pen on the desk.

I move to the bed, lean against the headboard, and reflect on the morning's ride. Recording our day might help. But first, I find the phone and punch in Benton's number. It goes to voice mail. Heavy hearted, I hang up, grab my notebook from the desk, and settle back on the bed.

Rooster was as solid as ever. He's predictable that way. Nothing tends to get him in a bind. They say a horse settles in at age ten. I know that's true. It is with Rooster and Stimteema. Hills were good. Cattle seemed to just lead us from one pasture to the other with little fuss. The heat seems to slow us all down. I made Rooster stand in the creek for a while. After a few minutes I jumped in and cooled off as well. I'm glad things are running smoothly, but I need to be challenged. In a big way. So I sit here and pray. Ask Creator to put something in my path that will make me grow.

I list my fears. The threats. All I've accomplished. My future plans. In bold letters I list all the reasons I deserve the chance to be queen of the hill. A knock rattles the door. "Char, I need to talk to you. I've got something planned!" Craig's tone sounds chipper.

"Come in." The door creeps open. "What's going on?"

He grabs the chair from in front of the fan and plops down, rubbing his hands together.

My gut clenches at his crooked grin.

"I've pulled together some riders and we're gonna have a mock race." He leans close, eyes round. "Tomorrow morning."

"Tomorrow?" I run a finger over the part in my notebook that refers to growth and groan. "How'd you pull that off?"

"Considering you have seven weeks to go and some of the guys were talking smack about you last night in town, I bet them."

"Bet them what?"

"Fifty bucks you'd win."

"What'd you do that for, idiot? I've raced flat tracks and smaller hills, but nothing like this. I didn't even race in Wellpinit last year." I cover my face in a pillow and scream.

He laughs. "I'm just kidding. About betting that is. I'm serious about the race, though."

I heave the pillow at him. "You're sick!"

"If that's all you got, better quit now." Craig lobs the pillow back at me. "For what it's worth, I think you'll win."

"Who's all racing?

"Some of the usuals. Plus one."

"Who are they?"

"You'll find out in the morning." Craig grins. "I hear the plus one's a real ringer."

"Who is he?"

"Not sure." Craig walks to the door and grins. "Benton almost got jumped last night sticking up for your scrawny hide." He steps out the door and turns around.

"Where's this race taking place?"

"Southeast end of Omak Lake. When we're done, I'll take you to Kartar, show you my roots."

I pick up the phone and punch in Benton's number. His voice mail comes on again. I slam the phone on the bed. My hand hovers over it for a moment and I dial Tone.

His mother answers. "How are ya, Charnaye? I hear you're tackling the big hill this year after all," she says. "You're full of surprises, aren't you?"

"Yes, ma'am," I say. *After all?* I wonder what Tone's been telling her. I ask for him.

"He's outside. I'll get him. You take care now."

A screen door slams over the line and Tone's mother hollers his name.

"Hello?"

"Tone, it's Char."

"Hey, what's up?"

"I'm in Omak with my aunt and uncle, training."

"So I hear."

I make a face to the phone. "From who?"

"You're the talk of the rez, man. One more chick tries to outrun the guys. Ya know." he chuckles.

"Whatever. I have as much chance of winning as the next guy, and you know it." I march to the window.

"Holy, simmer down. You know I'm on your side."

"Yeah. I know. Sorry. Did you hear my cousin's putting on some kind of mock race?"

"Yeah. I'll be there."

I pace the bedroom. "Who called you?"

"Craig didn't let you in on all the specifics, did he?" Tone sighs.

"No, he didn't." I drop to the bed. "What's going on?"

"Craig texted a bunch of us, asked to meet him at Rancho Chico's last night."

I go to the window. Craig's hooking the trailer to the truck. "How many?"

"About five of us. You sound worried."

I glare out the window at Craig. "I'm not worried. I just wish he'd be straight with me. He only told me Benton would be there. He wouldn't say who else."

A deep sigh straggles over the line. "Ya, Benton, me, Jarrod, Billy, and Franco."

I pace the room. "I don't understand why all the secrecy."

"He's not hiding anything from you. In fact, he's doing everything he can think of to prepare you, Char." The sound of a screen door slamming rings over the line. "You should have seen how intense he was last night. A couple of the guys were talking crap about you. I thought some big brawl was gonna break out. He's got some kind of control, though. He kept his cool, like some kind of CSI dude on TV."

"I know he's preparing me." I try to hide my shaky voice and give Tone a weak laugh. "I'm looking forward to whippin' up on you slowpokes." The more we talk the harder my gut twists.

"Well, got to run my mom to town. She twisted her ankle last week and has a doc appointment. See you tomorrow."

The phone clicks off. I stand by the window. Craig is loading tack. I put the phone away and go help him.

"What all do we need?" I hold the trailer's tack door open for him.

"I've got everything loaded. "Get ahold of Benton?" He leans against the truck.

"Whatever. He didn't answer. I did talk to Tone."

He takes a long look at me. "Figured you would. You girls have a need to 'talk things out.' "

I punch him in the shoulder. He lifts me into the air and walks to the corral. He's walking to the trough at a brisk clip. "You better not," I holler.

"Better not what?"

I kick and scream and laugh.

He keeps walking.

I kick some more, pushing my arms against his chest.

He tosses me in the water. The surprise on his face when he realizes I have a hold on his shirt and drag him in with me is priceless. He lands on top of me, pinning me to the bottom of the 390-gallon tank. I push him off and surface. He dunks me. I claw my way to the top and lean against the steel tank. I laugh so hard my gut hurts, for a good reason this time. He splashes water on my face.

"You pass the swim test," he says.

I splash him back.

"Time to eat." Timmy appears, looking at us as though he wants in on the fun.

We glance at each other, shoot out of the water, and drag him in. What seems like a short time passes before Auntie hollars at us to come and eat. I hop out of the tank, heavy clothes dripping. I glance at Craig and say, "We haven't had this much fun at our place in a long time. Not even sure when the last time was."

The next day I rise at the crack of dawn and do my chores. As we pull out, pink, the color of a salmon's belly, streaks the sky. I unroll the window and let warm air slide in. A half hour later we reach the south end of Omak. After unloading the horses, we saddle them, and I walk Rooster to the sandy shoreline. Most of the terrain surrounding the lake is rocky. More like one big, jagged rock cut in the shape of several hills.

"The rocks are granite and carved by glaciers of the Pleistocene," Craig says. "The Columbia River gouged this eight-mile river when lava flows moved it about."

"I can't even begin to imagine that happening. What that looked like. The rubble it made." The tropical blue water draws me close to its edge. I scoop cool liquid into my hands and rub them together. "Why does this feel soapy?" I rub some of it on my arms and neck. The breeze cools my skin.

"They say because there is not water flowing out of the river, it became saline. See those white deposits?" He motions to the rock lining the river. "That's sodium carbonate."

He talks like it's supposed to mean something to me.

"Do fish live in here?"

"The only ones that will survive are Lahona cutthroat trout."

"Eww, I wouldn't eat them."

Craig laughs. "They're okay to eat. I think."

"We shoulda brought some poles." I walk back to Rooster and hoist myself into the saddle.

We ride to the top of the hill. Even the blue sky looks brilliant against the yellow and brown landscape. "Where is the one boulder-sized rock?" I squirm in the saddle to a sharp poke in my thigh. I reach in my front jean pocket and pull out the last letter from my secret attacker.

Craig's focus drops to my hand. "What's that? A letter from Benton?"

I gulp. "Yep."

Craig gives me a dirty look. "Where's your helmet?"

I shove the letter in my back pocket.

I run my fingers across the top of my head and shrug. "In the truck. Or trailer. Where did you put it?" My tone is sharp.

Craig lifts a brow. "Where did I put it? It's your job to keep track of that helmet and your vest, not mine."

"I'll wear it next time." I nod to the truck. "It's in my bag."

"You forget it next time, you're done."

He motions to my chest with his chin. "Where's your vest?"

"In the truck." I say with a hint of sarcasm.

Craig shakes his head. His gaze shifts to a large boulder on a hill to our left. "It's called balanced rock. See it? Looks kind of like a haystack." He stares at me. "Not sure what's up with you, but you better leave your personal life at home."

If you only knew. I shade my eyes and squint against the sun.

"You hear me?"

I clench my jaw. "I hear you."

"When we're done, we can hike to it. Provided you win." Craig spins his horse around and rushes down the hill.

I crouch forward and kick Rooster.

Most of the way down we're on their tail. Then on the last turn, I pass him and win. "Looks like we're hiking to the rock after our mock trial. Better yet, let's go fishing."

"You have to win the 'mock trial' first."

"Like I said before, it's in the bag." I twist around at the sound of trucks pulling in, dismount, and tie Rooster to the trailer. Dirt from the rigs swirls around me. I wave it away, cover my nose, and go into a coughing fit. Benton waves from one of the rigs and parks. He jumps out, a wide grin covering his face. I grunt and fetch my helmet and vest out of Craig's pickup. The others park where they can find a spot and start unloading horses.

Pick in hand, I check the bottom of Rooster's hooves for rocks. When I straighten back up Benton is standing beside me. He swoops in and plants a lingering kiss on my lips, holding me tightly in his arms. I stiffen.

He frowns and backs off. "Be careful out there."

I narrow my eyes. "You didn't call me back."

"I've been working nights and sleeping days. I'm helping with the weir on the Okanogan," he says. "I knew I'd see you today."

I eye him like a snake I want to crush. "We'll talk later."

When the guys have their horses ready, we gather by Craig and form a semicircle, Tone on one side of me, Benton on the other. I give each one a sideways glance and shake my head. Take a step forward and cross my arms over my chest.

Craig fiddles with his video camera, rattles off a few rules, and we head to the top. *Know your surroundings.* As we climb the hill, I keep my distance. To my left, Benton stays between me and the others, Tone flanking my right side. Do they realize what they're doing?

"You ready for this?" Tone says.

I bite my lip and keep silent.

"I think she's so scared, cat's got her tongue." Billy twists around and sneers.

I wink at Billy and kick Rooster into a trot and come alongside him. I lean over and say, "Is that the best you got, cowboy?" I get ahead of everyone and enjoy the peace.

I hear Tone's and Benton's voices, but not their words. We make it to the top and ride on for thirty yards before turning around. *Don't race or you'll regret it.* My teeth clench.

"Let's make this a fair race." Tone waves an arm horizontally in the air.

I'm between Benton and Billy. Billy's still talking crap. Could he be working with Hagan? Would two guys team up? How do they know each other?

Tone hollers to Craig and it's only seconds until the pop of the gun cracks the air. We kick our horses and dart down the hill. I find a spot to the left of Craig and race for that. Billy and Tone are ahead of me. The sound of hooves on hard ground pounds my ears. We veer to the right and crash into the water, our pace slowing. Rooster lunges a few yards then swims. We're about thirty of fifty yards out when Jarrod leans toward me, takes his crop, and whips me. It makes contact with my face. I scream and grit my teeth.

I reach for the whip. My foot slips out of the stirrup, and I lose my balance the moment Rooster lunges forward. Before I know it, I'm in the water, rolling to the current. Hooves kick my sides and helmet. Even though it feels a whole lot longer, I'm under for only seconds. I fight my way to the surface, gasping. Rooster follows the herd and circles around. He swims close enough that I'm able to clutch onto his mane, somewhat hanging over the saddle, and ride back to shallow water. I holler from the force of the drag, my fingers clinging to the saddle horn, and recoil against the pain in my side. Once my feet touch the ground, I slip from the saddle and plunge into the water, horses jumping over me.

Benton and Craig rush toward me, Craig screaming my name. Their arms under mine and around my waist, they drag me to dry ground and lay me on the sand. With ragged breaths, I struggle to suck in enough air. I roll onto my side and cough, spitting up water.

Craig leans over me. "You all right?"

I nod.

Benton lays a gentle hand on my head. "Anything broke?"

"No. I just got the wind knocked out of me." Once I catch my breath, I roll onto my knees and sit back on my heels.

"Maybe she should stay home," Jarrod says.

Benton sprints to Jarrod and pulls him off his horse. Tone rushes over to break them up. Benton has Jarrod in a headlock. Craig drops his video camera at my side and sprints over, helping Tone break Benton's grip. Jerrod's face blooms a dark red hue as he struggles against Benton's rage. Billy wraps his arms around Jarrod and pulls him away.

"Why did you whip her?" Benton says as he lunges toward Jarrod.

Craig and Tone step in front of him, hands up.

"You said to keep it real," Jarrod says. "What, don't you think your little woman has what it takes? Is that why you're so protective?" He elbows himself away from Billy's grasp. "Maybe she should just stay home. Watch from the sidelines." He turns to me and glares, fisting his hand in the air. "This is a man's tradition. Our right of passage. You have no place in it. Stay home!"

"Shut your face!" I take a few wobbly steps toward them and bend over. Tone rushes over and takes hold of me. I flinch from his grip. He cradles me in his arms from behind and walks me to the truck. I ease down onto the trailer's running board.

"He's right. If she can't handle this…" Billy holds out his hands, palms up.

"She'll do just fine," Craig says. "This is why I had this. So she can get a taste of things before the real event."

Billy nods. He turns to Jarrod and says, "Let's load."

We watch the two drive away, eating their dust.

"What hurts?" Craig examines my head.

I knock his hands away. "My neck, legs, and sides. Nothing I can't handle." I ease my back against the horse trailer. "Glad I had this on…" I lift my helmet a couple inches above my leg. Wincing, I unzip the vest.

Benton marches to the lake, kicking rocks out of his way.

"I agree with him." Tone watches Benton.

"Oh sheesh. Nothing's broke." I fiddle with my helmet. "What was that up there?" I nod to the hill.

Tone and I lock gazes and he says, "What?"

"You and Benton."

"What about us?" Tone straightens, hands on hips.

"You know what I'm talking about."

"What happened up there?" Craig says.

Tone rubs the back of his neck. "Nothing. We care about you is all."

"You better start focusing, Char. These distractions are nothing compared to what lies ahead." Craig unties his horse and loads him.

I rise as a ninety-year-old woman would and make my way to Benton. He tosses rocks into the lake. He doesn't understand. But how can he when he has no idea? I want to scream. Tell him about the threats. I open my mouth but nothing comes out. Would he be that much more protective? Or try and stop me? The pain on his face makes my heart clench. "Hey." I lean against him because it hurts to stand straight.

He wraps both arms around me and pulls me close. "You scared me." His thick tone is just above a whisper. He kisses the top of my head and cradles it in his palm. "This was supposed to help you, not hurt you."

"Sorry." I wince.

He strokes my hair, brushing loose strands away from my face. I lay my head on his chest, gathering the fabric of his damp T-shirt with stiff fingers.

"Let's sit you down." He guides me by the small of my back as we creep to the pickup. He opens the door and helps me scoot in.

I lean back and sigh, eyes squeezed shut. "This is only a minor setback." I give him a small smile. "A little Tylenol and ice will get me back in the saddle in no time."

He rests a hand on my leg. "Next time someone strikes you, let them. It may sting, but he won't kill you. Then hang on like your life depends on it because it does." He rubs a finger down the side of my face. "He left a nice welt."

I finger the raised strip. "I can feel it."

Craig climbs in. "Best get her back."

Benton nods. "Call you later." He kisses me and shuts the door.

The truck creeps away. The side mirror reflects Benton and Tone having what looks like a heated conversation. They talk. Watch us. Benton stabs the air in our direction. Talk some more. Benton shakes his head and stomps off. Tone kicks the dirt.

CHAPTER 32

A week later the bruises have turned into a faded green-yellow hue. I rub some of the Indian medicine Aunt Jamison had given me on my skin. Not sure what's in the medicine and not sure my auntie knows, but between that, the willow bark and other bitter herbs to kill the pain, and Arnica she'd given me I'm ready for the next round.

"You about ready?" Craig hollers from outside my bedroom door.

"Ready for whatever Jarrod and those other fools throw my way." I stuff the cream in my bag and head to the barn. In the tack room crops and lunge whips hang from the wall. I pluck a rope quirt from the wall and flick it against the palm of my hand. It leaves a red mark. Next I try a quirt with a popper on the end. Not much of a sting. I hang it back on the hook and finger one of Auntie's leather over and under whips. I lift if off its hook and snap it against the same palm. The sting makes me flinch. "Perfect." I shove it in the bag along with my helmet and vest, drop the bag in Craig's pickup, and head to the house.

The smell of pork greets me at the door. The kitchen table is covered with eggs, bacon, pancakes, and fruit. I settle in a chair and lift up a strip of greasy bacon. "You sure this is on my diet?" Before Craig answers, I take a bite and fork a pancake onto my plate, top it with the rest of the strip, a spoonful of eggs, and a touch of syrup, roll it into a burrito, and take a bite. My taste buds dance. I wave it at Craig. A long swallow of cold milk washes it all down. I take another huge bite.

"Ready?" Craig glances at my breakfast burrito and follows suit. "Mmm. This's delicious."

"Don't talk with your mouth full." Auntie snaps him with a towel.

Uncle Buck sets his newspaper down. He clears his throat. "Just a minute." He drums his fingers on the table. "Char, tell me how you're gonna stay safe today."

Stay safe? Did he see the letters? I stop chewing.

Craig rolls his eyes. "She knows what to do, Pops." He heads for the door.

"That may be, son. However, she's in my care and I need to know she's not going to be hauled out by ambulance."

I finish chewing and swallow. "I'm not going to let anything distract me this time." I wash the lump in my throat down with the rest of my milk. "I've watched his video over and over until my eyes cross, Uncle. I'll be fine."

"And you're up to it?" Uncle says.

"Yeah." My fingers play with my braids.

"Come on, Char." Craig opens the door and waves me over. "Don't fret, Pops. It only takes coming off once to keep a person stuck to the saddle.

We head to the barn and brush the horses. I toss a saddle on Rooster's back and pull the cinch with rough hands. We lead them out to the truck. I load Rooster first.

Craig loads his bay gelding and latches the trailer door. "What's up with you?"

"Nothing." I hop into the pickup, take a bite of apple, and roll down the window.

Craig slides under the wheel, slams the door shut, and heads down the drive. "What aren't you telling me? You're edgy. Almost seem afraid. What's going on?"

Should I tell him about the letters? I open my mouth and snap it shut. Shake my head. "The closer it gets…I don't know." I hang my arm out the window. Cool air brushes against my skin.

"You better figure it out." Craig turns up the volume and sings to Randy Houser's song, *Like a Cowboy*.

I finish my apple and toss the core out the window. Forty-five minutes later we pull into the south end of Omak Lake. We unload the horses and warm them up.

Rigs pull in. Horses unload. Ten minutes later a familiar truck rumbles down the road and stops near Craig's rig, whipping a cloud of dust in our faces. Chase jumps out and dangles the key. "Got my license!"

I drop the reins and run to him, pulling him into a bear hug. "How'd you know we were here?"

"Craig. I convinced Dad to let me come, reminding him I'm your gopher during the stampede. Told him it was a safety issue." He smiles.

We head toward Rooster.

"Of course. How are they?" I hand the reins to him. "Haven't heard from Mom in a while."

He shakes Craig's hand. "Good. Sshapa's getting stronger every day." His gaze drops to his cracked boots. "They've hauled most of the bulls to Davenport." At the sound of the guy's loud voices, Chase's head jerks up. "Who's that?" He snickers.

I squint at the spare. "Not sure. Thought this was supposed to be the same riders as last time." The spare looks to be about Chase's height only with a few more pounds on him. He wears a baseball cap, jeans torn at the knees, and a tank top a size too small. After giving me the stink eye, he spits a stream of snoose on the ground and wipes his mouth with the back of his hand. I snort. "Another rogue cowboy. This should be entertaining."

"He must've come with Jarrod and Billy," Craig says. "I'll go check it out. Hey, Chase, congrats on the license."

"Thanks!"

"I'll warm up Rooster," I say.

"That's my job." Chase climbs into the saddle and walks the horse around the trailers.

Benton strides over, pulls me into a hug, and lifts me off my feet. He sets me down. "How you feeling?"

"Fine." My belly clenches.

He leans in for a kiss.

I let him give me a quick one and step back. "What happened to no distractions?"

He takes a step forward. "You don't distract me at all." He pulls me into his chest and places his lips close to my ear. "Be careful today. I mean it. Not sure who the new guy is…Something tells me he's not fond of chick jockeys."

I step back and nod. "I've watched Craig's stupid video a hundred times and know how bad I sat in the saddle. Don't worry. I'm prepared this time." I spin on my heels and beeline to Craig, curious who the spare is. Benton's on my heels. By the sound of his boots on gravel, he seems as anxious as I am.

"Back for more?" Billy smirks.

Jarod sneers, sweeping his gaze over my body.

I straighten my spine, chin up.

Franco smiles and nods, shifts his weight.

Tone hugs me. "Watch your back," he whispers in my ear.

The spare, thumbs hanging from his belt loops, surveys me as though I'm a piece of garbage.

"This is Robert," Craig says. "He's from Inchelium."

The spare's gaze darts from Benton to Chase and lands on me. "Kinda puny, aren't ya?"

Benton takes a step forward. I stop him with my arm. Jarod and Franco snicker.

"She's as tough as they come," Chase says from on top of Rooster's back.

Robert eyes Chase. "Who's he?"

"The kid who's going to keep you honest." Craig waves Chase off and has us draw numbers for placement. He then gives us a quick reminder of the rules. We mount our horses and head up the hill. Chase tosses a stick to the side of us. We move in sequence behind the stick according to the number we drew. Tone and Benton seem to have made some kind of pact because they are both keeping their distance from me.

I'm wedged between Tone and Robert. The horses wiggle and Billy's rears. Robert's horse bumps into mine. A wave of nausea comes over me. I bite my lip. Taste the blood.

With a shaky hand, I lean over and stroke Rooster's neck. Talk to him while zeroing in on where I think Craig is standing. A blast from the gun cracks the dry, hot air, creating an echo down the rock walls that line the lake. We take off. I fumble for the back strap on my saddle and find it halfway down.

We're in a tight pack and when we hit the water, it sprays my face. I lose a stirrup while wiping my eyes. Riders bump into me from every direction. Robert, slightly ahead of me, reaches down and tugs off Rooster's bridle and yanks the slippery reins out of my grip. I grasp a hunk of mane with one hand and the saddle horn with the other and hold on tight.

The pack hits the thirty-yard mark and arcs to the right. Billy and Robert pin me between them. Robert grabs my shirt and pulls. My arm pounds his until he releases his grip.

Rooster follows the pack as his herd instincts kick in. I grit my teeth and rein Rooster toward a pile of rocks straight ahead. I kick him as we come out of the water and he jets ahead, placing us second. Tone twists around, his gaze dropping to my horses head. He leans over, grabs a handful of Rooster's mane, and turns into us. It takes a bit to spiral down to a stop. I pat his neck and let out a deep, guttural whoop.

Robert rides over to me and throws me the bridle. "Nice job! You passed the test."

I snap my head to Tone, sending him a fierce gaze. "Test? Is that what you and Benton have been planning?"

"What? No!" Tone says. "Where'd you get that idea?"

"I saw you two talking as we drove out of here last week. Looked like you were planning something."

Tone shoots me a defensive laugh. "No. We weren't."

"What were you thinking?" Benton grabs Robert's shirt, his jaw clenched.

Robert shoves Benton away. "Figured if she was serious about coming off the hill, she needed to prove it and stay on." He reins his horse around and heads for his two-toned Chevy. He pulls back and stops his horse, twists around in his saddle. "You guys are too close to her." He glares at Tone, Benton, and Craig. "You're protecting her. But from what? Guys like me? Herself? You're not doing her a favor. She's gonna get hurt. I think you guys know it." He spins his horse around and trots away.

I fight the urge to yank him off his horse and kick his face.

Billy and Jarrod come closer.

"His sister tried to qualify a few years back. She got messed up pretty bad," Billy says. "Sounds like he'll do what it takes to either scare a girl off or make sure she can survive it."

"Looks like you can handle it," Jarrod says. "At least for now."

At least for now? "What the heck?"

Billy and Jarrod nod to Craig, load their horses, and drive out. I dismount and rub Rooster, watching the back of their trailer rumble down the road through a haze of dust.

"What's going on?" Chase says.

"Not sure." Should I thank him or shoot him? I hand Chase the reins. "I'll let you cool him off."

"That was unexpected." Craig motions down the road with his video camera.

Benton takes hold of my hand and raises it in the air. "You rode him like a mad woman!"

We all laugh. Is his sister all right now? Was there lasting damage? A shudder shimmies down me.

"What else was I supposed to do?" I turn to Tone. "So what were you two talking about?" I jerk my hand out of Benton's and step aside.

Tone and Benton exchange a questioning look, Tone fidgeting.

"You think we set this up?" Benton shoves his hands on his hips.

"All we talked about is whether we should let you either sink or swim," Tone says. "We know if you are to do this, it needs to be on your terms. We realize we can't protect you out there. So we made a deal to ride with you, not around you."

I toe the dirt with my boot. "Thanks. Robert apparently thought I should sink." A wave of dizziness swirls in my head and I bend over, hands on my knees. "I need some water."

"Who cares what he thinks. He's an idiot." Chase jogs to Craig's pickup and brings back a cooler.

Craig hands his camera to Chase and playfully shoves me into Benton. He catches me, holding on tight. The others join in and carry me to the lake.

"That's not what I was talking about!" I laugh. Struggle. Wiggle. Feel my body float through the air. Giggle. Feel the smack of water against my back.

Then Tone, Benton, and Craig jump in and we splash around. I laugh and drown all fear, worry, and tension in the lake. After awhile I trudge out, clothes and hair dripping and heavy and settle on the shore, trying to touch as little sand as possible. Benton stretches out, his head in my lap.

A war whoop breaks out and Chase rips by in socks and underwear and jumps into the water. "Last one in gets all the evening chores!"

"Still no sign of intelligence," I mutter. Doesn't he realize he's the last one in? We watch him swim while our clothes dry out. I run my fingers through Benton's damp hair, curling a loose strand round my pinky.

"Anyone hungry? Want to fish?" Craig motions to the truck with his head. "I brought poles."

All eyes turn to me.

"What? No way. Get 'em yourselves." I prop myself in the hot sand on my elbows. "I'm one of you." I close my eyes and let the sun bake my brown skin darker. Rooster's bridleless run skips across my thoughts. Who could it be? Time's running out. How can I figure out who's writing the threats and stop him? Them?

"We've created a monster," Tone says.

Footsteps from behind grow louder. My eyes barely open to Craig standing over me with a fishing pole.

He holds it out. "Here, you've earned it."

That evening, Benton meets us back at the Twisted Arrow. After a quick visit with my aunt and uncle, we slip into his pickup and head toward town.

"I want to show you something." Benton takes my hand in his.

I scoot next to him. "Where are we going?"

Benton grins. "You'll see." He pulls out of the driveway and turns left. We head into Omak and wind our way to Dewberry Avenue, stopping in front of a wire fence. "Get ready for the most beautiful view you'll ever see." The empty lot is bookended by homes. We get out, climb over the locked gate, and stride to the lip of the World Famous Suicide Hill. A high-pitched chirp of crickets surrounds us.

"Oh, my goodness." My hand sweeps over the sixty-two-degree slope. "This is steeper than I thought." I tap thick, soft dirt that spills down the hill with the toe of my boot. "This is nice soil. Solid footing." The Omak Stampede Arena grounds spreads out southwest of the hill and across the Okanogan River. Covered stands horseshoe the arena, leaving the chutes exposed. "I've never seen the grounds from this point of view before. It's amazing." I turn around. "How many feet is it from the starting point back there, to the point of the ledge of the hill?"

"About fifty feet." Benton says. "This is a 225-foot drop and once you cross the river, it's another 500 feet to the arena."

"It's one quick race." I swallow the lump in my throat. A sense of accomplishment—no pride—that wraps me in a light blanket. A cool breeze rushes between us and swirls down the hill. I shiver and rub my arms.

"Seconds, really. At first it all seems like slow motion, especially as you plow through the water, but then as you climb up the dike and into the arena, everything races by. The roar of the crowd will give you an adrenaline rush."

I shade my eyes with my hands and point to a grassy area southeast of us. "Is that where the Indian encampment will be?"

"Yep."

"And that's where we'll be." I point to the dirt paddock east of the arena jockey's begin from.

He nods. "We'll ride out of the horse paddock and follow the outrider along the river, over the bridge, and swing around to here." He sweeps his arm in an arc to his left.

I stare at the bridge west of us. It towers over the snake-like Okanogan River as it disappears and swings north. Trees line the riverbank, which lays below rock cliffs. Already the terrain is taking on its desert appearance. "I assume they'll have someone stopping traffic for us."

"Yep. TOSHA will be manning the bridge on both sides."

"I'm glad you brought me here. It's not as scary now. The beauty of it…it's like a sunset mixed with Carlos Nakai's flute music and my favorite flavor of ice cream."

"Which is?"

"Carmel fudge." I rub my arms. "What's your favorite?"

"Cookies and cream." Benton's smile broadens to a quarter moon.

I chuckle. "Never thought you for a cookies and cream kind of guy."

"To me, coming off this hill is Rolling Stone's *Start Me Up* meets Northern Cree with a twist of lime."

"You're the twisted one."

"One week, Char. We'll be coming down this in one week. I know you're ready. Be strong. Be prepared and focused." From behind Benton wraps his arms around me and we sway. A slow, gentle movement.

I lean my head back against his neck and inhale his scent. "I'm ready." I rub his arms.

We spend the next fifteen minutes or so listening to the cricket chorus. Something lightly brushes my arms. Perhaps it's Creator's protective spirit swirling around us. We watch His beauty streak across the evening sky as the sun lowers.

I pray I make it down safely.

CHAPTER 33

It's the first day of qualifications and I can't find my favorite socks. I braid my hair and rummage through my bag and suitcase for a third time. I slip on a pair I hate. They make my feet hot and itchy. I have four shirts lined out, trying to choose something that won't hook on the saddle horn. Something light. Snug. I select a plain lime green sports shirt Aunt Jamison bought me that matches my bandana and saddle pad. For the swim test, shorts or pants? I pull on pants and stuff shorts in a bag.

"Where are my socks?" My pitch rises with each word like a scared songbird. I throw clothes out of my bag and tip it upside down. I hurl my bag across the room. Benton gave them to me for graduation. "I need those socks!"

"Char, you in there?" Aunt Jamison taps on the door.

"Yeah, come in." I tug my shirt down.

Her eyes roam the room, mouth hanging open. "I washed these last night. Didn't know if you need any of them for today." She holds out a bundle of shirts and underclothing, my lime green socks poking out from the jumble.

"Yes! I've been looking for these." I seize the pile and toss them on the bed, picking out the socks.

"You hungry? You haven't eaten but a few bites all day."

"No. I'm good. I had a cup of fruit salad a while ago. Been snacking on those." I point to a bag of almonds. My stomach is like a helium-filled balloon someone has just released. It darts inside me, bumping into my ribs and kidneys.

"Once you get on top of the hill, you're gonna be fine. Probably once you get to the grounds. Don't worry, you'll qualify. You've worked hard."

"I hope so." I pull on my socks and boots with shaky hands.

"There will be plenty to do to get you and Rooster ready. Especially Rooster. Remember, he's a veteran. Trust him. Craig's loading him now."

I peer out the window and sure enough, Craig's shutting the trailer door. The phone rings and Timmy hollers for me. He bounces up the stairs and hands me the phone. "Hello?"

"Hey Charnaye, this is Hope. I have a few minutes and I just wanted to call and let you know I'm here for you and will try to break loose to find you before you head to the hill. You hanging in there?"

I glance at Aunt Jamison and point to the phone. "Thanks for calling. I'm pretty frantic right now. Probably just adrenaline, and I'm sure once I get there, I'll feel better. I'm always a little jittery before a race."

"You'll do fine. I was the same way. I've sent a few prayers your way."

"Thank you. I look forward to seeing you, even if it is from a distance."

I hand the phone back to Timmy. "I can't believe she called me." I shake my head. "She's pretty amazing."

Timmy shrugs. "Don't really know her. She's Mom's friend." He leaves the room.

Aunt Jamison has a quizzical smile. "Why are you surprised? She's your mentor."

"I don't know."

"That's the kind of person Hope is."

I watch Aunt Jamison's back as she disappears out of my room.

"Char, time to rock and roll," Chase shouts from the bottom of the stairs.

I stuff my helmet into my bag and bound down the steps. I stumble on the bottom two and Chase catches me.

"Slow down," he says. "You're worse than normal."

"I'm fine." I give him a crooked smile.

We proceed to the truck and climb in.

Craig's got the engine running and the AC on high, a grimace on his face. "Got everything? Helmet? Vest?"

"Yep…hold on." I check my bag for the over and under whip.

"I doubt you'll need that today. It's just a test," Craig says.

"Never know." I stuff the whip in my helmet, zip the bag, and toss it in the back seat with Chase.

A couple foals run, buck, and kick in the pasture as we pull out of the driveway. Most are sprawled out near their mothers. A couple bottle calves rest in soft grass under the shade of a few catalpa trees. My mind drifts back to the slump of Sshapa's shoulders. The loss of our cows. The tone of Mom's voice when she'd told me—relief mixed with sadness.

On our way to the stampede grounds, Chase and Craig talk and sing. I stare out the window, my throat in my gut. I think about last week's sweat with Craig. The calm feeling I had that night is what I wish I felt right now. I grab the beaded eagle feather off the dash Craig used to smudge me and Rooster with. I twirl it in my fingers as if it were gold. Then hold it close to my heart and pray, thanking Creator that because Craig and I are cousins, I can sweat with him. I pray for the safety of all of us jockeys. Pray for our horses. Pray for peace and wisdom. Most of all I pray for self-control over all the rotten carcasses who will try and destroy me.

Rows of cars park on the lawn near where the Calcutta auction will be, come elimination races in three weeks. Craig crawls up to the horse paddock. Jockeys, horse owners, and family of both settle in. I swear if someone lit a match I'd explode. A gatekeeper with a clipboard stops us, only lets jockeys and their families in. With a firm expression, he checks us off and opens the gate. We pull in and back into a spot closest to the river side of the fenced off area and unload Rooster.

I tie him to the trailer, run my hands over his back, and lean my head on his neck, inhaling his scent. The edginess melts away like ice on a hot day. It's pushing ninety degrees and sweat soaks my shirt. I dip my hands in Rooster's water bucket and splash the back of my neck. It's not enough, so I find a bandana and soak it with melted ice from the cooler.

"What's first?" I say to Craig and check out the competition, wondering who could be sending the letters.

"Vet check. Then swim and hill test, in that order. I want to wait until next weekend to do the hill test, let the water recede a few inches." Craig studies his watch. "Let's get him to the vet. You'll have the swim test soon after, which Rooster is familiar with and will pass. That's the least of your worries."

"The least of my worries. I agree with you on that." After Rooster passes the vet check, I tie him back to the trailer and find a bucket for water.

"What do you want me to do?" Chase says.

"Nothing yet." Craig fiddles with a bridle.

Chase sinks into one of the camp chairs we brought.

I fill the bucket with river water and weave my way back to the trailer, wondering where Craig is. "Chase, do you see a black box with vet wrap and stuff in it?"

Banging comes from the tack room. "Here's a black box." He extends it toward me.

"That'll do." I pull out lime green vet wrap. Aunt Jamison is sure persistent in making sure I match. I chuckle. It must be a barrel racing thing. I wrap one leg with a layer of vet wrap, add cotton batting to the back of his leg from below the hock joint to the fetlock, and wind another layer of vet wrap around. I dig in the black box. "Where's the tape?"

Chase extends his hand. "Here."

I pluck the white tape out of his hand and tear off three strips, wrapping two around the top and bottom and one just above the fetlock.

"You did a great job, Char," Craig says.

I stand. "Where have you been?"

"Watching you." He points to the back of the trailer. "I was fixing your bridle."

I peer around him. "What's wrong with it?"

"I replaced a Chicago screw," he says. "Nothing big. Give me some vet wrap and I'll help."

Chase lobs a pack to him. Ten minutes later we finish wrapping Rooster's legs. Benton and Tone wander over to us as I stick on the last strip of tape.

"How's it going?" Benton says.

"He's about ready." I tip my head toward Rooster. He kicks the trailer. Chase strokes his neck.

"I see his nerves have kicked in," Tone says.

I nod. "I'm not sure if he's excited or what."

"How many times has he come down this hill?" Benton walks over to him, runs his hand over his back and down his hind quarter.

"This'll be his fourth run." Craig checks a wrap without looking up.

"He'll give you a good ride," Tone says.

Benton drapes an arm around my shoulder. "Let's say a quick prayer then me and Tone have to get back." We all form a circle and pray for safety not only for the riders, but the horses as well.

Benton seems stiff as he walks away. Is he hurt? Did he get into a fight with someone who doesn't want me here? Who? Everyone seems to be focused on their horses, laughing, joking, talking about how they'll win this year.

"No distractions, Char." Craig scowls.

"When are *you* gonna get a woman?" Chase says.

"When I can support one." Craig ruffles his hair. "Let's get him saddled."

Chase unties Rooster and I slap the lime green pad and saddle on his back. The gelding stands quiet as I tighten the front cinch. Other horses dance around, one bucking as if he's here for the bronc riding event. Rooster eyeballs the other horses. I slip the bit in his mouth and check his headstall for any other loose ends. It appears to be in good shape. I slip into my vest, tie my headband behind my head, and snap my helmet into place. The sun's hot and blinding.

"Here's your sunglasses," Chase says.

"You can wear them. I don't want to see spots crossing the river." I hop into the saddle and circle Rooster around.

We make our way to the edge of the river for the swim test. There are a few ahead of me, so I wait in the shade. When it's our turn, Rooster creeps into the water and we swim across with no hint of refusal. As we drift downstream, I lean into the current, urging him forward. Even with the swollen river, he swims hard and fast.

Once on dry land, we climb the hill a few yards, circle around and gallop down, plunging into the cool water, and swim back across. He makes a flawless run. I dismount, wade back into the water, and offer him a drink. He sniffs the river, sips, and sighs.

I lead Rooster to the trailer and hand him off to Chase. "I hope he comes down that smooth next weekend."

While Chase puts a halter on my horse, I fetch a brush. In the bucket is a white, lined slip of folded paper. "No way!" My gut clenches. I step around the trailer. No one appears suspicious.

"What?" Chase peers around me.

I elbow him back. "Nothing, just a spider. I got it." I slip it into my back pocket at the same time I hand Chase the brush. I rush to the river and drop to the sand.

Congratulations on qualifying. If you enter this race, the odds of you making it down alive is next to none! If you think I'm joking, you better keep an eye on your tack.

I shove the letter into my back pocket, run into the middle of the paddock, and turn in a slow circle, my hand shading my eyes.

CHAPTER 34

Voices buzz the paddock. To find a quiet spot to meditate, I slip away to the river and wade in. The icy current numbs my ankles, but not my anxiety. The hill seems steeper today.

Chase joins me. "If you don't tell me what's going on, I'm telling Dad and Mom."

"Drop it! Someone's trying to get into my head, is all." I turn to walk back to the trailer when Chase picks the note from my back pocket.

"You shouldn't leave this hanging out." He waves it in the air. "What ever it is, it's getting to ya."

I spin around and reach for the note. "Give it here. I'm fine!"

He snaps his hand back. "Bull crap! You act like you're gonna rupture." He shoves the note in his front pants pocket.

"Give it to me!" I clench my teeth.

"No!" He spins on his heels and sprints down the beach, zig-zagging between dogs and kids.

I kick sand into the water and wade back in. *I'll deal with him later.*

The river has receded an inch or two since the swim test. I skip a few stones, ripples spreading over the surface. A few riders barrel down the hill and swim across. So far all have qualified and are moving on to eliminations. I swirl my bandana in the water and tie it around my neck. After a long moment of alone time, I traipse back to the trailer and check on Rooster.

Craig rests in a camp chair in the shade of a truck.

"Have you seen Chase?"

"Not for a bit," he says.

"What about Sshapa? He here yet?" I slowly spin around, frowning. *Where did he go? I need that letter.*

"You think I'd miss this?" Sshapa steps from the truck's tailgate, water bottle in hand.

"You're here!" I hug him, squeezing tight.

"I had to come see you. Tell you how proud I am of you." Moisture forms in his eyes.

"I'm glad you did. You look better than the last time I saw you. That nurse treatin' you right?" I give him a playful smile.

"We've had coffee a time or two." He winks.

"Where are my parents?"

"In the shade." He points to the south side of the paddock, where the Calcutta auction will be held in a few weeks. "I want a moment with you before everything starts." He lays a shaky hand on my shoulder. "You look like your Stimteema. She came down the Keller hill safe and sound, honoring our people. You will do the same." He takes a moment to pray over me and hobbles away.

"He looks old." I say to Craig.

My cousin nods and catches up with our grandfather, guiding him by the elbow.

"That's why Dad and Mom are selling all the cows come fall," Chase says. "Guess they want to fatten them up and get a good price." He walks by and whispers, "Tell me what's going on or I'll show Craig." He brandishes the note.

"Freakin' weasel." I glare at him and open my hand. "Give it to me."

He darts behind the trailer.

"Knock it off. We need to keep him calm." I nod at Rooster.

"Ready?" Craig says.

I flinch at the sound of his voice. "Yep." Eyes narrow, I shake my head at Chase. "We need to check the tack."

He examines Rooster. "I did. Everything looks good."

"I'll do it again." I fetch the bridle out of the tack room.

"It's just like practice at Omak Lake. Just steeper," Craig says.

"Way steeper." My fingers inspect the Chicago screws and buckles on the bridle. I untie my horse and climb into the saddle. Benton and Tone ride close and wait for me near the gate.

"Stay calm and focused. You're not timed today, so keep him steady, give him his head."

I nod and head out with a small group of jockeys.

There is no outrider for qualifications. Starting with the elimination races, we will have one to escort us down the highway, across the bridge, and to the hill. Sshapa and my folks wave from their camp chairs as I ride past. I smile at them. Mom presses folded hands against her lips. Dad pats her leg. Sshapa tips his cowboy hat.

Benton comes alongside me. "You're holding your breath. Let it out."

I nod, blow air past clenched teeth, and pin my gaze to the rider's vest in front of me. I take my hands, one at a time and shake the tingle out of them.

"You know what to do," Benton says.

"Yep." Throat tight, I swallow what little saliva's in my mouth. We ride alongside the sea of people to our right. I blink against the sun and wipe sweat from my face. Cheers and words of encouragement fill my ears. I mentally run through the drill: Lean back. Hang on. Lean into the current. Hold tight. Breathe. The river's high, will Rooster catapult us in? I finger the saddle horn and release a held breath.

Before I know it, we're to the bridge. Tribal TOSHA SUVs block oncoming traffic. The click of horseshoes on pavement resounds through the evening air, carrying the sound on the wings of the breeze and making my braids slap my back. *Click. Click. Click. Click.* Without pads on, the horses' shoes are slick on the pavement. Once off the bridge, my muscles relax. I find relief in the daylight. Thursday night, first day of the race during stampede, we do this in the dark. Will I be able to see?

We turn left, travel down Dewberry Avenue, and pass houses. Some are empty, some have elders waving at us from the shade of their porches. We make our way to the dirt lot. I dismount, walk through the gate, and head straight to the hill's lip. A tribal park's boat is in the water to the right as is a Jet Ski. They circle in the water like ravens spiraling down for a dead carcass.

A handful of men on horses standby in the river to the left. Spectators behind them wade in the water. Family and friends of the jockeys line the dike. I shift my weight and dirt rolls down the hill. A photographer points his lens up the hill from near the pine tree straight across. A hot sun beats down from an azure sky. *Breathe.* I wipe sweat from my brow, pray, and rub Rooster's neck, thanking him for the journey he's about to take me on. For a single moment I'm calm. Until another jockey comes to the edge. Ripples of fear from my toes work their way to my belly, swirl around, and lodge in my throat.

"Easy as a sunset mixed with Carlos Nakai's flute music and caramel fudge ice cream," Benton whispers, leaning in to my ear from behind.

Shivers dance down my back. I rub my arms. I give him a small smile.

Officials call for the next person. Since there is a first time horse who needs the support of a veteran, that jockey and horse, Benton and I, and Billy Beck file into a group. Tone will follow us by himself. There is no start gun, so we just line up like we did at Omak Lake and trust everything will be fair. I rein Rooster into a spot.

A jockey waiting for his turn spits at me, "You shouldn't be here."

Another agrees. And another. I circle Rooster and keep to myself. Benton watches from a few feet away.

Billy Beck tells them to shut their mouths or he'll do it for them. "She's earned her right to be here."

I nod, a small smile forming on my mouth. He nods back. I scratch him off my list of potential offenders. My legs feel Rooster's muscles contracting. He paws the ground. Other horses rear, side step, or dance in place while the jockey holds them back. Even though it's not their turn, the horses seem to know the drill.

"I'll be coming after you," one guy says. "Eventually."

The others laugh and give me cat-calls.

"If you can catch me," I say, without looking at him. I talk to Rooster in a soothing tone, one hand on the rein, the other on a hunk of mane.

I find myself sandwiched between Billy and the rookie horse. We glance at one another, nod, and kick our horses forward. We surge off the hill and I reach back, my fingers fumbling for my handle. I find it and hang on, leaning back. I manage to stay centered as we soar down. I sink deep into my saddle, heels down and toes out. At the bottom Rooster plunges into the river.

Water sprays in my face and blurs my vision. Rooster jumps and lunges until he can no longer touch the riverbed. At that point he rocks as he swims. I keep my concentration pinned on the pine tree. I'm bounced around by Billy and the rookie. The horses don't seem to know this is merely a trial. We are all in a tight pack. I lean low and spank Rooster with my over and under quirt, urging him on with the shriek of my voice.

"Keep going," Billy shouts to the rookie. "All the way in."

The path is clear up the dike and into the arena. Once Rooster's hooves hit the rocky bottom, he lunges and we surge onto dry ground. I glance back. Benton has a wide grin plastered on his face. We are almost hip to hip. We charge up the dike and into the arena and spiral our horses down to a walk.

"You made it." Benton dismounts and rushes toward me, his horse jogging beside him.

"I'm in!" I wrap my arms around his neck and press my lips hard against his.

"How'd he feel?"

"Strong. Sure-footed. I can't wait for the elimination race. I know we'll make the top twenty."

"Yes, we will." Benton releases me and we walk to the gate.

I hand Rooster over to Chase and scrunch my nose at him. My body trembles as adrenaline leaks out. "I'm starving."

"We'll get Rooster settled in then get something to eat. I'm sure the folks are eager to see you."

"I'm ready to see them." My voice cracks. We make our way to the horse trailer. I round the corner to see my father sitting in his wheelchair. He wrings his hands, eyes searching. When he turns his head to me, we lock eyes. He waves. I imagine him popping out of his chair and racing toward me, wrapping his arms around me. Instead, I rush to my father and encircle him from behind.

"I'm proud of you, Char. You scared me half to death, but I'm proud of you." He pats the back of my head.

I hold him tight. "Creator takes care of me," I softly say.

He nods again.

I hug Mom and Sshapa. Worry in my mother's eyes causes doubt to bump the cracks of my armor. *She can never know about the threats.* They are puffy and it makes me second guess my choice. An old woman's face stares back. After hugging me, Sshapa sinks back into a chair. He's quiet, staring at the palms of his hands. I scan the creases in his face. His sad eyes. His pale skin. I offer him a cool bottle of water. Hug him again. Is my racing taking a toll on them? But if I pull out now I go against my beliefs. What would everyone say if I do? What would Billy Beck say? Or Benton and Tone? What about those guys spitting at me? Would whoever's threatening me win?

Those who didn't qualify plod past, cussing as they mill around like a bunch of cattle in a holding pen, wanting to know what happened and seeking a name to blame. A name other than their own. One of the jockeys marches by, soaking wet. He must have fallen off his horse, an automatic disqualification. My one true fear.

Mom and Aunt Jamison spread the food out on the tailgate of Uncle Buck's truck. We eat our supper, say our good-byes, and load Rooster. I watch my family drive away. As for tomorrow, we hit the trail once again.

CHAPTER 35

Today I officially enter the race.

Even though it's late afternoon on Friday, it doesn't seem like the weekend has begun. But it's ramping up fast. My stomach twists to the point of puking. My body shakes as I wipe my mouth.

I'm the only girl. Talk about being out of place. This shouldn't take very long. Sign a waiver, fill out the entry form, and pay the fee. The other riders glare at me as they walk by. I lift my chin, square my shoulders, and hope no one can see me quivering. Every nook and cranny seems suspicious. He's got to be here.

"Hey, Char," Benton says. "You ready for this?"

I take a step, intending to leap into his embrace, but remember to keep it cool and give him a small hug instead. "Yeah, I'm good."

Benton drapes an arm around me. "Tone's on his way. I talked to him a while ago. We both got tied up at work." He watches me. "Why do you keep looking around like a scared bunny?"

"Nothing..." I smooth my hair, try and relax, but end up wringing my hands. The horse paddock is full. By the looks of it, there will be elimination races for the top twenty to go on to ride during the stampede. The walls of the arena tower over us. I see myself galloping in—first place. The crowd cheers. I take a couple steps forward and say, "It's surreal."

"You *are* nervous." Benton pulls me close and leans into my ear. "Waiting in line is the easy part. Once you sign the papers you're committed. That's when it sinks in. Just remember, you can handle this. You've trained hard. Proved yourself. You've earned your spot."

"Yeah." I finger the hole in the knee of my jeans.

"That's not convincing. Come on, Rooster passed his vet checks, hill and swim test. He qualified for the race, or we wouldn't be standing here. Practices have gone well, except you keep losing your stirrups. Have you figured out a fix for that yet?"

"Rubber bands."

"What? No way. That's dangerous. We're in water."

"Why? Aunt Jamison used them barrel racing."

He shakes his head. "Please don't—"

"Hey guys." Tone approaches us, holding hands with some blonde, Barbie-like girl. She's got fancy boots, tight jeans, bling from head to toe, including her belt.

I raise a brow at Benton then say to Tone's plus one, "Hey."

Tone points to the tall, toothpick of a girl hanging off his arm. "This is Julie."

I extend my hand, chest burning. She pulls the spaghetti strap of her tank top over her shoulder and gives me a schoolgirl kind of smile. Long, sparkly earrings dangle from her ears and five silver bracelets slid up her arm as she gives us a three-finger wave. I find myself staring, mouth open. I close it. Stuff down a snigger.

Jarrod swaggers over to us. "You really gonna do this, huh?"

"Yeah. Really, I am." I glare at him, lengthening my spine. He's got to be the one.

He looks me over as if I'm a sizzling steak, grunts, and saunters off.

"Who is *that*?" Julie says to Tone.

"Just some lowlife," Tone says. "This is Benton, Char's man."

They exchange greetings. We move up in line. Benton and I lock gazes. It appears we are thinking the same thing. Why Julie? Benton grabs my hand, weaving our fingers together.

Another guy with a hard look to his face who's just signed his waiver saunters by, giving me the stink eye. We move up again.

"So Tone, when did this happen?" I wave my hand in front of him and Julie.

She giggles and hugs his arm.

"A week ago. I met her at a family function," Tone says.

Benton squeezes my hand.

"She's family?" I know she's not, but can't resist. The tension is too thick.

Tone frowns, eyes narrow. "No, Char. She's my cousin's friend. They moved to Okanogan a few months ago. She just graduated, too."

"Oh? Where'd you move from?" I say, truly interested.

"Montana. A small cattle town in the southern part of the state."

Benton motions me to take a few steps. "Your parents ranchers?"

"No. They're both teachers. Well, my mom is. We moved closer to family and my dad's the new superintendent of Okanogan High School. My mom's hoping to get on as a teacher this fall somewhere there or in Omak."

"What about you?" Benton says. "What are your plans now?"

"I'm headed to Central this year. I also want to teach elementary, minor in reading." She smiles at Tone who is a foot taller.

Pants tucked inside roper cowboy boots doesn't quite say school teacher. Maybe that's what they wear in Montana. Actually, would they dress in cattle country. I shrug.

Another jockey walks away. A couple more and it's my turn. "Guess a lot of us had the same idea. Sign up tonight and get it over with." I give Benton a nervous chuckle. My shakes are back and so are the monkeys doing acrobatics in my belly.

Benton nudges me. I step up to the tailgate of someone's rig, sign my entry and waiver, and hand over the cash. Benton does the same and we walk out of the paddock.

"You did it!" He says, taking hold of my hand. "How does it feel?"

"Like there's no turnin' back."

We find a shady spot on the grass outside the paddock and wait for Tone and Julie. Only a few rigs remain. Someone's music blares from the softball field nearby.

"I think we should go celebrate," He say. "I'm starving. Want to grab a bite to eat? Should we invite Tone and Julie?"

"Sure. She seems like a great girl. I'm happy Tone found someone." Him having a girl at his side should douse any trace of rivalry. One less distraction.

"Me, too." Benton squeezes my hand.

I nudge his shoulder with mine, still trying to figure out why he chose me. He's smart, talented, drop-dead gorgeous. I'm plain. Nothing special. A tingle scatters over my skin as his ebony eyes peer into mine. Could I love this man? Be with him? Forever?

We meet at Rancho Chicos and order. The more we visit, the more I like Julie. She talks with a sense of confidence about her future plans. With quick wit, pretty green eyes, and a smile that shows straight, white teeth, she's bound to tantalize eager little students.

Julie clears her throat and looks at me. "So, what makes you want to enter this race?"

I take a sip of water. "Because I can."

"Is that the only reason?" She fingers her glass.

"Not really. For men it's about being a warrior. For me it's the same. Yet different. I've prayed about this and feel Creator has given me the same privilege and means to respect the culture. In the past, mostly men have raced. But it's not just for them." I drum the table with my fingers. "There's no reason why women can't have tradition in the same ways as men. I love horses and racing. It's who I am. It feels right, ya know?"

Julie shakes her head. "I'd never have the guts to ride a horse off that hill. Not even at a walk."

"It's not about guts. It's about honor."

"I believe you."

I smile at her, hoping our friendship will grow. And hoping she can't see my fear.

CHAPTER 36

Today is elimination day.

I wake before the roosters announce the morning's entrance. The fabric of my T-shirt sticks to my damp skin. This is going to be a long day. I jump in a cool shower, dress, and braid my wet hair. Feed Rooster, plop on a bale of hay, and lean against his stall door, hugging my knees.

Three weekends of qualifications wasn't too bad. The top twenty move on. Will I make it? Will the heat of late afternoon drain me? I trudge back to my room and try to rest, but my belly is in such a tight knot I end up tossing and turning. I walk to the window. Cross the room and sit on my bed. Lie down. Get up and peer out the window again. Drop to the carpet and do some push-ups and sit-ups. Jump rope for five minutes without a rope. Unable to choke down much food, I find myself at the door of Rooster's stall. He paces. I put on his halter and lead him out. I don't know why he's patrolling his stall. From what Craig says, he doesn't know it's race day until we pull onto the Stampede grounds.

We meander to a shady spot and he drops his head. Rips mouthfuls of green blades with his front teeth and chews, eyes half-mast. I sink to the ground, lean against a catalpa tree, and think about how far we've come. How we've grown as a team. I close my eyes and cover them with my arm.

After I don't know how long, the kick of a toe to my foot wakes me. Timmy announces lunch is ready. I jump at his voice, looking around for Rooster. He's gone.

"Chase put him back a while ago." He extends his hand.

I take hold and let him pull me up.

The phone rings as I walk through the screen door. Uncle Buck hands it to me. "Hello?"

"Hi, Char. When are you coming home?" Kari's voice sounds small.

I take the conversation to the living room and sink into the leather lazy chair. "I'll be home after the race." Should I ask if anyone has bothered her? Touched her? Wiped tears from her face? I grit my teeth.

Deep breaths scoot across the line.

"Kari?" I wish I could hold her. Not wanting to scare her, I keep my concerns to myself. She's been through enough. He could be lying about talking with her. Touching her. I swallow a boulder in my throat.

"I'm here," she says. "Mama's worried sick about you racing."

My heartbeat pounds against my ribcage. "Who told you that?" How can I convince my sister that everything will turn out fine?

"I heard them talking in their room last night. They thought I was asleep. But I wasn't. I miss you." She pauses. "Are you gonna die?"

"No!" I flinch for raising my voice at her. "I'm not gonna die, Kari," I say in a softer tone. He must have talked to her. "You have to trust me. I'll be home in a couple of weeks and we'll do something special. We can go to Spokane and see a movie and eat lots of ice cream."

She sighs, blowing her breath over the line. "You promise?"

"I promise." The ticking of the clock perched on the mantle over the fireplace pulsates in my ears. I tap my fingers on the armrest. "I have to go. I'll call you tomorrow, okay?"

She sniffles. "Okay," she says weakly. A click sails over the line. The coolness of the phone soothes my forehead. I should've pressed her about why she thought I was going to die. Ask who told her. Will she revert back to silent whimpers? I say a quick prayer for her before wandering back into the kitchen. She can't slide back into that dark place she hides. She's got a full life ahead of her.

"Everything all right?" Aunt Jamison hands me a glass of ice water.

"Yeah," I say. I'm able to choke down a piece of ham and a little coleslaw. I make myself a to-go cup of fruit salad. The Greek blueberry yogurt mixed in with strawberries and grapes and bananas should help with protein. I take a bite before fastening on the lid, hoping it settles my roiling stomach.

"Your parents aren't able to make it this time, so there will be no after-race dinner party. At least at the grounds. I'll have burgers ready when we all get back. I understand your grandfather needs his rest. He had to have his medication changed again."

"Years of hard work on the ranch…it's left him worn out. Mom too."

Aunt Jamison examines me. "They're going to be okay." She pulls me into a tight embrace and says a quick prayer.

What would I do without my family? Without my auntie? I finish what food I can and head outside.

We load Rooster and bounce down the gravel driveway. Every pothole makes me want to puke. When is Uncle going to fix his driveway? My fingers cling to the armrest, knuckles white.

We pull into the grounds and creep behind a line of rigs waiting to enter the paddock. Craig slinks us through the gate and backs into an open spot. Rooster rocks the truck and trailer and whinnies. He seems as excited and nervous as I am. I'm glad we give him Bio-Mos for his gut or he'd probably have ulcers. I pop a Tums in my mouth and wash it down with purple Gatorade.

Chase unloads Rooster and grabs a brush. I examine my tack.

"I'll take you to the hay trailer slash announcer's stage slash prize area after a bit. That will spur you on." Craig studies his watch. "Actually, come on, we have time now. Let's check out the saddles and jackets you'll be winning next Sunday."

We make our way through the swelling crowd to the grass area south of the paddock where the Calcutta auction will be. I study the saddles and jackets on the make-shift stage. It's a gooseneck Dressen Custom Trailer. No big surprise it has a Big R banner running across the bottom. One saddle and jacket perches on the gooseneck and a second saddle and jacket is on the opposite end. King of the Hill is stamped on the saddle fenders. *They're gonna hate to have to change that king to a queen.* I chuckle. Family, friends, and unknown onlookers sit in lawn chairs under the shade trees, waiting for the auction to begin.

After Craig talks to someone with a clipboard, he strolls toward me. "Time to grab Rooster. Let's go see what kind of bid he can get."

Eyes probe me in the paddock as I lead Rooster through. Some ignore me. Others scoff. *He's got to be here.* We circle in front of the stage. People talk loud enough that I can hear them say things like, "I'm betting on the girl just off her sheer anger of having to put up with the guys," and "She's too scrawny, I'll pass," and "I'm betting on that gal." I recognize Hope's loud voice. She points a clipboard at me from the stage. Onlookers surround me in a semicircle. Rooster allows me to lead him around, eyes wide, ears forward, yet calm. An auctioneer's voice hastens and after about ten minutes, stops at eight-hundred dollars. Not bad for a first-timer. A girl to boot. I'm sure last year's winner, who happens to be Billy Beck, will top a couple grand or more. Whoever wins the pot at the end of the race will be one happy camper.

I lead Rooster back to the trailer. At the east gate, I'm intercepted by a middle-aged woman with a camera around her neck, clutching a notebook and pen. Dressed in shorts and tennis shoes, a wide-brimmed sun hat, and red, sparkly sunglasses perched on top of a wide nose, she asks, "As the only woman rider this year, how do you think you will stand against the boys?" She arcs an eyebrow, pen ready.

"I'll hold my own." I try and step around her. She moves with me.

"What's your name?"

"Please move out of my way. I need to get ready."

"What's this big guy's name?" She extends a well manicured hand to touch him. "Isn't it cruel to ride these animals down that hill? Do you know how many have died so far?"

"No, it's not." The muscles in my jaws twitch. "We train these horses for several months, feed them a special mix of grain, vitamins and minerals, wrap their legs, take extra care to rub them down afterwards. Cruel? Not in the least. These horses live for this," I motion to the hill with a finger. "The hill is soft and groomed. Some of the best footing around for these athletes. Many of them fail at other events, or are rescued from slaughter. Bet you didn't know that!"

I squeeze my fingers round the lead rope and take a step to shove past her when I hear a voice behind me.

"If you have any questions about the race, you can talk with me. I'm Hope Bradeen." She nods to me, gently pulling the woman aside.

I slide past, giving Hope a look of appreciation. After handing Rooster off to Chase, I rush to the bathroom one last time before we draw for our numbers. I push past a crowd of spectators and wait in line. Once finished, I catch up with Craig. I drawn number seven. Lucky seven. Craig slips it over my vest, with the number showing on the front and back. He shoves the vest in my hands. "It's yours now, cousin."

We head back to the horse trailer.

My name rings in my ears as I approach the gate. Julie rushes toward me, waving her hand. Several other girls trail behind her.

Craig keeps walking.

"Charnaye, how are you doing?" Julie's Omak Stampede T-shirt fits her nicely. Better than the slinky tank top she wore the day we met.

"So far so good. It's nice to see you." I hug my stomach. "Actually, I'm super nervous."

"You'll do great." Julie glances about as if she's trying to avoid someone. "Don't tell Tone, but we all bet on you, too. You're the only girl I know who's ever run this crazy race." She introduces her four cousins to me and has me autograph five photos of me and the other jockeys. It's a clear shot of us half way down the hill.

"Where did you get these pictures?" It feels weird signing autographs.

"We took them with Stacie's camera," Julie says.

Stacie holds up her Canon. I admire the telephoto lens.

"We printed them out this morning at Wal-Mart," one of the cousins says.

"Can I have a copy of the pictures?" I study one of me and Rooster fighting our way through the river.

"Sure," Julie says. "We can print you off some from tonight, too." She peers at her cousin, who nods her head.

"Thanks. Well"— I glance over my shoulder—"got to get going."

I hug the girls and pass through the gate. The gatekeeper nods. "It's good to see a woman back in the race."

I nod back. Because of floundering thoughts, no words come out. I trip over my feet, act like nothing happened, and keep walking, heat creeping up my neck.

We have time to kill while the rest of the horses are Calcutted, so I sneak to the river and soak my feet. I've had enough of the guys talking smack. I skip rocks on the water's surface and pray. Pray for guidance. Strength. Focus. I meditate on what the gatekeeper said and agree. I do have the right to be here. Times have changed. If only they had a separate girls' race. More females would surely enter. The guys would have their time the first three days. All we would need is one run. *We'd get it done right the first time.* I chuckle and toss another flat, smooth rock and watch it skip several times. One for every woman who's entered this race. I skip another rock for those who are still to come.

"Time to wrap," Chase says.

I pull on my boots and socks.

"Can I help this time?" His voice sounds more confident, yet a hint of doubt laces through it.

"No." I shake my head.

He frowns and drops his chin. "Any more notes?" His tone sounds defiant.

"No. And don't tell anyone. It's only drama. Mom, Dad, Sshapa, they don't need to know. They have enough on their plate. Got it?"

"I won't!"

"Listen, we just have a routine is all," I say. "Besides, I need you to hand me the tape and vet wrap, it makes things go fast and smooth."

"Whatever."

Rooster kicks the trailer with a hind foot as I approach. I run my hand down his neck and across his back. "It's all right, boy." I take a minute and scratch under his belly, close to his front legs. His lips quiver.

Craig and I wrap his legs while Chase gets the saddle. I slip on my vest and helmet and hand the Crafty Dab Window Writer to Chase. A smile blooms on his face. He paints the number seven on each side of Rooster's rump and stands back to admire his work.

"You're a real artist," I say.

He slaps my shoulder. "You know it."

This time, I'm riding with Tone. Benton is in the next heat. I say a little prayer and mount.

Uncle Buck, Aunt Jamison, and Timmy stroll toward me. Timmy and Chase wave to each other and take off. Uncle Buck pats Rooster's neck. "How's he doing?"

"Fine."

"How are you holding up?" Uncle pats the calf of my leg.

"I'll make it." I give him a weak smile.

Aunt Jamison gives me a crooked grin. "You'll be fine. Seen Hope yet?" Her gaze explores the crowd of horses and jockeys.

"Yeah, over there." I point toward the auction site. "She saved me from a protester. Or a reporter. I'm not sure which she was."

"Okay. We're going to go nab a good spot." She and Uncle weave through the crowd and disappear.

"How's it going?" Benton says as he and Tone stroll toward us, leading their horses. Benton wears a purple ribbon shirt with a black cowboy hat against his dark skin. He could be one of those models on the cover of *Native Americans* magazine.

"All right." I take a deep breath.

Benton lays a hand on my leg. "Let it out. You're stiff. And shaky."

I gush air between pursed lips. "So are you before a race."

"True."

Craig hands me my over and under. "Keep your head on straight out there." He pats Rooster's neck and makes his way toward the river.

The walk to the hill is slow, but it gives me time for reflection. I talk to Rooster. Rub his neck. Ignore the crap talk. I imagine myself tossing the threats in the river, watch them float downstream and drown. But then they just bounce back and settle in my gut. I have to figure out a way to get rid of them. For good.

Tone and I ride side by side. Seems like he and Benton are still babysitting me. Yet at the same time, I like the comfort of their closeness and draw from their strength. Tone is quiet. I have a feeling he is running himself through each leg. I do the same.

I twist in the saddle. Billy Beck is staring at me. He nods. I give him a small smile and turn around.

We make our way to the landing. I make the usual trek to the edge, my horse at my side. Tone remains back near the line. I silently pray over Rooster one last time. The rescue boat, Jet Ski, and rescue riders wait in the water. The bridge stands against the cloud-scattered sky in all its grandeur. I allow the July breeze to whisk my fear away. Confiscate threads of doubt. I amble to the line and mount. Tone and I take a moment and gaze at each other, sending one another the usual good thoughts and prayers of speed and safety. I pray for the safety of every rider here. Even the ones who've made it clear they despise my presence.

The official calls out our numbers. Tone is the second one called. His expression twists, as do the red ribbons of his red and white ribbon shirt in the breeze. Again I'm toward the east end. The outrider disappears over the ledge. I grip my rein with my left hand, leaving my right ready to reach toward the back of my saddle. Rooster dances and his front legs hop up.

The gun fires and we blaze down the hill. A few second later I kick Rooster and he reaches with his front legs, leaping into the water. The *swoosh* of horses crashing into the water's surface is one I'll never forget. A curtain of water drops blind my vision. But as the water falls, a path clears. The pine tree sticks out like an eagle feather in a toddler's roach at a powwow. I nudge Rooster with the whip. He swims harder. Faster. When his feet touch the ground he digs in and we fly up the dike. Two horses are ahead of us. Billy Beck is in the lead. I lean forward and reach back with the quirt. Rooster's breaths sound like a freight train. Hooves pounding the dirt drown out all other noise. Until I'm in the arena and through the poles.

Billy Beck's the winner of this round. We'll see about next week. I know I can inch past him. He rides past me, holding up a hand. I slap it. He war whoops. The second place rider follows suit. As does the third-place jockey. Everyone else glares as though I'm bad medicine. I hold my chin up, chest out. I circle Rooster around and hop off, leading him to the gate. Chase runs toward me, Craig on his heels.

Chase lifts me into a bear hug, shouting, "Top five!"

I hand him the lead rope.

"How do you feel?" Craig says.

"Like the wind on fire." I shake my head. Did that really just happen?

Craig sweeps dirt off my back. "That's about what you looked like, too." He holds up his palm-sized camera. "I got great footage. Can't wait to watch it tonight. You should be easy to pick out in your shiny green outfit." He elbows me.

A lone horse jogs with a limp into the arena, and once everyone is almost cleared out, Tone stomps through the gate. My heart plunges. I wait for him, waving the others off. Craig waits with me.

"What happened?"

"He came off and hit the water hard. May have a stone bruise. I'm not sure." Tone's jaw clenches.

His wet clothes tell me he fell in, too. "I hope he didn't pull a tendon," I say.

Tone's nose wrinkles as he watches his horse favor a leg.

Craig helps Tone. They walk in front of us, Tone's head hanging.

"Fifth place. Nice!" Chase says as I walk through the gate. He puts his fist out.

"I'm in." I bump it. "He felt good. Solid. I've never known a horse with this much soul. I thought Stimteema had heart, but man, does this little guy fly." Half of me is thrilled, the other sad, knowing I'll have to return him once the races are over. The paddock buzzes with congratulations and excuses. A couple young women, maybe in their late twenties, clap me on the back as I walk by.

"Four more days till eliminations," Chase says.

I gulp. *Four more days.*

CHAPTER 37

I wipe my mouth with shaky hands. "I can't believe it's here." I circle Thursday with my finger on Craig's calendar. I star it with a red Sharpie and print QH in the box.

Aunt Jamison looks at me from across the kitchen table. "Eat up. You'll need your strength." She motions to my food with her head. "Oh, I almost forgot, this came in the mail yesterday." She hands me an envelope with no return address.

When is this gonna stop? "Thanks. Must be from Kari." I hold Chase's stare, praying he keeps his mouth shut.

Craig takes a bite of spaghetti and sits back in his chair. He drums his fingers on the table. "Tonight's gonna be different. You've raced only in the daylight. You know the race will start in the dark. You'll go into the arena during the day, in between the rodeo events, for introductions. Once out, the outrider will escort you to the hill."

"Yeah, but we've been riding in the dark since we were kids. Remember all the midnight races and hide and seek games we used to play? The dark doesn't bother me. Rooster's run in it." I fan my hands out in front of me, sneer at my unsteady fingers, and sweep them under the table.

"That's true. Those were great old days." Craig leans back in his chair. "The thing is, we didn't run off a cliff, so to speak, at breakneck speeds with twenty other guys and drop into the Okanogan."

I take a bite of chocolate chip cookie. Craig reaches over in order to seize the sugar-coated enemy, but I pull back before he can and give him the evil eye. He retreats. I take another bite and hold the cookie above my head, grinning. "I've earned this." I wash it down with ice-cold milk. "What's it like? What should I expect?"

Craig shakes his head. "I don't know. Never have done it. I figure you would have asked Benton or Tone by now."

I run my hands over my braids. "I'll do that today. "We're supposed to meet at the Ferris wheel and take one ride before saddling up."

"When were you gonna tell me? It'd be nice to know we need to leave early, considering I'm your ride."

"Just did." I smile and shove the last bit of cookie in my mouth.

"The previous jockey who rode Rooster did mention that he saw only darkness when first crowning the hill. I'm not sure if this happens to everyone," Uncle Buck says.

I shrug." Maybe it doesn't happen to Benton and that's why he hasn't said anything."

"Trust Rooster, Char. He knows what to do," Aunt Jamison says.

After lunch I rush upstairs to double check my bag. My helmet feels heavy as I twirl it in my hands. I stomp around the room, wondering why Craig hasn't told me in detail about the dark before today. I stuff my helmet in my bag, gaze at the cattle in the field out my window, and open the letter.

It's over. You lose. Rooster dies today!

"What the…" I crumple the note in my lap. Go back to the window. Take a few steps back. Maybe I should show the cops. That would keep my family out of it. Now that I'm eighteen, I don't have to involve anyone. I fold the letter and stuff it into my pocket. I'll show the next cop I run into.

We pull into the parking lot, and Craig stops so I can meet with Benton. I push through the crowd and wave as I approach the Ferris wheel. No cops so far. Benton hands me a ticket. We slide into our seats and wait. Benton drapes an arm over my shoulder and kisses my head. Once everyone is aboard, the Ferris wheel moves forward. Our seat gently rocks. Benton pulls me close. The calm before the storm. My tummy roils as we climb higher. The noise of the carnival floats to the top. My tummy twists, and I giggle. Then turn serious.

"What's it really like crowning the hill in the dark?" I say.

As we rise back over the top, the desolate hill comes into view. Would he really hurt Rooster? I shouldn't be on this ride. I should be with my horse, protecting him. *I need to get off.* I lean forward as if to wave down the operator. The chair jerks forward.

"What are you doing?" Benton pulls me back.

"I…uh…" I shake my head. "Sorry."

"You need to calm down. What's gotten into you?"

"Nothing!" I lean back in the chair and grip Benton's leg. "What's it like?" My voice is softer.

He sighs. "It's kind of like riding this Ferris wheel. But at night. And faster."

I used to ride the Ferris wheel as a girl at night. Stars lit the black veil. They seemed huge back then. Tons of them filled the darkness like a massive sea of twinkling diamonds. "Can you see anything?" I squint against the sun.

"Not at first because I'm looking straight ahead. The other riders glow from the lighted path. I hang on, knowing it will be over as quick as it starts. My horse can see, so I just need to trust him." He jerks the chair.

I scream and slap his thigh.

"That's what it feels like." He laughs and rubs his leg. "Now close your eyes."

After a long moment, I close them.

Benton gently rocks the chair. My stomach drops as it sways. I hold my left hand out as if I'm holding on to Rooster's rein. I keep them closed as the chair comes to a stop and switches direction. I squeeze them tight. My stomach hits bottom and I let out a yell. My voice releases the butterflies. I feel them flutter up my throat and out my mouth. I snuggle close to Benton and open my eyes. *Rooster dies today!*

One more rotation and we're done. We unload and I practically drag Benton to the paddock. Is he okay? Is Craig with him?

I press a hand to my chest and feel the rush of my heart. I let go of Benton and hug Rooster. "You're safe," I whisper.

Benton heads off to look after his horse. After Craig and I wrap Rooster's legs, I get the saddle and toss it on his back. The front cinch looks like someone had cut part way through. I finger the tear. Craig's gonna find out about the threats. How can I change this without him finding out? *Crap! Crap! Crap!* I can't.

"Craig, there's a tear in the cinch. We need a different one."

"What? I checked the tack earlier." He comes around and takes a look. He combs his fingers through his hair, hunts for a different one in the tack room, and changes the cinch. I bite my lip. Barely making it through the Calcutta auction and arena introductions, I wait. Watch rodeo participants and royalty ride past. At dusk, we hook up with the outrider and make our way to the bridge. The horses walk calmly, straggled in single file as though they are soldiers going into battle.

"You okay?" Benton says.

I nod, unable to swallow, my mouth is so dry. Instinctively, I reach for water but have none. I stiffen to the click of steel shoes on pavement. The river meanders below us like a shadow as dusk blurs the view.

Once we are at the top of the hill, I get off and walk Rooster to the ledge. Lights mark the path. The boat's light glows circles. The dirt on the hill is faint. We wait as they finish bullriding. The music blares from the arena. I drum the beat with my fingers on my hip, pacing. I lead Rooster back and mount. I circle my horse around until I'm given my number and take my place, holding him back behind the line. *Rooster dies tonight—*

The gun blasts.

Rooster bolts forward. I reach back and clutch my handle, letting him have his head. I'm jerked back as he leaps off, hugging the hill. Even though my eyes are open, only blackness surrounds me for the first few strides. My gut rolls as we rush down. It seems like Rooster has only taken a few steps before we plunge into the water. I lean forward as he swims across, water drops flicking my face. 2, 15, 8, 11 bounce into view. I give him a few taps with my quirt and he surges ahead. I tighten my grip on the reins.

We climb up the dike and round the corner, blinded by bright arena lights. We are through the poles. Three jockeys are ahead of me, which means I'm in the running. One point. All I have to do is climb the leaderboard and I have a chance at winning. Billy is second. Jarod's beady eyes pinned on me.

The crowd is on their feet. Camera's flash. A high-pitched voice screams my name. Jill is jumping up and down, waving like a mad woman. I raise my arm and point to her, noticing half of my high school is sitting in the front section with her. They hold up white poster board with "Queen of the Hill" written in thick black letters across the front. Some have feathers painted on them. Others horses. Or a girl and a horse and number seven. Even with no signature attached, the signs have Jill Lamore's style written all over them. They wear matching white T-shirts with some photo ironed on them. I'll have to catch Jill as soon as I can.

My eyes blur. I wipe a hand across them so no one will see tears. Jill must have rounded up her posse once school was out. Everyone needs a best friend like her. I motion for her to go the gate that leads into the horse paddock.

Craig and Chase meet me at the gate. I slide off and hug them both.

Craig lifts me off the ground, squeezing me tight. "You kicked butt!" He lets me down.

"Yeah, but I need a smoother ride. I felt like a monkey on a donkey."

"Tomorrow will be better. You know what to expect now," he says. "This is your first Suicide Hill race. Give yourself a break."

"Chase, will you meet Jill at the gate?

He nods and leads Rooster back to the trailer.

Once out of the way, Jill runs toward me, screaming. She hugs me and steps back. She points at her shirt. It's a picture of me coming off the Omak Lake hill.

"Where did you get the picture?" I say.

Jill points to Chase.

He crosses his arms. "She called and asked for a picture. Got one from Craig. She swore me to secrecy or she promised to find someone to make my junior year a nightmare."

Jill hands me a shirt. "We made one for you, too." Team Toulou is printed on the back.

I take it from her and slip it on.

"Did you see Old Lady Sherman is here?"

"No way." My gaze darts past her as if I'd find her mixed in with the jockeys.

"Not in here," Jill says. "I saw her checking out some western purses. Guess she had to come and see if the rumors were true."

I grab a bottle of water and take a long gulp. Pour the rest over my head. "I hope I bump into her." I wipe my eyes.

Jill glances around. "Where's Benton?"

"Probably taking care of his horse," I say. "I'm glad you came and I love the shirts!"

"Thanks. It took me a month to raise the money to make them. I can't wait to see how you do tomorrow. Maybe we can meet sometime and catch up."

I agree. Jill takes off to find her friends.

Chase watches Jill sidestep horses and jockeys and horse poop in her baby blue tennis shoes. "Mom and Dad are coming Sunday. It's easier on Dad."

"If I can keep this up, they'll be here to see me win." I jerk away as Craig pours a cup of ice water down my back.

"Don't flatter yourself." He laughs. "You haven't won yet."

CHAPTER 38

I meet Jill late morning at the Indian encampment. We check out beaded jewelry and T-shirts. Jill enjoys an Indian taco while I choke down a few bites of one. She buys her mom a pair of green and red earrings with a geometrical design. Even though I'm with my best friend, a heaviness hovers over me, gripping my chest with gnarled fingers. Each breath feels labored. Most of the time I find myself cradling my stomach. I can't shake it.

We wander around and I try to hide my distress. But Jill is too savvy for that. She makes a great attempt to distract me with whimsical toys and funny jokes. It's not working. I find Chase and Timmy by a booth with water toys and ask Chase to hang with Jill for a minute. He takes one look at me and says that Craig is back with Rooster shooting the breeze with other horse owners.

"I'll be right back," I say to Jill.

I rush away and find Craig and wave him over. Concern creases his face and I ask him to come with me. We step behind the trailer which sits closest to the river and in the east corner of the horse paddock. I tell him about my concerns, all the while hugging my midriff. He fetches his eagle feather and a bundle of sage and after lighting the sage, smudges me. The smoke swirls around me, blessing me. We pray for protection and guidance. Strength. A sense of peace covers me like a warm blanket on a January night.

The sound of the river calls me over and I sit with my bare feet in the cool of the water. I skip a rock. Ripples fan out and slowly fade.

Craig brings me purple Gatorade. "You'll be fine."

"How do you think the cinch got cut?"

"I'm not sure. Nothing real sharp in the trailer." He arches a brow. "Got any ideas?"

I shake my head.

"Hey," Jill says from behind me.

I pat the ground beside me, relieved she showed up. I shouldn't have asked Craig. Now he's suspicious. "Sorry for running off like that."

"I'll look into it." Craig hikes up the embankment.

I stiffen.

"You okay?"

"Yeah. I just…I felt like I couldn't breathe. So Craig prayed with me and we smudged." I reach down and swirl my bandana in the water and wrap it around my neck. Eleven in the morning and the sun is already beating down on us.

"Does he know about the notes?"

"What?"

"From school?"

I exhale. For a minute it sounded like she knew about the ones that keep showing up around here. Could she? "No."

"Have there been more?"

I shake my head.

"I can't imagine what you're going through right now. But I'll be praying for you, too. This has got to be a lot of pressure."

You have no idea!

Jill takes her flip-flops off and soaks her feet. "I got your back."

"And I got yours." I toss a few stones in the river and soak in the silence of the moment. Up river, children and their parents cool off, playing in the current. A few people with inner tubes float by. I lie back, cover my eyes with my arm, and attempt to blot out my fear. *Maybe I should pull out before something bad happens.*

I don't know how long I'd been asleep when drops of water pelt my face and stir me awake. I blink away the sun. Benton stands over me with a wet fist over my head. Jill is lying beside me, still as a rock.

"Time to rise and shine before the sun bakes you stiff." Benton claps his hands.

Jill pops up. "I can't believe I fell asleep."

I close my eyes. "Give me a couple more minutes." I don't get them. The shock of frigid water on my hot flesh jerks me to my feet.

Jill giggles and splashes water on her pink arms. "I better let you get ready."

"Get a water first," I say.

We make our way back to the horse trailer.

"You must be feeling better," Craig says. "The vet's already checked Rooster. He's good to go."

The scent of liniment lingers in the air. "He's not drinking much." I snatch two bottles of water off the tailgate, hand one to Jill, and take a sip of the other.

"He'll be fine." Craig holds out a small cooler. "Dig in. You need your strength. I'll worry about Rooster." He nods to Jill. "Get her to eat. She's gonna need her energy." He waves us away.

Jill plucks the cooler out of my hands and opens the lid. "Here's the problem."

Benton peeks in. "What? She's got a banana, muffin, milk, cheese sticks, carrots, celery…there's nothing missing." He thinks a minute. "Wait, I know what's missing."

I peek in. "What?"

"Caramel fudge ice cream!"

"Get her out of here," Craig says to Jill. "Go find her some if that'll get some food in her." He glances at his watch. "Have her back in an hour, belly full."

Benton heads to his trailer and Jill and I head for the food court.

The hour passes quickly and I'm ready to get back to the paddock. With some food in me, I'm raring to go, eager to scrutinize the tack. Nothing's out of place, torn, or cut. I sigh. After the Calcutta auction and wrapping Rooster's legs, I tack him up and turn him loose with Chase. Jill and I sit in our camp chairs behind the horse trailer and listen to the rodeo. We watch contestants whiz by as they come in and out of the arena, zeroing in on barrel racers. "I bet my aunt was fast in her time."

Jill nods as she chews on a bite of Indian Taco, watching me.

I tap my boot with a crop, flinching at every bang of the trailer from Rooster's hoof.

Time slows for a while, until the racers are called into the arena. Jill and I hug and she heads to the stands. I ride with the others into the arena and circle around as the announcer makes introductions. My classmates are in their same spot, holding up Jill's signs and sporting the white shirts. She waves. I circle in front of them, drawing courage from their affirmations. They make me feel like I could ride to the sun and back and not have one hair singed on my head.

It's time to go.

We approach the starting area. I watch each rider and their horse, guarding my space. I stay clear of the ones I've come to know as trouble makers. We line up as our names and numbers are called out. Horses rear, lunge forward, smack into their neighbors. Rooster prances. I talk to him. Lay a hand on his neck. Assure him we'll make it down.

The gun fires and Rooster lunges forward, knocking me to the side. I gasp and recover before he crowns the hill and hang on, leaning back. I fumble for my handle and can't find it, so I clutch the cantle of my saddle. I rein Rooster toward the middle, veering left as a couple of horses lose their footing and tumble. Legs mixed with dirt slide down the hill. A horse's cry for help resounds in the night. It's an eerie sound. One I don't care to hear again. I stay left until we pass the wreck, saying a quick prayer for them. *Help* is all I have time for.

Hands shaking, I squeeze the reins and stiffen my body. Rooster stumbles. *No!* I'm jerked forward. I find the back of my saddle and hang on. We manage to stay upright and keep going. I force myself to breathe.

Water pelts my face as we leap forward. Sounds I've never heard before escape my throat. I urge Rooster forward with my boot heels and my quirt. I'm not sure how many of us are left, but as we surge up the dike, Rooster passes horse after horse. His breath is fast and loud. We pass the second horse as we turn into the arena. A dizzy wave comes over me. Seconds later we're neck and neck with Billy Beck.

It wasn't good enough to take the lead. But we've moved up. For the first time I think Rooster and I might have a shot. A girl has never taken the title. That's because she's never had my horse. Billy raises a fisted arm and whoops. This time I follow suit. We ride past one another and Billy raises his hand. I slap it. My cheeks hurt from smiling. Confidence replaces dizziness.

Where's Benton. *Oh, Creator, no!* My throat tightens like a noose around a cowboy's neck in an old western. I whirl around in the saddle, searching. Chase runs to me and I jump off and hand him the reins.

"Benton's horse went down. He's hurt."

"Where is he?" I say, trembling.

"They're getting him to the ambulance." Benton's dad leads his horse out of the arena. It must be a good sign. Why else would his dad find the horse and not someone else? Two more riderless horses jog into the arena. The crowd cheers.

I rush over to Mr. Marchand and find out my boyfriend may have broken his leg. Other than that, he's fine. His mom is with him. They'll take him to the hospital. I give his dad Craig's cell number and he promises to call.

Between the threats and now my boyfriend, I'm numb. What else can happen? Tears threaten, but I blink them away, pretending dirt is in my eyes.

Craig finds me and leads me to the ambulance. I'm allowed to see Benton for a moment before they haul him off. Dirt covered, he gives me a crooked grin, eyes heavy with pain. I don't even know what to say, so I give him a hug. Tell him I love him. The ambulance lights fade into the crowd. I send up prayers of thanksgiving. Another rider is whisked away with a possible broken collarbone.

Cracked bones are a long way from one's heart. Both jockeys are alive and the horses are safe. All in all, it's a good night.

I go back to the trailer and lean into Rooster's neck. I soak in his smell. He's already unsaddled, so I cut off his leg wraps, sponge his back with diluted rubbing alcohol, and wash the river sand off him. After searching every inch of him for cuts, Chase takes over and walks him until he's dry. It's late when we load everything and head back to the ranch. Uncle Buck and Aunt Jamison left once they saw me in the arena. She has grilled burgers, green salad, mac salad and cake spread out on the table. They dig in. I pick at my food.

CHAPTER 39

My mind relives the race all night long. Dirt spraying in all directions. Horses legs and hooves kicking in the air. The horses' screams. *I warned you, you can't hide, check your tack, it's over!* Did he mess with Benton's tack trying to get to me? Eyelids heavy, I struggle to crack them open, even with the sun blinding me through the window. I roll over and groan. My muscles are stiff and my head hurts. Never did get that call from Benton's dad last night. I'm guessing they were pretty busy between Benton and his horse. My stomach is taut with hunger.

I try and sleep longer, but all I do is toss and turn. The threats churn in my thoughts. I pull on some shorts and a T-shirt, down a couple Tylenol, lather on Sombra, and straggle outdoors. After jogging for a half-hour, I turn back and walk most of the way through cow country, dodging sagebrush and inhaling its scent. *Be strong and courageous; do not be frightened or dismayed, for the Lord your God is with you wherever you go.* I suppose that means down the hill too. When I get back I'm able to eat a few bites of a pancake and Auntie's canned peaches before gathering my helmet and bag. I stuff the letters in my bag so no one finds them.

Craig loads Rooster. You'd think he'd be tired by now, but he's raring to go. He hops into the trailer and quickly settles in.

I glance around. It's too quiet. "Where's Chase?"

"I let him sleep in."

I groan. "You got to be kidding me. He has a job to do."

"He'll come with my parents and Timmy later." Craig teasingly whips my leg with a crop. "Cut him some slack. He's been your little servant since the day he arrived. Let him have some fun. He even hung with Jill didn't he while you had a little meltdown? He should have stayed with Timmy and his friends…"

We slide into the truck and unroll the windows. "He still needs to be here." I scowl.

"Not everything's about you." Craig pushes the gearshift into first and steps on the gas.

"You're right. It's not." The bitter taste of crow swishes in my mouth. "I'll talk to him later."

The trailer sways to Rooster's shift of weight as we head down the driveway.

My nerves tingle once we reach the stampede grounds. Sweat beads down my back, my shirt sticking to my skin. I wave the bottom of my shirt with one hand and grip the door handle with the other. We creep into the paddock and claim an empty spot. We seem to have the Creator's favor as we always find a space riverside. Today neither the smell of the water nor its sparkle do me any good.

Craig's cell phone chimes. "Hello?" He hands it to me.

I give him a questioning look. "This is Charnaye?" My gut tightens.

"Hey, Char—"

"Benton, oh my goodness. I need my own phone. I wanted to call you. Your dad promised to call, but when he didn't I figured he was really busy. How are you feeling? How bad is it? Where are you?"

"Glad you miss me." His tone is laid back. Slightly slurred.

"You're on pain meds aren't you?" I shake my head at Craig.

"Yep! They work well, too. I'm on the couch, cool soda in hand. Flipping through TV channels. Thought I'd call and wish you luck."

"The easy life must be nice." I get out of the truck and find a camp chair.

"It is. I broke my leg, so I'm out. But that's okay. I'd rather watch you take it all from the stands than from behind you on Archie. Although I'll miss the view." A laidback chuckle wiggles through the line.

I sink to the chair and frown. "You're in no shape to come down here."

"Whatever! The doc said I can come. No one can stop me from being with you, Char. It'd be worse to sit here, wondering how things are going."

Part of me wants him here, but how selfish is that? He needs to rest. I shake my head. "No."

"My dad's bringing me down. I'll be there in a few hours. I have a cast. Don't need surgery. Have crutches and pain pills. That's all I need."

"Hey—" The line goes dead. I grab a brush and start in on Rooster with short, harsh strokes. "What's he thinking? What an idiot. He needs to rest! I can see him after." Each swipe gets more forceful. Rooster pins his ears and nips my side.

I lean back against the trailer and catch my breath. What am I doing? I've let him totally get me off track. I throw the brush in the tack room and plop down on the floor of the tack room. After a few moments to calm my nerves, I lead Rooster over to the vet. He checks him over and gives me a thumbs up. I walk him back to relax and get a drink. I check the tack again, combing over every centimeter.

"Why don't you go for a walk?" Craig says. "Walk off your nerves."

I jump at his voice. So does Rooster.

"I've been watching you. You're a mess. Go find something…get a grip."

I agree and march off to the gate. At this point, there is no reason to be in a hurry. I wander around, looking at the vendor booths outside the arena. My mind mulls over the threats. What would he try next? Or who? I spot Old Lady Sherman and grunt. Slink over, pretending I don't see her. She reaches for a bag. I snatch it first. She glares at me, her face forming a judgmental grin.

She searches my face. "You really are doing this, with no regard to your safety?"

I nod, handing her the bag. "Yes, ma'am. I am."

"Well, you certainly fooled us." She lifts her chin and slithers to the other end of the booth.

I snicker while running a finger along the vendor's bling-covered table and walk off. When making my way to the next booth my eyes fixate on a figure with red hair, weaving in and out of the crowd that's already gathering. *Hahoolawho*. I step out into a clear spot. He sees me and glares. He walks a straight line and stops in front of me, nose to nose.

"I bet by now you think pretty highly of yourself." Hagan scrutinizes every inch of me with his steely gaze.

I push him backward. "I've had enough of you." I curl my fingers into a fist.

"You won't finish. They'll make sure of it."

I push past him.

Jill shouts my name, waving at me. We greet with a hug, my body quivering.

"Was that who I think it was?" Jill says, eyes wide.

"Yep. Still a jerk." A bird circles overhead. "I can't let him or any other hater get to me."

"You never have." Jill grabs my arm. "Let's check out that booth!"

We amble over to a stand covered with colorful dresses. Jill picks through a line of above-the-knee dresses and holds one up, brows arched.

I wrinkle my nose. "I saw Old Lady Sherman a minute ago." I cross my arms, fighting the urge to puke.

"No way!"

"She was her usual rude self." I croak out a chuckle. "Thinks I should pull out."

"No way!"

We rake over a few other booths before weaving our way back to the paddock. Craig has Rooster ready for the Calcutta. His coat shines in the afternoon sun, and I swear this horse is strutting. I point to the saddle and coat on the stage. "Can you see me wearing that Pendleton jacket with the white spotted Indian horse embroidered on it?" I ask Jill.

She squeals. "For sure!"

I spin around and come nose to nose with Hagan, who's glaring at me. I push past him and grab Rooster's lead from Chase and circle him around.

Bids come in. They climb higher. When the auctioneer says, "Sold," it's at three-thousand dollars. My head spins. Jill screeches. Who took the bid? A middle-aged man dressed in snakeskin cowboy boots and a black Stetson hands an envelope to the cashier. He tips his hat at me. Winning half that money will help with Dad's medical costs. Rooster continues to strut as we walk away, calm as an eagle floating on a soft breeze. The next horse spins around, pulls away from his jockey, and careens into Rooster. Rooster kicks him. The horse jerks out of his rider's grip and runs off, splitting the crowd.

I reach the gate and sigh with relief. The protesting woman is nowhere in sight to insult me with her opinions. Hope must have given her what she wanted. She has a way of smoothing things over in a gentle and professional manner. Something I have yet to learn. Or maybe I don't need to. I might need all that grit to pull this off. If I win, there's a chance I go to college. If I lose, I stay home, get a job, and help with the ranch.

Chase meets me at the gate and takes the lead rope.

"Have a nice rest?" My tone is snarky.

He hangs his head.

"Sorry. Stakes are a little high today."

He shrugs. "The carnival was worth staying up for. Thanks for letting me sleep in."

I wave him forward. "Thank Craig. I was ready with a water gun to your face." I laugh. "But really, I appreciate all you've done."

Chase stares at me, mouth open.

I bump his shoulder with mine. "Just want you to know."

His face turns pink.

We wrap Rooster's legs. I offer my horse one last drink. He sniffs the bucket and kicks the trailer.

"Just like his owner."

Benton leans against his crutch, a sloppy smile across his face. I give him a gentle hug. He pulls me in tighter. Kisses the top of my head. I drink in his scent, lingering in his embrace.

He holds out a permanent marker. "You get to be the first to sign it."

"Thanks." I grab the marker out of his hand. "Yeah, I had to beat off the other girls so you'd get the chance…"

"Always the comedian." I sign my name and draw a heart by it.

Craig sets a chair out for him as Chase hands him a bottle of water. I give him my chair so he can prop up his leg. I fix a saddle on my horse's back. Chase bridles Rooster, marks a number seven on his rump, and walks him around. My horse eyeballs the other horses as if to size them up. Warn them he's the king. Horses whinny, tossing their heads. It feels like an invisible lightening storm has just hit the paddock.

We do our usual arena show and tell. Once again Jill has friends rallied, signs bobbing in the air. It looks like there are more in the group, teens and adults. I bite my lip. Jill sees me and leans forward, shouts louder, leading the chant, "Queen of the Hill." I fight to keep my composure.

We exit the arena and snake our way to the top. Tonight seems extra dark. It's the last night race, as tomorrow's will be late afternoon. In the background, kids pop balloons as they walk by the staging area. Horses bolt forward, rearing as their jockeys try and rein them back. One rider falls off and his horse speeds down the hill. The jockey swears, sprinting after the kids. Some of the bystanders hold him back. There's a lot of shouting. I keep my distance. Circle Rooster around. I'm not sure if the race committee will let him take his run anyway. *Stupid kids*. I'd like a go at them.

It takes a bit, but once everyone is as settled as can be, we keep behind the line and wait for the blast. I'm in the middle this time. A straight shot to the pine tree. I whisper to Rooster, reminding him he's my king. The gun fires and we blaze down the hill. I have to make this count. I only have one more chance.

I quickly take the lead as we plummet into the water, yelling, whipping, kicking. No one will swipe the lead from me. I won't let them. Billy's on my left. I swat at him as if I could reach. He cackles, shouting something I can't translate, but know the meaning. I spur Rooster on, kicking like a crazy woman, and he pushes forward, stretching his neck, nose out. He digs up the dike and into the arena. Billy's horse pounds the dirt beside me.

We bolt past the poles and I circle right. The announcer screams, "It's Charnaye Toulou. She's done it. Her first win. Placing second overall. If she can hold the lead and win tomorrow, she'll take it all. The first woman to win the World Famous Suici-i-i-ide Race. Ladies and gentlemen, Charnaye Toulou, the first woman to take the lead."

The crowd is standing, arms pumping. A sea of cowboy hats wave in the air. A little girl in the stands plugs her ears. A few others cheer and wave as I ride past.

I circle Rooster down to a walk. Billy comes toward us from across the arena, pointing at me. I rein my brown ruler over to him, hand up. He high-fives me. "I'll get you next time." He grins as he passes me.

Chase races toward me, not paying attention to the other horses. I stand in my stirrups, waving and shouting for him to stop. He keeps coming, oblivious to the danger. I dismount and yell, "Did you hear me?"

He lifts his hand to high five me. I slap it harder than I should. It doesn't faze him. He leads Rooster away, pumping a fist in the air and making a high-pitched whooping sound. Aunt Jamison appears as Chase moves to the left. Arm in arm, she walks me to the gate. Although my breathing slows, my body shakes.

Benton waits at the gate with pride covering his face. He leans in and kisses me. "I knew you could do it." He crutches beside me as we walk.

"Once I had the lead, I couldn't give it away. I've never spurred Rooster that hard before."

"You were great! One more day."

I nodded. "One more day." I rub a knot out of my arm. Pain shoots up from the back of my neck. I reach back and massage the knots. When we get back to the trailer, I sit in front of Benton and he works the kinks out.

"I'm good for something," he says.

I sag back into him. The warmth of his arms around me releases my tension. It's nice just to be with him. We don't require anything of one another. Just our presence is enough. Our time. No pressure. It's safe.

Or so I think. A flicker of doubt creeps in and hovers around me. The voice surrounds me. It laughs, taunting me. *You can't do this. You're a girl. You are not good enough. It takes more than a talented horse. It's not your rite. You. Will. Lose.*

CHAPTER 40

It's Sunday, the final day. With the hill towering over me, I consider how Creator places confidence and power in us, not fear. But a strong mind. Power. That's what I have to cling to in order to grab the title. It's the only way. I can't let fear creep in. It will only destroy me.

I unload Rooster. He nudges me as if to let me know he can be trusted. I stroke his forehead and stand a moment longer. Once I have him tied to the trailer, I fill a bucket with water, hands shaking the entire time. I try and choke down nausea with sips of water and Tums. It doesn't work. I pluck a brush out of a bucket and run it down his back. He cocks a leg. I use slow, even strokes.

You can't win. It's over!

I stop brushing. I pray for wisdom and strength.

Go home. You shouldn't be here.

"I am here." I massage Rooster's shoulders with my fingertips. "I'm staying."

You're going to get hurt.

I squeeze my eyes shut. "I won't get hurt. Creator's protecting me."

He's busy. He doesn't care. He doesn't have time for you.

Gentle, familiar hands claim my shoulders.

"Spirit of doubt and fear be gone. Creator, fill my daughter with your peace. Give her strength. Wisdom. I pray, Creator, You protect her. She's here to honor you. The woman you created her to be. In the traditions you have allowed our people to have." My mom's voice sounds like an angel, her breath on my neck. The peace she asks for bathes me. I lean into her, allowing her to embrace me.

"Thank you," I whisper and grip her wrists.

"You have everything you need. Just believe, Char. Trust Him."

For the first time in months, confidence shines in her eyes. She smiles, her face soft, and runs a finger down my cheek. "Win or lose, you're always my daughter."

"Kari heard you guys, ya know. She thinks I'm going to die."

Mom nods. "Sshapa overheard her talking to you on the phone. We told her you would be safe." She pauses. "She knows Creator's protecting you."

"Does she?"

Mom picks a brush from the bucket and we work together to make Rooster's coat shine. When it's time for the Calcutta auction, she leaves to meet Dad, Sshapa, and Kari. I walk Rooster to the roped off section and circle him. A balloon pops and he sidesteps into me. I elbow him over. *Stinking balloons.* Benton and his family sit with mine. He gives me a thumbs up.

The bidding starts.

I stand a little taller when my parents' and Sshapa's hands rise and fall to the auctioneers call. Others bid against them. The dollar amount rises. My stomach roils with each call of the auctioneer. Sshapa wins the bid at four thousand dollars.

In their cheap, straw cowboy hats, Mom and Dad look like a couple of little kids who've just won a carnival prize. Sshapa struts over, black felt cowboy hat, Wrangler jeans with the front legs creased, black boots shined, and hands the keeper of the funds a wad of cash. All three of them wear the white shirts Jill made. Across the backs announce "Team Toulou." Benton's family wears them, too.

Chase meets me at the gate. "Nice load of bills the folks have, huh?"

"No kidding! Where did it come from?" I hand him the lead rope.

"Auntie's been keeping Mom in the loop, and she's been bragging pretty heavy on you. They've scoured the rez and donations from around Republic and all four districts have poured in. Aunt Jamison has also rounded up a bunch from her friends. If you win, Dad will have a hefty wad of cash. No one else wants a cut of it."

I swallow back a lump in my throat, thinking about all the house repairs. "No way!"

I take my usual calming walk down to the river, fumble for flat stones, and toss them in. They skip across the smooth current. The ripples fan out. They remind me of the cash that's come in for my family. The sun illuminates the hill. Fear and doubt tumble down and land in my throat. What if I don't win? They lose all that money. The generosity of those more fortunate with their cash, time, and art skills makes me want to win even more. If others believe in me this much, I need to rise and meet them at that level. I can't lower the bar. Not now.

Back at the horse trailer, I scour through the bucket and pull out a cotton roll and lime green vet wrap. "Where's Craig?"

"Haven't seen him." I toss supplies to Chase.

Footsteps tap down the floor of the horse trailer. It wobbles. I catch of glimpse of long blond hair cascading out of a brown baseball cap through the trailer windows. "Hey!"

Chase sprints to the front of the trailer, I dodge Rooster and slink behind it. When I round the corner, Chase has a girl pinned against the trailer with his forearm to her throat. In her hand is a folded slip of lined paper. She glares at me with snaky, blue eyes.

"What's this?" I pluck the paper out of her hands and unfold it. "Last day. Last ride for you. Ever!" I crumple up the paper and throw it at her. "You? Why, Carla? What did I ever do to you?"

"What's going on?" Craig picks up the note and reads it. He turns to Carla. "Did you write this? Who are you?"

"She's from Republic. We went to school together. She's Hagan's friend—"

"I told you before, we're not friends. I hate him." Carla fights Chase's grip. Craig pulls him back.

I raise a hand to slap her, but Craig grabs me around the wrist and pulls my arm down. "Have you been the one sending these?" I step closer.

Craig puts an arm in front of me. "How many have there been?"

"This is the eighth."

Craig holds out the letter. "Eight?"

"Who did you have sneak them around for you?" Chase says. "I know you don't have the guts to do it yourself."

Carla laughs. "That was easy. I knew you hated Hagan, so I made it look like he wrote them. His idiot friends were more than willing to help me get them to you. As for sending the letters to your aunt, all I had to do was contact your mom and tell her I wanted to mail over some support money and I had the address."

"How did you get the letters in the tack room?" I said.

"I paid some low-life jockey. It's not hard to figure out who supports you and who wants to see you fail. Besides, you're predictable, Charnaye. I knew when you were here and when you were off with Benton or Jill."

I got in her face. "What about Kari?"

Chase pushes his way to Carla, forearm back at her throat. "You touched my little sister?"

"No." Carla kicks Chase off her. "We were out of school by then. I knew how sad she was at graduation. It was an easy play. I knew that'd get to you." She smiles. "It did, didn't it?"

I sneer at her. "Why'd you threaten me?"

"Why?" Carla's lip curls. "All this queen of the hill crap at school. You have to idea what that means. I train every day. My parents don't care if I'm sick, tired, have a test the next morning. I have to ride. Western, English, trail, hunt seat. You ride in the mountains, run a few fairs." She grunts." "All your free money, claiming some rite of passage that you don't have to work for. Have no idea what it means to earn something."

I shake my head. "You have no idea how hard I've trained for this. What it means to our family. What we've been through the last couple of years. What the money's for."

"You get everything free. We work, train in the rain, heat, snow. We pay for what we have!" Carla tries to shoulder past us.

Chase slams her against the trailer, his hands pressed against her face. "You freakin'—"

"Chase!" Craig pushes him off Carla.

"Really?" I stare at her, open mouthed. I almost feel sorry for her—typical jealous rich girl. "You get everything handed to you by your parents. What do you work for?"

Chase grabs her by the arm. "I'll deal with her, you guys finish getting ready.

"What a witch." Chase says.

"Forget it." I shove my brother toward the back end of the trailer. "Let's go."

With trembling fingers, I wrap to the hum of the paddock. Chase wraps the left legs, I take the right. When done I stand and admire his work. I'm about to comment how well he's done when a jockey stalks up to us.

"Give up yet?"

"You the one who delivered the notes?" I say.

His sneer sweeps my body. "I'm gonna make sure you don't finish." He turns on his heels like some kind of Army soldier and marches off.

"You touch her and I'll kill you!" Chase starts after him but I stand in his way. Push him backward.

"Leave it alone! We got work to do."

Chase glares at me until his breathing slows. He nods. "Still, he touches you, he's dead."

"Fair enough, little brother." I hand him a bottle of water. "Let's get this bad boy saddled."

Because we're behind schedule, I'm rushed to get Rooster ready, have to hop on without warming him up, and hightail into the arena for introductions. Once our arena parade is finished, we follow the outrider like a shepherd leading his sheep to slaughter. I struggle to find calm even though we've found Carla to be the one behind the threats. Soon someone will be crowned "King of the Hill." Or perhaps queen.

I ride in silence until the deliverer trots up beside us and taunts me. He rides to my left. Close enough for me to hear his words. "You won't make it through the water." He lets out a string of cuss words through brown, crooked teeth.

I stare at him, stone-faced. *Protect me, Creator.* It's all I got.

"I'm taking you out," he says.

I pray until his ugly rolls away. Carla must have paid him to intimidate me. I sink into the saddle and rock with Rooster's sway. The jockey's number two gently bobs in front of me. Clicks of horseshoe on pavement scratch my nerves like nails on a chalkboard. *Breathe. Relax. Focus.*

Clop. Clop. Clop. Clop.

"Your brother isn't here to help you. I'll get him, too." He swears some more.

Give me your peace. I let my mind drift to every inch of the course. *Breathe. Relax. Focus.*

"Turn back." His voice is deep. Scratchy.

My fingers twitch. *Keep us safe.* I stiffen. Tremble as if a hot wire is plugged into my saddle. Rooster prances.

"You're weak."

We turn down Dewberry Avenue. The jockey pulls back and circles around. The ribbons on his blue and orange ribbon shirt flutters. *You're weak….*

Bile rises and burns my throat. I swallow and pray as we ride the last leg. *I'm strong.* Before we reach the gate I dismount. With wobbly legs I walk Rooster to the edge of the hill and kneel. Where are the white shirts? Team

Toulou. Not seeing any, I spit what remaining saliva I have in the dirt. It's not even enough to create of puff of dust. They may have migrated to the stands. I'm sure my dad is down there somewhere with binoculars. He might be watching me now. I linger a moment longer just in case. I check the clip on my helmet, making sure it's tight. My tongue feels like it could curl up and wither away. The sour smell of sweat sickens me. I brace against a wave of dizziness.

The pine tree seems hidden behind the sun's glare. I talk to Rooster. Tell him I trust him. Remind him he's the king. And I'm his queen. I lead him closer to the starting line and hoist myself into the saddle. Missing the strength of his touch, I pray my boots stay in the stirrups. I circle Rooster a few times, release stray thoughts, focus on the ride. How he feels. His ears. *Know my surroundings.* Billy's in line. Jarrod's a few feet away. The deliverer is struggling to keep his horse calm.

He glares at me.

I avert my gaze. It's the same zoo. Horses rearing, jockeys attempting to hold them back. Eyes wild, they seem to want this more than we do. Rooster's coat shines from sweat. He prances, nosing the bit. The official draws for positions. I have the number ten space. The deliverer draws eleven. I purse my lips. He comes alongside me, ranting obscenities. His horse side runs, jamming into us. I beat him off. Rooster rears, front legs striking the searing air. I'm tossed to the side. Shaken and weary, I ride it out. We all manage to stay in a crooked line behind the guy with the starting gun. He slides it out of the holster and pulls the trigger.

Rooster snaps forward and in a few seconds, we are midway down the hill.

We surge into the river, water slapping my face and blurring my vision. Someone's whip strikes my arm, back, and head. I flinch and grit my teeth. There is the gentle sway as we swim across the swift current. After shaking the water out of my eyes, the tree flashes into view and disappears behind a curtain of water droplets. Someone's hand grabs my shirt, pulling me sideways.

With narrow eyes and twisted face, he shouts, "You're finished!"

I clutch the saddle horn with one hand and try and beat him off with the quirt around my wrist. My sleeve tears from my shirt. I reach back and spank Rooster, leaning forward. The rein slips from my grip as Rooster's hooves touch the riverbed. He lunges forward, forcing my belly into the saddle horn. A wild animal-like scream escapes my throat as fear turns to rage.

An image of my father in his wheelchair, eyes cast down, scrapes across my mind. *Keep going.* I reach for the rein, but it's too far forward, near his ears. *I can't.* With one bounce of his step, it's between his ears. I snap my arm forward, fingers out. It's too far away. My tormentor bumps his horse into mine as we soar out of the water. The rein flicks back and I'm able to wrap my fingers around it. Rooster gains speed, passing riders. I'm clear of the deliverer, but sandwiched between two other jockeys. They squeeze their horses against my leg. I kick and spank, hitting the jockey to my right. He slaps back with his crop and yells profanities at me.

Dust floats into my eyes. I squeeze them shut. Tears stream. I wipe them away, clearing my vision. I catch a glimpse of Billy Beck's back and one other just behind him racing up the dike. I have only a few seconds to make my move. Horses hooves pound as they dig into hard dirt. Rooster's body heat warms my legs. There's no way around them. An image of Sshapa smiling, holding a picture of Stimteema and the horse she rode off the hill in Keller years ago pops into my mind. Proud eyes stare through the glass picture frame, telling me there is a way. Creator is about to clear a path for me. This rite of passage flowed through her veins. It now flows through mine.

Daylight slips through a crack between the horses. I kick and spank and scream. Rooster surges forward, passing one. Then another.

We turn the corner into the arena. I rub elbows with someone. I don't know who because my eyes are again squeezed shut. I scream and kick and spank some more. Lean forward, rein arm extended, head down. I'm still hollering when we cross between the poles. I have no idea how close we are. The crowd is deafening. I open my eyes and circle left, examining the other jockey's expressions. Some smile at me while others glare, jaws clenched. Was it enough to claim the title?

A sea of white bounces in the stands. My parents cheer, Kari jumps on her chair, hands in the air. My heart sinks at the sight of Sshapa. He sits in the front row, hands covering his face. My eyes dart from jockey to jockey as they struggle to spiral their horses to a walk. They prance instead, noses high in the air. Rooster follows suit. The announcer hollers and chatters like when American Pharaoh won the Triple Crown. I can't make out what he's saying. I strain to listen, motioning for the crowd to hush. They get louder.

Billy Beck rides by, hand high. I slap it. Then another. And another. And then it comes over the loud speaker. I spin Rooster around and face the announcer. He points and nods at me with a wide smile on his face and screeches my name and "Queen of the Hill" in the same sentence. Shock buzzes down my arms. This must be how Victor Espinoza felt. Numb. Excited. Honored. The sea of white pumps their fists in the air, shouting "Girl Warrior" over and over and over…

The grass dance is to purify the earth for the rest of the dancers to come. Rooster's name now makes sense to me. He's helped pave the way, not for dances and celebrations, but for girl's journey into womanhood. So they too can follow their dreams into the circle of life, leaving a legacy for future generations.

Did you enjoy *Girl Warrior*? I hope so! Would you mind taking a minute and leave a review? https://amzn.to/2HXZ5ef

It doesn't have to be long. Just a sentence or two telling what you liked about the story!

To receive two FREE gifts and get updates when new Carmen Peone books release, click here: https://carmenpeone.com/about/

ACKNOWLEDGMENTS

Without the following people, this book would not have been written. Thank you from the depths of my heart:

Tarren Muesy for hopping up into the school library one spring day and inspiring me to write this story. You planted the seed and gave me insight into a high school contestant's view of the World Famous Suicide Race. Stephanie "Pete" Palmer for your insight as former Owners and Jockey Association president. You gave me a behind the scenes view of how the race works and added validation to this story. Debi Condon, your support, wisdom, and direction as a woman racer who's tackled the "Hill" is invaluable. Thank you for taking me on your personal journey. My editors, Heidi Thomas and Leo Brickner.

I interviewed many people for this project and I'm indebted to you all:

Chris Burch and Jack Hamilton for the Republic School District tour. The owner of five-time champion horse—Taz, Jim Phillips. Thank you for letting me see Taz's heart. Loren Marchand, Taz's jockey, thank you for teaching me what it takes to train and win. The courageous warriors who've proved their manhood in a tradition of rights of passage: Tony Joe Louie, Tarren Meusy, Dion Boyd, Scott Abrahamson, Austin Covington, thank you for taking the time to share this honor with me. Sylva Jane Peasley thank you for sharing the Keller race history. Rod Hergesheimer for the use and knowledge of AP History and Brenda Vanslyke for lending me a Precalculus book and checking my work. Kim Spacek for school suspension protocol. Christy Martenson, Violet Gulack, Caitlyn Aubertin, Becky England, Sue Jacobsen, Luann Finley for your hours of ideas, encouragement and proofing.

ABOUT THE AUTHOR

CARMEN PEONE is an award-winning author who has lived in Northeast Washington and on the Colville Confederated Reservation with her tribal member husband since 1988. She had worked with a Tribal Elder, Marguerite Ensminger, for three years learning the Arrow Lakes—Sinyekst—Language and various cultural traditions and legends. With a degree in psychology, the thought of writing never entered her mind, until she married her husband and they moved to the reservation after college. She came to love the people and their heritage and wanted to honor them with fiction true to culture and language as taught by elder Ensminger.

A horse enthusiast herself, she trains for and competes in Extreme Cowboy and Mountain Trail competitions with her horse, Cash. She is a certified NASP archery youth instructor and coach.

Carmen loves to hear from readers.

Connect with her online:

Blog: https://carmenpeone.com/

Facebook: https://www.facebook.com/CarmenEPeone/

Pinterest: https://www.pinterest.com/carmenpeone/

Twitter: https://twitter.com/carmenpeone

Instagram: https://www.instagram.com/jcpeone/

BOOKS BY CARMEN PEONE

Hannah's Journey

In the mountains of northeast Washington, sixteen-year-old Hannah Gardner fights for her childhood dream—to race horses with her adopted Indian Aunt Spupaleena. Frustrated with her daughter's rebellious spirit, her mother threatens to send her away to Montana to live with an aunt Hannah's never met. Determined to live apart from her parental grip, Hannah runs away and races with her adopted Indian aunt's horse against Indian boys who vowed to stop her at any cost. Will one young Indian man be her way out?

Delbert's Weir

In a time when the west was still untamed, sixteen-year-old Delbert Gardner leads two friends into the backcountry for a three day adventure. Little did they know three days of hunting and fishing would turn into eight days of near starvation, injury and illness. When hope of returning home seems out of reach, Delbert recalls watching his Native American friends construct a fishing weir and sets out to build one himself. To him, it is the only way out.

Coming Fall of 2018

Change of Heart

After fighting with her sister, thirteen-year-old Spupaleena bolted from their Arrow Lakes pit home into the dead of winter. Spupaleena didn't know where she was going but knew she could no longer live at home. Haunted by the deaths of her mother and brother, Spupaleena ran until she'd run too far.

Upon discovering Spupaleena's body, Phillip Gardner, a trapper, brings her home to his cabin. His wife, Elizabeth, does her best to help heal Spupaleena, although with a broken heart and a mangled body, she is not likely to survive. But when Phillip doesn't return from a trip into town, a pregnant Elizabeth and a weak Spupaleena are forced to find strength to keep going.

Coming in 2019:

Heart of Courage

Spupaleena was not about to back down. Knowing she encompassed the skills to race against young Indian men, Spupaleena begins her intense training. However, Rainbow, her middle-aged mare, would only carry her so far. She would need to find a new horse, but where? She was tired of her fellow racer's cruel insults, one young man's in particular. She was determined to not only race him, but to win. But at times, wondered if that was enough. Spupaleena's father was against her. Would she have the spirit to compete and win? If so, would her father ever learn to accept her determination to train and race horses?

Heart of Passion

Spupaleena will do nearly anything to make her dream of breeding the finest race horses in Indian Country come true. She and her relay teammates have been racing and winning, but one young man is resolved to see her fail. Spupaleena is passionate about her dreams and goals. Not any human nor circumstance will deter her–not poison, not injuries, and certainly not a pride-filled, vengeful male competitor. She's determined to have it all, but will the hunger to triumph steal the reins? Will Spupaleena find her place in a man's world and prove everyone wrong?

Made in the USA
Monee, IL
03 September 2020

R00215